Enjoy the mystery!

BLOOD AND BONE
By
Austin S. Camacho

Austin S. Camacho

Copyright © 1999 by Austin S. Camacho

Second Edition Published November 2004
ISBN 978-0-9762181-0-4

Cover Design by Cathi A. Wong

Published by:
Intrigue Publishing
10200 Twisted Stalk Ct
Upper Marlboro, MD 20772

Printed in the United States of America

BLOOD
AND
BONE

-1-

SUNDAY

"Wake up, Joey," Floyd said to his bodyguard. "You might have to kill this one."

The stranger drew Floyd's attention the second he walked into the club. Something marked him as a dangerous man, but it took Floyd a minute to figure out what. Like everyone else at The Tip Top that night, he was black—actually, light skinned for a black man, kind of a golden color, with wavy brown hair cut short. He was not particularly big, barely six feet and a little on the thin side. His clothes did not stand out. He wore a basic black suit and tie.

A man's eyes would sometimes draw Floyd's attention, but that could not be it this time. The stranger wore very dark wraparound shades. As the man moved around the crowded tables toward him, Floyd realized it was the stranger's attitude that had drawn his eye. This man carried a calm confidence seldom seen in a place like this in Northeast Washington D.C.

"You need something?" Floyd asked as the stranger stopped in front of him. He certainly would not rise from his chair for a nobody, and Joey and Lawrence would take care of any trouble, if anybody was stupid enough to start some. The stranger crossed his hands in front of himself, hands covered by black leather gloves. The man looked bored.

"Just to deliver a message," the stranger said. "It's from Jewel. She says she quits."

The music in the Tip Top was throbbing so loud Floyd could not make out the words, although he could feel the beat. It made conversation almost impossible. But he heard this man clearly.

"And you are?"

"Jones," the stranger said. "Hannibal Jones."

Floyd leaned forward to make sure Hannibal heard him. "You know, around here pimps don't go around trying to rip each other off. But I'll tell you what, Slick. You tell that bitch to drag her narrow ass in here in the next ten minutes, and maybe I won't mess her up too bad."

"You've misunderstood," Hannibal said. He dropped a card on the table. It bore his name, phone number and the word "Troubleshooter" in block letters. "The woman is under my protection," he said. "Let it go. She's gone. Get over it."

The music lowered, and Floyd noticed every eye in the place was on him. All of them, drunks, whores, drug addicts, and a few real people who wanted to relax for a while. They all smelled of liquor, or drugs, or cigarettes, or desperation. This Hannibal Jones did not smell of any of that. He was an island in this place, isolated and alone. Floyd glanced to his left with a wry smirk.

"Look here, stud. This here's Joey. He takes care of my light work. And that guy behind you, Lawrence, he cleans up the messes Joey leaves behind. If I was you I'd get to stepping before I pissed somebody off. You getting my message?"

"Look, can't we talk about this?" Hannibal said. Floyd's only response was a blank stare. Hannibal glared down at the floor for a moment and curled his lips in. "The hard way he said. "It's always got to be the hard way. "Then he looked up and Floyd saw his own smile disappear in Hannibal's lenses. "Okay, who's first?" Hannibal asked.

Joey was good. There was no telegraph, no warning body language. But somehow, when his big right fist reached its target, Hannibal's face was no longer there. Floyd saw his bodyguard take a hard snap kick in the gut and a back fist across his face before Lawrence got his arms around Hannibal, locking his arms down. Somebody stopped the music but nobody spoke. It was a private hassle, but everybody wanted to watch.

"Not bad, stud," Floyd said, "but you can't expect to come in here with that Jackie Chan shit against the big boys."

"Uh-huh," Hannibal said. He smashed his head back, bloodying Lawrence's nose. Then he snapped forward, grabbed Lawrence's ankle and jerked up. Floyd heard Lawrence's head thump the floor behind Hannibal. Joey moved in again, but black gloves blocked both his best punches. Then two crisp jabs and an uppercut put Joey over Floyd's table, spilling his scotch. More confused than scared, Floyd reached for the nine millimeter at the back of his waistband.

"Don't even go there, stupid." Hannibal pulled an automatic from under his right shoulder and shoved its muzzle into Floyd's cheek. "You get your piece out, it's pure self-defense and I turn your face into abstract art."

Silence gripped the room and the Tip Top became a still life while Floyd watched himself sweat in Hannibal's Oakleys. He thought about business and his rep and his honor. Mostly he thought about dying.

"It's your world," Floyd said. "What now?"

"Now we negotiate and come to an agreement," Hannibal said, sitting on the table and pulling his gun back an inch. "My terms are simple. Let it go. One girl less. No comeback."

Floyd sat taller and straightened his face. No fear, he told himself. Back to business. "Who you work for, stud? New player coming in?"

"I work for me," Hannibal said. "Solve other people's problems. Jewel had a problem. She wanted to get off the streets. I solved it. Now, is this over?"

Floyd considered himself a good judge of character. He could negotiate a position with this one. The man was leaving him an out, so it would not look like he was getting ripped off.

"All right, if the bitch wants out, she's out. But this better be for real. I find out she's working the streets I'll kill her. I mean anywhere, dig? I got friends all up and down the coast, and they know every whore out there. She starts hooking, her ass is mine."

"Fair enough," Hannibal said. "I'll pass that on. As long as she's out of the life, I'll keep her safe. Otherwise, I'm out of it." Then he holstered his weapon and stood up. "Pleasure doing business with you. When your two friends wake up, tell them I said practice."

-2-

Hannibal pulled into his parking space and killed the engine of his white Volvo 850 GLT. There were no markings, no sign or label, but the space was universally recognized as his.

He was on the move since early Saturday morning and his long day ended with a bar fight and a half-hour drive down to Anacostia and home. Weary as he was, Hannibal scanned the area before he opened his door. The cone of a street light covered his car's hood and peeked in through its windshield. His street looked quiet as he eased out of his white leather seat and set his anti-theft device. He smiled at his neighborhood's split personality. He had come home at a rare quiet moment, too early for the hip folks to be coming home from the party, or for the church crowd to be heading out.

His rubber soles fell silently on the red sandstone steps leading up to the front door of his red brick, three-story building. He used two keys to open the outer door. Once in the hall, he faced the central staircase but instead of turning left to his own flat he veered right. The front room of this apartment was his office. His heavy oak desk faced the door, flanked by a pair of file cabinets. A smaller desk stood beside the door on his left. He stepped across the oval broadloom rug, but before he could even riffle through the papers in his IN box he heard footsteps from the far end of the railroad flat.

Her perfume preceded her, the sharp sting of Patchouli. "Did you talk to him?" Jewel asked in a nasal New Jersey accent. Her high-pitched voice always sounded to Hannibal as if she were about to cry.

"I took care of it, on condition you stay off the street," Hannibal said, but his casual response did not remove the fear from Jewel's cat-like eyes. She was Hannibal's height, model thin and very black, a Nubian princess whose beauty was marred by the wear showing at the corners of her eyes. A thoroughbred, Hannibal thought, passed through too many owners and broken down by being ridden by too many jockeys.

"You won't go back on our deal?" she asked, smoothing a hand down her straight black hair. "You said if I was nervous I could stay here a few days."

"Jewel, I'm a businessman and you know my rates. If you're willing to go the fee you can stay right there in my guest room until you feel safe. I just don't think..."

"Well I do." Her fingers pressed into his right arm with disturbing familiarity. "You don't know Floyd. Anyway, I got plenty of money stashed away and I don't mind spending it staying alive until I figure out where I'm going. You want cash?"

"Any way you want to pay," Hannibal said, dropping his messages back into his IN box. Nothing pressing. He would file these and check for email messages in the morning. His eyes were starting to droop.

"Any way?" Jewel asked, pressing her thumping heart against his. Hannibal stared into her frightened eyes, and they dropped closed, even as her lips

6

parted, inviting his tongue in. His tired mind reeled. She was beautiful, exotic, and certainly talented. She was also a client.

"Let's stick to negotiable currency." He gently pushed her shoulders away with his index fingers. "Something I can put on my books. Besides, it's so late it's early and I'm beat. Why don't we call it a night?"

Across the hall, Hannibal walked back to the fourth door from the front and unlocked it. Loud beeps reminded him to cross his living room, reach around the bathroom door and punch in his four digit code, disabling his alarm system. Too tired to think further, he walked through his flat to the front room, dropped his clothes in a pile and crawled into bed. He silently thanked God it was Sunday morning before his eyes slid shut.

-3-

"Morning, lover," Cindy said. "You still in bed, sleepyhead?"

Hannibal checked the absurdly expensive Porsche titanium watch Cindy gave him for Christmas. Eight fifteen. He had slept for more than four hours, but it felt like five minutes.

"Worked late," he said, trying to pull his mind together. "Isn't it Sunday? Why're you up so early? God, I need coffee. Something going on?"

"Well, this might sound weird but I've got a job for you."

Work? Hannibal spun onto his back to get his brain into focus, then sat up quickly. His hand hit something beside him.

"You're not mad, are you?" Cindy asked. "I feel kind of guilty talking business on Sunday morning, but it's kind of important to me."

He was listening with only half his mind. What his hand had hit was a body. Jewel's body. She must have crept in while he slept. He watched her eyes open dreamily. He knew what was next. In Hannibal's experience, a woman's eyes opened only seconds before her mouth. As Jewel prepared to speak, he clamped his free hand down over her mouth.

"Nothing to feel guilty about," Hannibal replied, sensing the irony of his remark. "If it matters to you, it matters to me. Somebody in trouble?"

"That's your business, isn't it?" He could hear Cindy's soft chuckle. "It's one of Mister Nieswand's personal clients. Kind of a delicate situation. I told him you could handle it and he asked if you could make it to his place for brunch."

"Brunch?" Hannibal asked to fill time. Jewel started to sit up and the sheet fell away. She was naked. Actually, THEY were naked. "Sounds good. How should I dress?"

"Well, it is business. Better make it suit and tie. It's out in Oakton. They dress for snacks in that neighborhood."

"Oakton? I better get going then. Give me the address." Hannibal glared a threat at Jewel before he removed his hand. She froze in place while he found a pen and pad by the phone.

"No, pick me up," Cindy said. "He wants me there too. I'll be ready when you get here, so we can make his place by eleven, okay? See you later. Love you," she added, throwing a kiss into the receiver.

"Me too," Hannibal said, forcing a smile into his voice. "See you soon." He settled the phone gently into its cradle, but in the time it took him to turn around, his expression turned to rage. "What the hell are you doing in here?"

Jewel shrank back against the headboard as if struck. "I was lonely. You were alone and I thought, I mean, I figured..."

"If I didn't think that pimp would kill you, I'd put your ass in the street right now," Hannibal snapped. "Now get across the hall, lock the door and get some clothes on." Despite his anger, he watched her dancer's behind squirm into a too tight miniskirt and admired her legs in motion until they reached the other end of his apartment and slinked through the

9

door. As the door latch clicked he leaped to his feet and headed for the kitchen. He did not have much time to get his act together and he had a stop to make before he left.

At eight-thirty, Hannibal knocked on the door directly upstairs from his own living room.

"Yeah, who?" came a grumbly voice from inside. Already up and in the living room, Hannibal thought.

"It's me, Sarge."

The door popped open and a stocky black man wearing only boxer shorts thrust his head out. He looked Hannibal up and down, taking in the black suit and tightly knotted tie. "You going to church?"

"Cindy called with a job," Hannibal said, "but I've already got one. Want to make some money?"

Sarge rubbed a hand across his scalp, past his hairline, which had receded halfway back on his head. His flexing biceps made the fouled anchor tattoo jump. "Well, you'll be coming for October's rent pretty soon and the place I been playing bouncer in looks like it might go belly up soon. Sure, I can use a few extra bucks."

"Good. Got a client down in the office side. She's paying my full daily fee to have a safe place to crash while she sorts out her life. It's worth my usual subcontractor pay if you'll keep an eye out for trouble next couple of days."

"Two fifty a day?" Sarge grinned. "I hope she never leaves. Is she cute?"

"Beautiful."

"Then for three hundred she can stay up here with me," Sarge said, smiling even broader.

"Actually, she's used to getting money for that," Hannibal said. Sarge's face fell. "But she's trying to break that habit, if you get my meaning."

Sarge nodded and a new alertness showed on his face. "And somebody don't want one of his meal tickets taking a walk, right? Okay. She's safe long as she stays in the building. You and me, we chased whores, junkies and who knows what all out of this building before we moved in. I guess I can hold off a pimp."

"Sarge, I trust you more than the FBI, but I got my pager and phone just in case something comes up."

"You going far?" Sarge asked as Hannibal headed for the stairs.

"Another world," Hannibal called back. "Oakton."

* * * * *

"Look, I'm sorry if I ruined your Sunday morning," Cindy said as they eased into the wooded cul-de-sac, then rolled slowly up a long blacktop driveway toward a three-car garage. "You've hardly said a word."

"Sorry, honey. I'm not mad, just tired I guess, and the weather isn't helping." Not really a lie, he thought. It was the kind of overcast day that made you think you could reach up and touch the gray cloud ceiling. Drops sprinkled down slowly enough to cause his windshield wipers to make that awful noise, even at the lowest intermittent setting.

Hannibal had driven from Southeast Washington, D.C. across the Fourteenth Street bridge and down to Old Town Alexandria to pick up Cindy Santiago in front of her home. Then he drove ten miles west on Route 7 in sluggish Sunday morning traffic to turn down the equally congested Route 66, to reach a Washington suburb where people bought homes for what the realtors called "gracious country living." But half his mind was occupied by the houseguest who had sneaked into his bed, a guest he had somehow failed to mention to Cindy.

He pulled his Volvo to a stop and stared up at the stately colonial in which Gabriel Nieswand stored his life, barely outside the beltway. It was exactly the type of brick monstrosity he knew Cindy aspired to. And he would love to give her one, the next time he found himself with three quarters of a million spare dollars laying around.

Hannibal was out of his car and planning his long stroll up the flagstone path when he heard an engine roar to life and a long Mercedes came screaming backward down the center of the wide driveway.

"Whoa!" he shouted, waving his arms. The limousine's brakes locked, filling the air with the smell of burned tread. He caught a glimpse of a woman in the back seat. Fortyish, with blond hair that did not fit with her complexion and a pleasant face which was losing the battle with gravity.

Then the driver got out, a beefy black man in chauffeur's livery, curling and opening his huge hands. His nose showed he had not won every fight in his life, but his eyes said he did not particularly care. He seemed to take a second to appraise Hannibal, deciding they were in the same class.

"Move it before I push out of my way."

Hannibal straightened his jacket and stepped forward. "Look, I'm not somebody's driver here. That car's my baby. You put a scratch on her I'll break your legs."

The chauffeur spit out of the side of his mouth. Hannibal heard Cindy in his right ear say "You're tired. Don't do this," in a pleading tone, but he was in no mood for taking crap off some servant.

"Them shades supposed to scare me?" the chauffeur asked. "You don't look like one of the lawyers, so I don't have to take your shit. Move the frigging car."

"I'll bet you been in a lot of fights," Hannibal said, pointing at the horseshoe-shaped scar on the back of the chauffeur's right hand, "but that don't mean jack to me."

The bigger man's eyes flared open. He swung his big right fist at Hannibal's head. Hannibal blocked that punch, then the left, and drove his own left into the bigger man's stomach. The driver grunted but swung a right cross that connected this time. Hannibal's ears were ringing, partially with Cindy's scream. He let two more hard punches bounce off his upraised forearms. Then he managed a pair of jabs into the other man's already broken nose. Seeing an opening, he drove an overhand right into the man's jaw. The driver staggered against the Mercedes and Hannibal saw one more good shot would do it.

"Paton!" the shout turned Hannibal's head. A man was trotting down the path from the house, moving like he was unaccustomed to anything more than a mild walk. He wore an expensive sport coat and a less expensive toupee.

"Miss Santiago, what is the meaning of this?" he asked. Hannibal lowered his hands, realizing how stupid he was being. Cindy stepped forward, turning on the smile she used to calm both clients and prosecutors.

"Mister Nieswand, may I present Mister Hannibal Jones. I'm sorry, but there was some misunderstanding with your driver."

"Paton, I don't believe this," Nieswand said with an air of superiority Hannibal found stifling. "Now you go on and take Mrs. Nieswand on those errands. Mister Jones, I am terribly sorry."

"My fault," he said, suddenly not wanting to get Paton into more trouble. "As Ms. Santiago said, a misunderstanding." Then he faced Paton. "You've got quite a right there."

"You got a pretty mean punch yourself," the driver said, extending his right hand. "I'm Ike. Sorry about this. I'm kind of sensitive about..."

"I understand." Hannibal saw Paton's eyes cut to Nieswand and realized it was important to shake Paton's hand, showing no hard feelings, which, in fact, was the case. Paton had shrunk back into his servant's role. With an insecure smile he got back in the limo, pulled it forward a bit and eased it carefully around Hannibal's car.

"I know he's a little rough," Nieswand said, "But he looks out for the Missus. And I use him as a courier sometimes. You give a package to Paton, you know it's going to get where you want it to go." Hannibal judged Nieswand to be in his mid-fifties. Lawyers, in his experience, came in three brands. Crusaders, like Cindy. Honorable businessmen, like her other boss Dan Balor. And slippery, legalized con men. While he smiled and nodded, he placed Gabe Nieswand into category three.

Once inside, they walked across a marble floor through a two-story foyer, and out onto a custom redwood deck. Soft classical music leaked out to the deck from the house. The table was set for four. A nameless woman in modernized maid's attire poured coffee and delivered Belgian waffles with fat, brown sausages. Actually, Hannibal assumed she did not have a name. She simply had not been introduced; a sign of her unimportance, which he would have expected to offend Cindy.

"I must say, you're looking lovely today Miss Santiago," Nieswand said once they were settled in their chairs. She smiled and nodded, and Hannibal had to admit the man was right. His woman was stately and slender, with a high, narrow waist. Her deep brown hair was carefully waved in a contemporary style a couple of inches beyond shoulder length. Yes, she knew how to wear that expensive navy business suit, but her real beauty was born to her in her Hispanic heritage. It was in her smooth, clear skin, her sharp cheek bones, her dark eyes and broad smile. It was the face of an angel and, because he preferred women with ample brassiere filling, he thought her body blew Jewel's away.

Why had he not noticed her beauty when he picked her up today? Was he taking her for granted? It was too late to say anything now, after her boss had already complimented her.

"So, Mister Jones," Nieswand began around a mouth full of waffle, "Miss Santiago tells me you help people in trouble."

Hannibal pushed whipped cream up onto the bit of waffle on his fork. "Cindy is familiar with my business," he said. "But so is the other senior partner in your firm, Dan Balor. Surely you spoke with him."

"Of course. I know how you cleaned out that apartment building of his that turned out to be a crack house. He tells me you live there now and act as building superintendent. Like Miss Santiago, he raves about your ability to get things done. In fact, I've checked you out rather thoroughly. Your police career, both as a patrolman and a detective. And your time with the Secret Service. Everything I know now makes me certain you're the right person to help a client of mine named Harlan Mortimer."

"You're careful about your client's welfare," Hannibal said across the top of his coffee cup.

"He's also a friend."

"He's also black," Hannibal said, slicing the end off a sausage. "That why you want me?" He ignored Cindy's dagger eyes.

"What else do you know about Harlan?"

Hannibal gathered his thoughts while he chewed, then cleared his mouth with coffee. "I know he started out buying real estate in the district, then got real rich buying and selling land in northern Virginia. I know he's got a rep for being tough in business, but fair."

"Did you know his only son ran off eighteen years ago? That he was nineteen when he took off? That he left behind a wife and his infant son?"

"That the problem?" Hannibal asked. He was noticing how well the closely planted trees protected Nieswand's deck from the rest of the world. A brightly colored jay was chatting with his plainer mate on a branch a few feet from Hannibal's head. These noisy neighbors seemed to make the scene more peaceful.

"Yes, I suppose it comes down to a missing person's case."

The anonymous girl replaced their plates with new ones, each holding half a cantaloupe. "Not my usual type of thing," Hannibal said, bracing for the kick under the table and accepting it silently. Then the rapid-fire patter of footsteps drew everyone's attention to the house. The man who burst through the French doors had a round, sepia-toned face under a shiny pate. Gray cotton wool ringed the back of his head from ear to ear. An expensive suit hung loosely on his skeletal form.

16

"Ah, our fourth has arrived, albeit a bit late," Nieswand said, standing. "Cynthia, Mister Jones, Doctor Lawrence Lippincott."

"A pleasure," Cindy said, taking the older man's hand.

"That goes double for me," Hannibal said, shaking the doctor's hand briskly. "Your free clinic isn't far from my place in Anacostia. Got to admire a man who gives back after he's made it."

"Glad you know a little about Lawrence," Nieswand said as they all sat. "He's the Mortimer family doctor. As they are both my clients he's the one who brought the problem to my attention."

Hannibal pointed to his cup and the phantom girl refilled it. "I'm not sure I understand. Just what is the problem with Mortimer's son?"

"His son isn't really the problem," Lippincott said in a precise Harvard accent. "Well, perhaps after all he is, but the problem I must face is the son he left behind. A son now grown to his teens in Harlan's home. A boy who's spent the last five years wrestling with chronic myelogenous leukemia. An old man's disease, for God's sake."

The pain on Cindy's face made Hannibal's heart ache. Silence settled over their table in the peaceful woods. Even nearby birds became still. And the melon in his mouth was still pulpy, but not nearly as sweet as it tasted a second ago. Swallowing was difficult, but he managed.

"Excuse me, Doctor, but I always thought leukemia was a children's disease."

"Not this type," Lippincott said. "What you hear about generally is lymphocytic leukemia. It attacks children, but if we find it early we can usually beat it with chemicals and radiation. Myelogenous,"

17

Lippincott gulped a mouthful of coffee, "well, it's rather a tougher opponent. We've taken radiation and chemotherapy just about to their limits with Kyle."

Lippincott lapsed into silence and Nieswand picked up the ball. "Lawrence here thinks a bone marrow transplant could be the answer, but you can't get it from just anybody. Blood and bone marrow have to be the same type. Parents and siblings have the best chance of a match."

"I see it," Hannibal said, mostly to spare Nieswand having to say more. "The known family's been tested I assume, with no luck. That's why the manhunt."

Nieswand raising his left hand. The server appeared with a box of cigars. Only Nieswand took one. "It is, as you say, a missing person's case," he said, lighting his cigar, "but if I understand your business correctly, this is indeed your type of thing."

Hannibal turned to Lippincott who was clinking a spoon around in his cup. "How much time does the boy have?"

"We're clutching at straws here."

"Okay, I get it," Hannibal said, easing his glasses off. "Last chances are by definition what we try when all else has failed and time is running out. That's okay. Desperation is my business. How much time?"

"Two, maybe three weeks if his progress doesn't change."

Hannibal sat back in his chair. Lilacs and forsythia growing beneath the deck seemed inappropriately sweet. "Gone eighteen years. Three weeks to find him and bring him back."

"Money is no barrier," Nieswand said. "You can drop any other jobs you're working on and give this your complete attention."

The low clouds were breaking up, but instead of true sunshine, the sky cast a ghostly glow around objects. Hannibal slid his Oakleys back into place. "I don't drop prior cases. They are commitments just as this would be. And my fees don't change. I get five hundred dollars a day plus expenses, and my expenses are never questioned. Anybody I subcontract gets another two-fifty a day."

"This means you'll take the case?" Nieswand asked.

"Maybe. But I won't take a penny until I know there's some chance of success. I'll have to see what kind of leads the family can give me, then we'll see."

Cindy squeezed his hand, implying she knew his answer before he did.

-4-

Hannibal wished he could travel by helicopter. Great Falls, Virginia, where Harlan Mortimer lived, was about ten miles due north of Nieswand's home. But roads never travel due anything, so he followed Nieswand's Saab on a zigzag path for forty-five minutes, up Hunter Mill Road to Springvale Road then across the Georgetown Pike. The clouds blew back in during the drive, and an occasional drop dotted Hannibal's windshield.

Finally they turned into a subdivision aptly named Riverscape. The grade was not steep on Mortimer's cul-de-sac, but as they pulled into the driveway in front of his three-car garage, they could see the Potomac through the woods behind the house. Hannibal let Nieswand and Lippincott climb out of the doctor's Saab before he unhooked his own shoulder harness. He wanted to see who paid deference to whom. Nieswand waved to Hannibal and Cindy to follow him to the house, but he invited Lippincott to lead the way.

He expected to be greeted by a servant at the top of the brick stoop, but the woman who opened the door was too well dressed. A natural color mohair sweater suit showed off her well maintained shape, but straightened black hair and overly correct posture dated her. Her dark eyes roamed the four faces as if trying to make connections between them.

"We need to see Harlan, Camille," Lippincott said. "It's about helping Kyle." The woman backed away and the group entered. Lippincott and Nieswand obviously knew where they were going but Hannibal stopped to extend a gloved hand.

"Hannibal Jones. One nameless person per day is my limit."

"Camille," she answered, gently shaking Hannibal's fingertips. "Camille Mortimer. I'm..."

"She's Mister Mortimer's daughter-in-law." The new voice came from the direction the other men were heading, but it was neither of them. Hannibal turned to see a short, clean cut, Ivy League looking black man striding toward him. The navy blazer and rep tie said Harvard, the next generation. His hair was short, but already receding on a scalp that probably had not seen forty years yet.

"Malcolm Lippincott," the newcomer said, pumping Hannibal's hand. "Are you with Nieswand and Balor?"

"I'm the other attorney," Cindy said, pushing her hand forward for another solid shaking. "Cynthia Santiago. Mister Jones here is a consultant we sometimes employ."

"Sorry for the brisk welcome," Malcolm said, not sounding sorry in the least. "I didn't know your business here."

"Mal's a little overprotective sometimes," Camille said, her dark face blushing still darker. "but he's been my best friend through all this."

"Jones." It was Lippincott, calling from the next room. "Can I see you for a moment?"

Hannibal excused himself and joined Lippincott. The archway led to a two-story, bayed great room.

Lippincott leaned against the brick fireplace. Above it hung an ornately framed painting of a woman in a field of flowers. The name at the bottom was Monet. Coin display cases lined the mantle like toy soldiers guarding the painting.

"Nieswand?" Hannibal asked.

"Gone to make a phone call, which is fine. I wanted a moment with you alone." He paused until he realized Hannibal was waiting for him to go on. He seemed uncomfortable with the silence.

"Camille is rather distraught," Lippincott finally said. "With good reason. She's been through a lot. I saw what it did to her to be abandoned by her husband. And now it looks as though she'll lose her son as well." Hannibal stood quietly through another long pause, waiting for Lippincott to make his real point. When the doctor cleared his throat, he thought this must be it.

"This search for Jacob is Camille's idea, not Harlan's," Lippincott said, avoiding Hannibal's shaded gaze. "He'd clutch at any imagined chance because losing his grandson will kill him. But she's the one who wants to see Jacob again. I don't think she's ever gotten over him."

"You've been the family doctor that long?"

"Doctor and friend," Lippincott said.

"Okay, tell me about the missing son."

Lippincott began to pace back and forth in front of the fireplace, hands clasped behind his back, looking like a figure on a German clock. "Jacob was a bad seed, Mister Jones. Undisciplined. Ungrateful. Irrationally immature. Wanted to be a hippie, or a black revolutionary or something. The boy brought nothing but pain to those who loved him. His disappearance certainly helped his mother into an early grave. He left a woman who loved him and his own unborn son for a street girl. And he abused her."

"Abused her?" Hannibal asked, settling into a deep easy chair. He worked to stay relaxed, trying to counterbalance Lippincott's increasing agitation. "You mean physically?"

"I examined her once," Lippincott said, his eyes floating back into the past. "Just a child, a year or two younger than Jacob. She laughed about the scars, but I couldn't. Cigarette burns, Mister Jones. Scattered around her stomach, her buttocks, and the upper part of her legs."

"Pretty?" Hannibal asked to keep Lippincott talking.

"If you like that type. Half black, half Chicano. Small, but with big breasts and a big behind. Big, watery cow eyes." He suddenly stopped, as if he thought he had said too much.

"What was her name?"

"I don't remember, and it doesn't matter," Lippincott shot back. "This is about here and now. And you working for Harlan Mortimer. Look, I may still be able to find a suitable donor for Kyle in time. But Harlan won't have it, not while he thinks this wild goose chase has a chance of success."

"And what would you have me do?"

"Take the money and take a nice vacation to Florida, Mister Jones." Lippincott's face was rigid, but his hands were begging. "Send back a report in a couple of days saying there are no leads and it's hopeless."

"Fake an investigation?" Hannibal asked, slowly rising to his feet. Lippincott nodded. Hannibal stepped close to the doctor and slid his dark glasses away from his face. His eyes flared deep green and he pressed one fingertip deep into Lippincott's chest.

"Listen well, Doctor," he said through clenched teeth. "I might not take this case. If I figure it's hopeless I'll say so. Or, I might give it a shot, and if I do, I'll do my very best to find the boy. But understand there is no third option for me. I work in two modes. The best I got, or not at all."

"Sounds like you're the man I want."

Hannibal looked up to watch the source of that deep booming voice stalking toward him, very fast for a man his size. The handshake was fierce, the eyes crinkled points of brown fire. "I'm Harlan Mortimer."

-5-

"Will you find my son, Mister Jones?" Mortimer asked.

"I'll decide when I've got a little more to go on," Hannibal said, pushing his dark glasses back into place.

"Right," Mortimer said dropping into the chair Hannibal had occupied before. "What can I do to help you do your job?"

"Well, first you can tell me something about your son, like why he left."

Camille entered carrying a tray and walked straight to her father-in-law. He took a tall glass from the tray, after which she moved around the room, prompting everyone to a seat by placing a lemonade for them. Hannibal took his glass from its place on the coffee table but chose to stand. His eyes stayed on Mortimer.

"Jacob left my home because I removed him from my will," Mortimer said. Hannibal saw not a trace of remorse or guilt on his face.

"You cast him out."

"No, just out of my money," Mortimer said. "Jacob, his wife and his then unborn son would have been welcome in my home forever. He lost his inheritance because he got another girl pregnant."

"Ah, yes, the other girl." Hannibal sipped his lemonade and glared at Lippincott. "Do YOU remember her name, Mister Mortimer?"

"Jacob called her Dolly. I don't think that was her real name, but rather a nickname. A pet name. Don't know her real name. Girl looked like a whore. Acted like it too."

"I see." Hannibal stepped a bit closer to Mortimer's chair. "How about some of his friends? People he hung out with?"

A small grimace. "Never knew any of his friends. When he dropped out of George Washington University, he fell in with a bad crowd. Left over left wing drug types."

"Uh huh. Not much there." Hannibal gulped the last of his lemonade. Then he moved forward until only inches of gleaming hardwood flooring separated his toes from Mortimer's. "Where did he go? What were his favorite places to hang out?"

To his credit, Mortimer showed a glimmer of regret now. "Afraid I don't know any of the places he used to go."

Hannibal bent to place his now empty glass on the table beside Mortimer's. His head turned toward Mortimer and his voice dropped almost to a whisper. "Look. This kid we're talking about. Did you know him at all? Had you met this guy?"

Mortimer's voice returned to booming. "If I knew where he went, do you think I'd have let him just disappear with my coins?"

-6-

The copper disc glinted between Hannibal's fingers. Even in its fancy case it looked no more valuable than any other newly minted penny to him. He tried to imagine the pleasure in owning something so outwardly common.

"That's a nineteen fifty-five double die obverse," Mortimer said behind him. "See how the back is restruck off center? That's a minting mistake. There probably aren't a dozen of those around. I keep a few of my prizes on display. That night, before he left, Jacob..."

Hannibal turned to see Mortimer staring up at his painting, lips pressed together and turned in to his teeth, eyes closed, hands thrust deep in his pockets. "The bulk of my collection is in a locked cabinet in my study, in pull-out trays. That bitch convinced him to take a tray of my more valuable coins when they ran off. He stole from me, Mister Jones," Mortimer turned to Hannibal, conflict twisting his powerful face in odd ways, "but I'm prepared to forgive him even that if you can bring him back to me."

"You haven't given me much to go on, Mister Mortimer," Hannibal said. "I'll have to consider this, but I'll let you know before the day is out."

It was sprinkling again from a black sky which promised a real storm when it worked up the nerve. Hannibal supported himself with both hands on the hood of his car. Nieswand stood a couple of yards behind but Cindy stared into his face from a foot away.

27

"So what's the real reason?" she asked. Then she was quiet, as if she knew if she stood there long enough he would explain. He wished he knew how she could be so confident—and so right.

"He never once mentioned the sick kid," He finally said. Cindy nodded, confirming that was all the explanation needed. Nieswand just as clearly did not get it.

"You got to understand Harlan," Nieswand said. "He was on top of the world. Everything going his way. Then his only son just disappeared. Mrs. Mortimer died of a broken heart just months later. Doctor Lippincott said it was stress-induced angina, but I know it was a broken heart, and Harlan blames Jacob. Men do funny things sometimes when they love and hate the same thing. But it's not your job or mine to judge. Mine is to represent Harlan's interests. I'm prepared to hand you a retainer right now against your fee and promise you a fat bonus if you pull this off."

Hannibal turned and leaned against his Volvo with his arms crossed. "I'm still thinking about this."

"Well, I have to get home," Nieswand said. "My wife's not feeling well. If you decide to take the case, come by the house for your money. If not, let me know so I can try to get someone else. Maybe Cynthia knows someone more cooperative."

As Nieswand pulled away, Hannibal asked "Are you in trouble if I say no?"

Before Cindy could answer, Camille came out of the house. The light rain made her hair begin to curl at the ends, but she did not seem to care. Outside of her father-in-law's presence she seemed much more self-assured.

"Would you please come back inside? You don't have the whole picture." When Hannibal hesitated she turned to Cindy. "I see you're a team. Please, both of you come back in. Hear me out and then if you don't want to get involved with this family, I'll understand."

"May I ask a question?" Cindy said on their way up the long carpeted stairway.

"Of course. I think you'll find me a bit more open than Harlan."

"Good," Cindy said. "Do you want to see him again?"

Camille stopped at a door. "Eighteen years is a long time, girl. And Jake mistreated me, and abandoned his son. But I still love him and that part of my life's an unfinished story, isn't it? But this isn't about me. I wanted you to know, before you left, what this is really about."

Camille pushed the door open. The room was dim, the shutters admitting only narrow bands of light. Someone had sprayed vanilla scent recently. A hip hop beat played at such a low volume, Hannibal felt more than heard it. Cindy went in a few steps and stopped.

"Come on in," the boy said. "It ain't catching." He raised his head from his pillow with some effort. Hannibal walked in close to the bed. The bald head and skeletal form made the seventeen year old look like a man of fifty.

"Kyle, this is Mister Hannibal Jones," Camille said. The boy presented a hand, which Hannibal quickly took. Then, reconsidering, he pulled off his gloves and shook again. Kyle's dark skin was chalky underneath, Hannibal assumed from anemia. Or the chemotherapy. Or the radiation.

29

"Ma tells me you're a private "Dick," Mister Jones." Kyle's voice lacked energy, but his smile made it up. Hannibal pulled his Oakley's off.

"Sort of," he said. "A lot of people think I'm just a "Dick." And call me Hannibal, please."

Kyle laughed a genuine, but weak laugh. "So, you going to find my dad?"

"Well, I don't think I'm ready to make any promises." Hannibal crouched down beside the bed and looked at the portrait of normality the room presented. Boom box, comic books, television, and a stack of text books on Kyle's night stand. "What you reading?"

"Got to keep up with school," Kyle said. "No point getting better and then having to repeat a grade or something. See, I want to have some choice of the college I go to. I don't think I'll make it on an athletic scholarship. I mean, it's a little late for me to start developing a good hook shot, don't you think?"

"You know, Kyle, even if I find your dad..."

"Hey, I know it's not a lock," Kyle said, pulling himself into a seated position. His pajama top hung on his shoulders like the shirt on an understuffed scarecrow. "Bet I know more about it than you. See, what I need's an allogeneic transplant. That means a close family member. The donor takes an HLA test. That's human lymphocyte antigens. You follow?"

"I understand enough to know there has to be a type match," Hannibal said.

"Right. Well, the odds of a match are about twenty-five percent. Mom and grandpa already struck out, so that's two out of four. So when you find my father, we'll have a fifty-fifty chance. Now, don't you think fifty-fifty's enough to have hope?"

After a moment, Hannibal said "Absolutely."

"So, think you can find him?"

"I got one advantage, Kyle," Hannibal said, standing. "I don't think anybody has really looked for him yet. I'll report in to you as I go."

Kyle reached out his hand one more time. "Will you lie to me?"

"Kyle!" Camille snapped. The question was so direct it caught Hannibal by surprise. But the two men locked eyes and Hannibal clasped Kyle's hand.

"No, son. I know some people who love you have probably tried to make things look better than they are. But no, I won't lie to you. Now let me go get started, okay. I'm on a deadline here."

Camille's face was clouding up as she closed Kyle's door from the outside. Cindy patted her shoulder, blinking to keep her eyes dry

"Poor kid," Hannibal said. "Being attacked by his own blood and bone. Got a lot of heart though." Then, to center his mind, he performed the ritual of pulling his gloves back on and pushing his sunglasses back into place. When he turned to Camille his mouth was set in a grim line.

"You got a picture of Jacob?" he asked.

"In my room."

"Well let's go," Hannibal said. "Like I told Kyle, I'm on the clock."

In Camille's room, Hannibal stared at a photograph of a young lion. Jacob had his hair picked out in a neat natural style. A peace sign and a ceramic black fist shared a leather cord around his neck. His eyes were very light, at least in the photo, shielded behind tortoise shell glasses. His teeth were very even and very white. His nose was thin for a black man, almost pointed. But his lips were full and his chin aggressive. A face a person would not quickly forget.

"Can you find him?" Camille asked.

"God, where to start?" Hannibal said, almost to himself. He ran a hand back through his hair. While he memorized the face of the man he would be searching for, Cindy put a comforting hand on Camille's arm.

"Eighteen years ago this wasn't a mystery, was it?" Cindy asked. "If you really loved him, you know where he was."

To Hannibal's surprise, Camille knelt and pulled a shoe box from under her bed. He noticed there was no dust on its lid. When she sat on the bed, Cindy joined her. Camille took in a deep breath and let it out in a long sigh before lifting the lid from the box. From it she pulled a greeting card and handed it to Hannibal.

"A friend up in Baltimore sent me that birthday card. That address on the back is the place where he worked."

The address was for something called the Moonglow club. "You never told Harlan?" he asked.

"He'd have had Jake arrested," Camille said. "I wanted to let Jake come back on his own. I always thought Jake's fascination with that other girl would fade away and he'd come back to me. I didn't want anything bad to happen to him."

"Well, this is at least a starting point. Ever been there?"

"Kyle was a year old when I finally got up the nerve to go up there." Camille said. Tears started down her face, but she was not participating in the crying act. It happened all by itself. "Took Daddy H's car and got a map of Baltimore and drove myself up there. Me and my baby. But when I got there, he was gone."

"Gone?"

"Nobody had seen him for months," she said. "He just left one day and never came back."

"Quit his job, just like that?" Hannibal asked.

"Well, he was working but it wasn't really a job." Camille next produced a newspaper clipping with a grainy photo attached. It was Jacob Mortimer all right, under a huge afro and without his glasses. He was on stage at a small club, wearing bell-bottoms and three-inch shirt cuffs, bellowing into a microphone.

"Daddy H sent Jake to school to be a lawyer, but what he really wanted to do was sing," Camille said. "That's why he dropped out of school. He was gigging at the Moonglow regularly. Nobody who knew him could miss his face, or his voice, but Daddy H never heard about him because he sang as Bobby Newton."

"Jeez, the guy really longed for the sixties, didn't he?" Hannibal said. "That outfit, and taking the names of two of the Black Panther leaders for his stage name. How come you never went up to see him perform?"

"You kidding? I was too busy being a mom and studying. After Jake dropped out, Daddy H put me through college. Not that I ever did anything with it, but I owed him. I had to make up for Jake, didn't I?"

-7-

Ten minutes later, Hannibal was driving southward through the storm the sky had been threatening all day. It was almost too warm and muggy for his car's climate control system to cope with. The midday darkness was deep enough to force him to remove his glasses. He stared through his wipers whipping back and forth, straining to see what was ahead.

"I'm glad you agreed to help," Cindy said, almost shouting over the din of rain crashing on the Volvo's roof. She had squirmed out of her jacket and kicked off her shoes. "That boy needs to know somebody's really trying. And his mother needs comfort."

"Well, don't look at me," Hannibal said. "I don't go for the whiny type."

"She wouldn't have to look far if she'd only look. Malcolm's right there."

"I think he helps," Hannibal said, loosening his tie. "She said he's her best friend."

"Didn't you even see?" Cindy said. "The man's in love with her. I mean, wasn't it obvious? Some detective you are." She softened her remark with a kiss on his cheek.

"Hey, I find your boss as big a mystery as the missing heir," Hannibal said, slowing down and turning on his headlights in the growing storm. "I mean, I'll be real glad to get back there, get my

34

retainer and get to work. But some day I'd like to investigate him. I'd like to know how an old Jewish attorney comes to have so many black friends. And why he puts up with a chauffeur he can't keep in line. And how come he sends his wife away when he's got company coming."

"I can answer that last one," Cindy said. "He's tried to keep it quiet, but it's pretty common knowledge that Abby Nieswand has a bit of a drug problem. She's been in and out of treatment centers without much success. Hey, maybe he needs a tough driver to try to keep her under control. Makes you wonder if..." Cindy's hands suddenly slammed into the dashboard. "Oh my God! Over there!"

Hannibal had almost missed it. A car traveling in the opposite lane had veered off the road, into the wooded area Hannibal knew to be the Lake Fairfax county park. It had slid down the slight grade maybe fifty feet. It looked as if Hannibal's car was the only one on the road, but he slowed to a crawl anyway before pulling to the side. Then he signaled and flashed his lights before turning around. Even moving along on the shoulder on Hunter Mill, he almost overlooked the crashed car. It was a Ford Taurus in that dull gold color so many of them seem to be, its right headlight smashed against a tree.

"Should I call an ambulance?" Cindy asked, picking up the car phone.

"Let's see if there's still anyone in there first," Hannibal said. He climbed out of his car and slid down the embankment off the edge of the road, squinting against the rain. He was ankle deep in mud as he approached the Ford. Water poured down the back of his neck as he bent to look into the driver's seat. He hated getting wet with his clothes on.

The driver was alone in the car, hunched over the steering wheel. A big black man, casually dressed. Hannibal opened the door, and the driver moaned.

"Take it easy," Hannibal said. "You've been in an accident. Are you okay?" No response. Worried, Hannibal pulled the man into an upright position. The right sleeve of his light windbreaker was torn, and blood was caked around it. As Hannibal moved him, fresh blood flowed out.

"You're hurt," Hannibal said, looking around as if someone was there to help. He considered taking the man to his own car, but quickly abandoned that idea. Even up so small a grade, the man could be hurt getting to the road in a driving rain. Besides, for all Hannibal knew he could have other injuries to his back or neck.

"Listen," he told the man inside the Ford. "Sit tight and try not to move too much. I'm going back up. I've got a phone in the car. I'll have an ambulance here in a couple of minutes."

"Thanks," the driver said. Then he drove his left elbow into Hannibal's stomach. Half inside, Hannibal bent forward over the driver. The man's palm slammed up into Hannibal's chin, driving his head into the edge of the car roof. Hannibal slid in the mud and dropped, dazed, onto his back. Rain poured into his face, but it could not wash the blue dots away from in front of him. He rolled onto his right side, fighting to catch his breath. He considered reaching for his gun, but he saw that the man he tried to rescue also had one. It was already pointed at him. He lay still, trying to clear his head.

"Appreciate the kind thoughts, pal," the driver said, shouting over the crashing rain, "but I think I'll just take the car. That way if I need an ambulance, I can call them myself."

Hannibal managed to struggle to his feet but had to lean against the Ford to watch the other man back his way up the embankment. He could not let Cindy face the gunman alone. He managed five steps toward his own car before the world started spinning and he dropped to his knees. How hard had his head hit the car roof? Self-hatred mixed with his feeling of helplessness forced him back to his feet. Dizziness and nausea drove him back to his hands and knees.

He vomited, then watched the rain wash the evidence away. Water streamed down into his eyes. He thought about his ruined suit and his car being driven by a madman and his woman in mortal jeopardy and decided if he could just have a minute to get his mind back on track he could climb that hill and kill the man responsible for all that. All he needed was a minute.

"Oh God, Hannibal, are you all right."

Hannibal looked up to see Cindy, her hair hanging around her face, her nylon covered knees pressed into the grassy mud in front of him.

"Took a knock on the head," he muttered. "You okay?"

"Sure," she said, putting an arm around his shoulders. "That man, he waved a gun at me and told me to get out. He took off in your car and I came looking for you. Your eyes look funny."

"Yeah, I think a mild concussion makes your pupils dilate. Help me up."

Together they stood, and Hannibal instantly felt better. He held his face skyward to fill his mouth with rain water, then spit out the taste of his own vomit. His head seemed clearer now. And he thought he heard a car up on the road, but with the rain he could not be sure. Then he turned to Cindy again.

"Look at you. You're beautiful. But you're soaked. Get in the car, I'll go up to the road and get us a ride out of here."

The grade was slight, but the ground was slippery and it took Hannibal a minute to reach the shoulder of the road. He did see a vehicle pulled to the side about thirty yards on and headed for it. Before he was halfway to the car he was met by two men, both wearing rubber rain coats with caps on under their hoods. Hannibal was about to ask them for help when one man reached inside his slicker, pulled out a revolver and pointed it at him. Hannibal was considering diving back into the woods off the road when the first man spoke.

"Freeze right there. You're under arrest for murder."

-8-

Hannibal's hands went up slowly as he turned to face the gunman. His mouth was suddenly bone dry, the only part of him that was. While he tried to decide what to say, the shorter man, the one not holding the gun, moved in close. He smelled of chewing tobacco, never a good sign from Hannibal's point of view. He started to pat Hannibal down but got only as far as his shoulder holster. With an "ah hah!" expression on his face, he pulled the weapon from its sheath.

"This what you capped him with?"

Behind him, Hannibal heard "Do they teach you clowns about Miranda in this state?" He turned to see Cindy stalking forward along the road. Despite the seriousness of the situation he had to smile. She looked like a drowned rat, her hair pasted to her forehead and cheeks. Her white blouse, turned transparent by the water, clung to her body, highlighting her chilled, erect nipples. She was barefoot and her stockings were shredded from the knees down. Rage flashed from her dark eyes and right then Hannibal was glad he was the wronged party.

"Who the hell are you?" the taller man asked.

"My name is Cynthia Santiago. I'm this man's attorney."

"Well I hope you're a good one," the tall man said, pulling a badge from inside his raincoat with his free hand. "Fairfax police. Believe your boy here just drove away from shooting a man. Looks like the weather stopped him."

"You've got no evidence, no probable cause, and I can easily prove we just came from the other direction," Cindy said, pushing her face into the trooper's. "I ought to sue your ass for false arrest. Now put that damn gun away."

The officer hesitated, but could not quite let go. "Nope, this man's under arrest and we're taking him back to the chief. Rory, better read him his rights, and then cuff him."

"What you better do," Cindy growled through small clenched teeth, "is drive us to Gabriel Nieswand's house. It's not far from here. Back in Oakton at..."

"I know where it is," the tall policeman said. "You're in luck, lawyer lady. That's just where we're headed. Scene of the crime."

Cindy swallowed hard. "Nieswand's? Are you sure? Is Mister Nieswand all right?"

By the time the police car pulled into Nieswand's driveway, the rain had stopped. Hannibal and Cindy climbed out of the car, squishing as they walked. Their captors removed their raincoats, leaving themselves annoyingly crisp and neat. Hannibal was about to ask them to remove the handcuffs when Nieswand came jogging toward them from the house, followed by a strict looking man in a tan suit. He had a severe hair cut and dangerous blue eyes.

"What are you doing?" Nieswand blurted as soon as he was within hearing range. "Have you lost your minds? Miss Santiago, are you all right? Get those handcuffs off that man immediately."

"Sir, are you okay?" Cindy asked at the same time. "They said there was a murder. Your wife?"

"She's fine, just a little shaken up."

The other man stopped in front of Hannibal and looked him up and down. He was not in uniform, but Hannibal instinctively knew he was a police detective. He may have been born with a badge.

"You know these people?"

"The woman is in my firm," Nieswand said, almost hysterical. "The man is working on a private investigation right now for one of my clients, a Mister Harlan Mortimer. In fact, they were both at Mister Mortimer's home up in Great Falls when the crime took place."

The menacing blue eyes turned on the two troopers, who wilted under their gaze. A key was quickly produced and Hannibal's hands were freed. The troopers got back into their car, but the man they were avoiding held his hand out to Hannibal.

"Orson Rissik," he said. "Chief of detectives, Fairfax Police. City, not county. I apologize for those two knuckleheads. They may have screwed up, but their hearts are in the right place."

"No harm done," Hannibal said, shaking the detective's hand. "They just got a little overzealous."

"Overzealous?" Cindy said. "Ought to sue them. You've got a legitimate false arrest charge here."

"They got carried away, but they were just trying to do their job," Hannibal said, to Rissik rather than Cindy. "Probably weren't far off. The guy they're looking for is almost certainly the man who stole my car at gunpoint."

"You give the knuckleheads a description?"

"They weren't in a listening mood," Hannibal admitted. "Figured they already had their man."

One icy stare got the tall man out of the car without a word being said. Then Rissik turned back to Hannibal and the ice in his eyes turned to friendly sunshine. "Would you be kind enough to give these men a description of the man and your car? We'll try to return it to you as soon as possible."

"Sure." But as Hannibal turned toward the car, his eyes passed over the entrance to the garage. Under the police tape he saw the body, still there, face down. He recognized the man by his size.

"That Paton, the driver?"

"Yes, sir," Rissik said. "Right where we found him."

"Mind if I take a look?"

"Well that would be highly unusual, but," Rissik's eyes flashed to Cindy. "Under the circumstances, and your being so cooperative and all, I suppose it might be okay."

While Cindy went into the house to clean up, Hannibal gave the troopers a detailed description of his assailant and his car. Then he and Rissik walked up the driveway toward the garage. Hannibal noticed how similar their walk was. He figured Rissik must have noticed it too.

"Nieswand said you were working an investigation. You were a cop?"

"Three years on a beat in New York," Hannibal said. "Three more as a detective. Then they accepted my application at the treasury department."

"Secret Service?" Rissik asked. Hannibal nodded. "Well then, maybe you'll see something I missed. You know the deceased?"

"We'd exchanged some words," Hannibal said. Looking down on the still form gave him an eerie feeling. Was it only a couple of hours ago this guy had tried to knock his head off? Now he lay still, all the life drained out of him through a tiny hole at the base of his skull. Without thinking, Hannibal peeled off his sodden suit coat and knelt down for a closer look. Rissik followed.

"Mrs. Nieswand found him out here and freaked. I questioned them both. They were no help with the guy's personal life, even though he lived right here for a year."

"He lived in their house?" Hannibal asked.

"In the guest apartment. Servant's quarters actually. You can see by that pale patch on his wrist that his watch was taken. His wallet's empty too, but I'm not sure I like robbery as a motive. Did you know him well enough to have any other ideas?"

"No," Hannibal said, then "Well, maybe." He pointed to Paton's right hand. "See that scar, shaped like a horseshoe? Fifteen, twenty years ago that was a symbol for a small gang used to run around the East Coast. Omega, I think they called themselves."

"So you think it might be a gang thing?"

"Could be," Hannibal said. "That looks like a twenty-two wound. Neat, precise, very professional if you ask me. Any other signs of injury?"

"Medical examiner hasn't been out yet," Rissik said, standing, "but I did a quick examination. All I see is the lump on his head where he hit the floor in here. His jaw and his nose are a little bruised, but that could be from the landing too. And his knuckles are a little scratched up."

Hannibal smiled a small smile. "I think that happened earlier today. So, no real sign of a struggle. Yeah, I'd say it looks kind of like a mob hit."

"Well, that's one more idea than I had," Rissik said.

Hannibal stepped back out into the new sunshine. He wanted to be in dry clothes. He wanted to get a pair of sunglasses on. He wanted his gun back. Hell, he wanted his car back. He turned to Rissik, smiling at himself.

"Do you mind if I take a look at his room?"

Hannibal was on Paton's bed reading a letter when Cindy walked in. Her hair was clean and brushed out, her face glowing from a fresh scrubbing. The plain blue ankle-length frock she wore was a little too big for her, as were the deck shoes around her feet. She smelled of Jasmine, probably the scent of her shampoo.

"You look a lot better, babe."

"A shower can do wonders," Cindy said, kneeling in front of him. "And it turns out Abby, Mrs. Nieswand, is close to my size."

"You talked to her?"

"Not really," she said, pushing her hair back behind one ear. "Doctor Lippincott's got her under sedation. What brought you here? I figured you'd want to get home and change the second you could."

"I guess I couldn't resist the puzzle of Paton's death," Hannibal said. "His room says a lot about him." The flowered wall paper was certainly there before him, but the rest of the room was very masculine. Cigars on the chest of drawers. Playing cards and dice on the dresser. No spread on the bed to cover the plain wool blanket. And on the headboard, a clock radio and several racing forms.

"I think this guy made some kind of connection with you," Cindy said, stroking his nearly dry leg.

"Yeah, on my jaw," Hannibal said. "Truth is, I want his killer. Aside from wanting my car back, I owe that guy something and I'd love the chance to pay him back."

"And what you got there?" Cindy asked, tapping the pages in his hands.

"Found this letter under the bed," Hannibal said. "It tells me old Ike wasn't everything he led his boss to believe."

"Really?" Cindy slid up on the bed to look over his shoulder. The cheap box spring groaned under their weight. "What's it say? He a drug dealer? Victim of a mob hit man? Who was he?"

Hannibal leaned back so Cindy could snuggle under his arm. "Well Daisy, that's who this is from, thinks his name was Pat. Looks like she's his ex-wife, but he's still interested."

"Oh yes," Cindy said, trailing her finger along the page. "Look at this paragraph. I've found a good life, a real life, and you're not going to ruin it. Leave me alone or I'll have to tell Phil about the old days, and about what happened on the Westside. Hm."

"Sounds like a threat," Hannibal said, "but down here she said she still cares about him and says there's no reason for there to be any hard feelings between them. In her words, she just wants him to keep his distance."

"She sounds nice. Wonder if he was still bothering her."

"Wouldn't be hard," Hannibal said, standing and folding the letter back into its envelope. "The return address is Catonsville, Maryland."

"So here you are." At the sound of Nieswand's voice Cindy sprang to her feet. Hannibal dropped the letter on Paton's headboard and turned to pick up his jacket.

"Rissik told me you were up here, looking for clues or something," Nieswand said, ushering Hannibal and Cindy toward the stairs. "Did you forget why you were here? Or would you rather pursue Paton's death? No one will miss the man, you know."

Hannibal breathed deeply, his eyes fading into green on his way down the plushly carpeted steps. "The man was killed on your property. He lived in your house. Are you saying you don't care?"

"What I'm saying," Nieswand said when they reached his study, "is you can't help him now. But you can help Kyle Mortimer. Miss Santiago told me you decided to take the case. Will you now accept a retainer and make it official?" Before Hannibal could respond, Nieswand shoved a check into his still damp shirt pocket, the way a man jams a bill down into a stripper's G-string.

"Now, I suggest you get going," Nieswand said, easing Hannibal toward the door. "The car Ms. Santiago ordered is here and his meter is probably running."

Hannibal was startled to face bright sunshine as he opened the door. The clouds which blanketed the area all day had evaporated while he was inside. His next shock was the taxi waiting in the driveway and the short, bulky Latino at the wheel. He slid into the back seat and Cindy followed him in. The driver backed out of the driveway, speaking to his passengers without ever turning his nearly bald head.

"Hard day, Hannibal? Cindy told me they stole your ride."

"That ain't the half of it, Ray," Hannibal said. "But Cindy didn't tell me she called her old man for a lift."

"Hannibal, if not for you my little cab company wouldn't exist. Picking you up is a pleasure. Besides," he chuckled, "business ain't been all that good. Now where to?"

"How about my place?" Cindy asked Hannibal. "You can get cleaned up and you've got a change of clothes there."

Hannibal looked at her the way he always did when she discussed their personal lives in her father's presence. It was awkward enough for him living in the same building with her father. Ray knew what their relationship was, but Hannibal was still uneasy about being too obvious.

"I guess," he said, rolling down his window. "Listen, Ray, do you think I could hire you and a car for a couple of days? I've got a case and it shouldn't wait. The trail starts in Baltimore and I'll need to get up there."

"How far is Catonsville?" Cindy asked before Ray could answer Hannibal's question.

"It's right there, a suburb on the southwest edge of Baltimore," Ray said. "Why?"

"Yeah, why?" Hannibal added. Cindy sank back into the seat with him, nuzzling his ear the way she did when she wanted a favor and did not want to risk getting no for an answer. "Sweetheart, somebody ought to tell that nice lady that her husband's dead."

"Ex-husband," Hannibal corrected her. "And she didn't want to be bothered with him, remember?"

"She said she still cares about him," Cindy said, running a finger gently down his neck.

"So call her up."

"This isn't something a woman wants to hear over the phone," Cindy said. "Besides, Mister Nieswand was being a jerk. You ought to do this on his time." Her fingers moved to slide down his chest. "It'll make you feel better."

"Sounds like we'll be making a detour," Hannibal said loud enough for Ray to hear.

"Sure thing," Ray said. "When you think you'll want to get going?"

Cindy had reached Hannibal's knee by this time and his throat was tight. She answered for him. "Getting late in the day for starting a case, isn't it? Daddy, why don't you pick Hannibal up tomorrow morning? At my place."

MONDAY

Ray Santiago pulled his best limousine off the Capital Beltway at the College Park exit, and headed north on Interstate 95. The ride was smooth and he stayed within five miles per hour of the speed limit. But Hannibal knew Ray considered him more family than a customer. For one thing, Ray would never light up a Kent with anyone else in the back seat.

"So, you didn't tell me much, Paco. This is a missing person's case?"

The sky went up to infinity this day, with a sun so bright the light seemed to come from everywhere. After two weeks of intermittent rain, all of Maryland was the color of a new pool table. Hannibal smiled into the rear view mirror.

"I've got to find a lost father to save the son's life," he said in a matter of fact way. "Tell you all about it on the way up. First I've got to make a call."

Hannibal picked up the telephone in the back seat and pushed buttons. His mood was buoyed by more than the weather. Ray picked him up early enough to be at Kuppenheimer's as the door opened. He bought only working clothes today: a black suit, suspenders, and soft leather loafers. A white shirt and a subtly patterned tie from Structure. Soft gray kid gloves. And a pair of very dark wraparound Oakley sunglasses.

New clothes always made him feel better. Now he was doing a good turn, a freebie for no reason except his woman said it would be a nice thing to do. He got the number from Directory Assistance and he only listened to two rings before a woman's thin, squeaky voice said hello.

"Hello, is this Daisy Sonneville?"

"Yeah. You selling something?"

"No, ma'am," Hannibal said, "I don't want anything from you. My name is Hannibal Jones and I have some news for you about Ike Paton."

"Who?" Her voice was no less suspicious.

"Pat. Your ex."

Hannibal was not sure if the long silence meant surprise, fear, or simply a lack of interest. It ended with a long, ragged breath.

"Are you in Baltimore?"

"Will be in half an hour or so," Hannibal said. The way Ray was flying down the road, it would probably be less. "I'm headed up from Washington. I've got some business in Baltimore, but I'd gladly stop by your place if you want to give me the address."

"I see." her words were precise and measured, as if they were too precious to waste. "No. Not here. When you hit the Beltway get off at exit twelve and go over to Wilkens Avenue. About half a mile in toward the city there's a little shopping center. I work at the University of Maryland not far from there. I'll meet you in that coffee shop and we can talk, okay?"

* * * * *

"See anything?" Jewel asked.

"Nothing bad," Sarge answered, pulling one of his feet up onto Hannibal's desk, which he was sitting on.

50

She knew he was supposed to make her more relaxed, but sitting there, staring out the window with a baseball bat always in reach, he made her feel as though violence was imminent. She hopped to her feet and started pacing, but Sarge sat as still as before. Damn it. If she was nervous, anyone around her should be.

The sound of the doorknob turning made her spring to the next room. Through the half open sliding double doors she saw an old woman shuffle in, her stout, round form wrapped in a long red flowered dress. Sarge got to his feet, apparently out of respect.

"Well, good morning," the old woman said. "Looks like I got somebody to talk to today."

"Morning, Mother Washington," Sarge nodded with a big smile. "Yeah, I'll probably be around pretty much today."

"How are my boys?" Mother Washington asked, setting her purse on the small desk.

"Everybody's fine. Hannibal, he's out on a case. I think Ray's with him. Virgil and Quaker, they working a job for a local landlord."

"Praise the Lord," Mother Washington said, her face split into a broad smile. "Long as they all working, they ain't getting in no trouble. Suppose it's the same for an old woman, so let me get to the kitchen and get my supplies."

The woman took three steps toward the next room and came face to face with Jewel. It was a full face, Jewel saw, and very dark, topped with gray hair pulled to the back and held by a rubber band. Mother Washington turned to Sarge whose face fell into a guilty expression.

"I'm sorry," Sarge said. "This is Jewel. Jewel, this is Mother Washington. She's kind of adopted the guys

51

who live here." The woman turned back to look Jewel over. It was an uncomfortable experience. While Sarge's eyes on her made her feel sexy in her tight miniskirt, tank top and spiked heels, Mother Washington's gaze made her feel naked. The woman had certainly marked her as a street girl, but her eyes held pity rather than disdain.

"A girl in trouble," Mother Washington said with a knowing smile. "Well I'm glad to know you. I come by most days to straighten up and answer the phone."

"What do you mean by that?" Jewel whined, drawing her fists up to her hips. "A girl in trouble. You saying I look like somebody in trouble? What makes you think I'm in trouble?"

Sarge almost gasped, but Mother Washington looked at her the way she often looked at the mildly retarded.

"You hiding here in Hannibal's office," Mother Washington said. "The door to the street is locked in the daytime. You got Sarge here watching over you. Your eyes don't hold still for a minute. Don't take a genius to see you in trouble. But you got nothing to worry about, child. You found sanctuary."

With a nod she stepped off toward the kitchen. After a moment, Jewel followed. Mother Washington hummed an old spiritual as she gathered furniture polish, a feather duster and cloths from a cabinet. With those tools in a small pail she pulled a broom and dustpan from behind the refrigerator and headed back toward the front of the house.

"I know that tune," Jewel said trailing behind her.

"It's gospel," Mother Washington said. "Throw Out Your Lifeline."

As Mother Washington started dusting the desk, Jewel picked up Hannibal's IN box. "What did you mean by that? I found sanctuary."

"I mean you're safe here," Mother Washington said. "Once you got Hannibal Jones protecting you, you got nothing to worry about. People in trouble, that's his stock-in-trade."

Jewel stood with her arms crossed as Mother Washington dusted everything that was not permanently attached to the room and a few things that were. "You make him sound like some kind of saint."

Mother Washington looked at Jewel with a kindly light in her eyes and suddenly the younger woman felt calmer. Then she handed Jewel the dustpan and started sweeping. At appropriate times, Jewel would crouch to let her sweep dirt into the pan.

"Let me tell you something about Hannibal Jones," Mother Washington said. "See this here building? It don't look like much, do it? Kind of wonder why a man would have his business office here, don't you?"

"Now that you mention it," Jewel nodded.

Mother Washington looked toward the big desk and, without being asked, Sarge grabbed one end and swung it around so she could sweep beneath it. Jewel did not see a speck of dirt underneath, but Mother Washington swept there anyway.

"Not too long ago this place was a crack house," Mother Washington said. "Junkies and dealers just moved in here and set up shop. Everyday there was somebody trying to sell my grandson that poison. Police didn't do nothing. People who lived here didn't think they could do anything either. Then Hannibal Jones came around."

53

Sarge righted the big desk and slid the smaller one across the floor for cleaning. Shafts of sunlight coming through two big front windows illuminated the few remaining dust specks in the air. Jewel noticed she was catching the radiant calm the other woman generated.

"Hannibal said the man who owns the building hired him to clean it out," Mother Washington went on. "He brought this big fellow and a few other friends and they came in here with some big sticks and just cleaned house." Her broad smile revealed a gap between her front teeth. "Just spanked them and put them in the street. More than that, he involved everybody on the block, gave our men some pride again, brought our people together again."

Mother Washington began gathering her cleaning equipment. "Now, I was real glad to see the bad element go, but I knew as soon as Hannibal and his friends left, the trash would just come back in. That's the good part. He decided he liked this old building too much to leave. And the neighborhood liked him just as much. So he stayed right here, and his friends moved in too, upstairs. I think he made a deal about the rent, because his being here does keep the trash from coming back. And he's kind of the super for the building."

"So you're part of his company?" Jewel asked Sarge. "A professional troubleshooter like him?"

"Me? I'm just an old gunny sergeant who works as a bouncer in a few local clubs. When I met Hannibal I was homeless and jobless. We all was. He just hired us to help with that one job. And I pay rent for sure. But it's a lot better than a homeless shelter and Hannibal helps me keep working. Like now."

"So, he lives on that side, keeps an office on this side, and you," Jewel nodded toward Mother Washington, "You're like his maid and secretary both?"

Mother Washington stopped in her tracks. "No, dear. I'm his friend and I help him out."

* * * * *

Hannibal wondered how long Daisy had been waiting for him to walk into the coffee shop. She had chosen a booth which offered a certain amount of privacy, while giving her a clear view of the door.

He spotted her easily enough. She had not told him how striking she was for a woman in her forties, but she had described herself as a natural ash blonde. Her hair was straightened, then waved in almost a Marilyn style. It struck a stark contrast against her coffee colored skin, but her face was pretty enough to pull his attention away from her hair. Her body was trim, nicely filling her simple yellow shift.

After asking Ray to stay at the counter and asking the waitress to bring him coffee, Hannibal joined Daisy in the booth. Her posture was erect, her eyes bright and intelligent, her nails meticulously manicured.

"Good morning," he said. "Sorry to drag you out like this."

"Is this trouble?" she asked. "Will you be followed by the police?"

Hannibal accepted his coffee and waited for the waitress to move away before he answered. The fresh perked aroma both energized and relaxed him for the unpleasant job ahead. "I didn't want you disturbed so I didn't mention you to the police. I found your name and address among Ike Paton's effects."

Daisy's brows knit together and she leaned in on her elbows. Her carefully manicured voice formed careful, measured words. "His effects? Just what is going on here Mister Jones?"

"I'm afraid your ex-husband is dead, Mrs. Sonneville." Hannibal dipped his head to push his dark glasses more firmly into place. "I'm sorry to tell you he was murdered yesterday. I know you're not regularly in contact with him but I just thought you should know. I barely knew Ike, or is it Pat?"

"Pat, please." Daisy sat back, her arms wrapped around herself. "He was Patrick Louis all his life until about a year ago. My first husband was a criminal, Mister Jones. My present husband doesn't know the kind of people I used to associate with. That's why I asked to meet you here. Pat and I have been divorced for seven years now. Seven years, but this still..." she swallowed, and apparently decided she had said enough. After a moment she said "Thank you for this. You didn't have to come here."

Hannibal smiled. "My woman insisted I tell you, and not over the phone. But if you don't mind my asking, you were still in contact? Usually when a woman remarries that ends that."

"I left Pat, Mister Jones, he didn't leave me. See, Pat was one of those men," she glared defiantly at Hannibal as another member of a dirty species, "who believed who he slept with had nothing to do with who he loved. I could put up with his gangster friends, an occasional slap, but not that. So I left, but he never stopped chasing me. Then about a year ago he wrote me from Atlantic City saying he had finally found the perfect business opportunity and he was about to get rich. I wrote back to tell him I wasn't interested. I guess this plan was as risky as everything else he ever did." Her voice dropped with her eyes. "I guess it finally caught up with him."

Hannibal subtly checked his watch. He had done the right thing, but he was burning daylight, Kyle's time. Still he hated to waste a possibility, so he would gamble two more minutes.

"Mrs. Sonneville, I'm involved in an investigation here in Baltimore and if you have a couple of minutes you might be able to save me some time."

"Sure," she smiled, seemingly relieved to change the subject.

"Have you ever heard of Jacob Mortimer?"

Her eyes rolled up the way people do when they're pretending to search their memories. "No, that name doesn't mean anything to me."

"How about Bobby Newton?"

"Nope, sorry."

"The Moonglow Club?"

"Sure," she said along with the first genuine smile she had given him. "It's over on Fells Point. Place has been there forever. I've got to get back to the University, but if you've got a notebook I can give you good directions."

"Great," Hannibal said, pulling a pad and pen from his inside jacket pocket. As he had guessed, a glimpse of his gun did not bother a woman who had lived with Ike Paton, AKA Patrick Louis. She wrote in a script as precise as her speech.

"Math department."

"What?" Daisy asked, looking up.

"I've been sitting here trying to decide what you teach at Maryland. I think math."

Daisy raised a small hand to cover her squeaky giggle. Her eyes flashed at him, almost but not quite flirting. "Mister Jones, that makes my day. I don't teach at Maryland. I'm a cleaning woman."

-10-

The door was open but the place was obviously closed. Hannibal and Ray walked into a dark cavern filled with dancing shadows bounced off the long mirror behind the bar. Chairs were turned up on tables, their legs thrust toward the ceiling. The odor of stale beer rose from the tables, the chairs, the floor itself.

Quick footsteps violated the silence of the sleeping club. The man stalking toward them wore a plaid jacket and pants that, incredibly, did not match. Wire framed aviator style glasses shielded his eyes. Even in the dark, Hannibal could see the blond thatch on his head was not all his own hair. The man was two or three inches shorter than Hannibal, but he looked his visitors up and down with a hard eye.

"Sunglasses, as dark as it is in here?" the man said. "You the police or the mob? Don't matter. Got no use for either of you. Get the hell out."

"Not a cop," Hannibal said, offering his card. "Not the mob. Name's Hannibal Jones. You the owner?"

"Quentin Moon," the man said, examining the card closely as if he expected it to yield additional information, some deeper meaning. "Yeah, I'm the owner. I'm also the manager, part time bartender, clean up boy, bouncer, chief cook and bottle washer."

"Mister Moon, I just need five minutes of your time."

"I'm kind of busy," Moon said, tucking Hannibal's card into his shirt pocket. "Hit the road, Jack."

Before he could say anything else, Hannibal felt a hand on his arm, then heard the door open and close behind him. He imagined Moon had a woman meeting him, which would explain his inhospitable welcome. But it was a man who brushed past Hannibal on his way in. A man who Hannibal thought looked like an eerie, white fun house mirror image of himself. He was taller and broader than Hannibal, and wore cheap sunglasses with his black suit. And, of course, Hannibal had a neck.

Never willing to miss a possible conflict, Hannibal followed the bigger man into the club, with Ray at his side. The new man glanced at Hannibal, then removed his own glasses and focused on Moon.

"You know why I'm here," the newcomer said. "You ain't paid."

"And I ain't going to," Moon bellowed back. "You think you scare me? You don't scare me. I been hustled by experts."

"Uh-huh." No Neck threw a hand around Moon's neck and put his weight behind a right hook into Moon's belly. Moon doubled into a ball and dropped to the floor. Hannibal looked back at the door, to see No Neck's backup grinning there, no gun drawn.

"Wait a minute man," Hannibal said, smiling like an old friend. "You going to shake the man down with me standing here?"

"You a cop?"

"No," Hannibal said, hands stretched wide.

"Then piss off." No Neck stiff-armed Hannibal hard enough to send him into the bar.

"You getting to be a problem, Moon," No Neck said, kicking Moon in the chest. "Last guy had this beat was too easy, but I ain't allowing no exceptions."

"Maybe just this one." Hannibal's words made No Neck turn. Hannibal's gloved fist raked across his jaw.

No Neck shook his head to clear it, and his lips spread into a broad grin. "You ain't got enough ass, stud."

No Neck raised his fists like a seasoned boxer and bounced a couple of crisp jabs off Hannibal's forearms. As he stepped in to deliver an overhand right, Hannibal sidestepped and whipped a front snap kick into his gut. His enemy grunted, so Hannibal kicked him again. Backup Man had not drawn yet. Good.

No Neck lowered his guard and Hannibal jerked the man's head back with a straight left. Dazed, No Neck charged, but Hannibal easily moved aside, pounding the back of his head as he went by. When No Neck wheeled around, Hannibal put an uppercut through his guard. It put the mob man on his butt.

Now Backup Man reached to his waistband, but Hannibal filled his own left fist with automatic first. "Don't," he said. "I'd have to kill you, then your partner. Why don't you just come help him to his feet?"

When Backup Man came near, Ray slapped his head and took his gun. Then Hannibal motioned to him to help No Neck up.

"Now, I don't know either of you, and I don't want to know you," Hannibal said. "But I want you to know me. Call your friends down in DC and ask them who Hannibal Jones is. Then cross this place off your list, understand? Because, my friend, if I have to come all the way back up here to talk to you, I will seriously fuck you up. Understand?"

The action had taken less than two minutes. Hannibal was not even breathing hard. After the two shakedown artists backed out of the room, Hannibal put his gun away. Moon regained his feet, using the bar for balance. His breathing was deep but ragged.

"Now, five minutes of your time?" Hannibal asked as if the unpleasant interruption had not happened.

"You kidding? After that, you can have all the time you want. Come back to my office."

Quentin Moon's office was brightly lit and colorfully decorated. Money was scattered across his desk, mixed in with cash register receipts and small notes, probably IOU's. Moon lurched to his chair and waved Hannibal and Ray to two others.

"Those bent nose types been hassling me since I opened the place twenty years ago," Moon said. "They come around every so often to slap me around. I learned long ago that if you say no and stick to it, they eventually decide you ain't worth the hassle. But thanks for saving me some lumps."

"My pleasure," Hannibal said, his eyes following Moon across the floor. "So this was your place from the beginning?"

"You got it," Moon said, returning with three beers and glasses. He handed Samuel Addams bottles to his guests, keeping a Miller Lite for himself.

Hannibal shared a smile with Ray while they opened and poured their brews. "So, Quentin, do you remember a kid named Bobby Newton?"

"Do I?" Moon pulled an Alka Seltzer packet out of his desk drawer and dropped the tablets into his beer. "That kid made me more money than anybody I ever had in the club, before or since. Everybody was looking for the new Al Green, and I had him right here in my place, three times a week for eight months. He had the soul, man, but when he wanted to, he could turn around and be as funky as Sly."

Moon's eyes drifted into the past while his beer threatened to boil over. The fizzing sound dominated the room for a moment. Abruptly he grabbed his glass and swallowed half its contents. Hannibal turned his head to hide his disgust.

"I know it's been a long time, but his family's lost track of him and I'm trying to find him. Did you know him well enough to have an idea where he went?"

"Hey, I knew Bobby pretty well," Moon said, starting to search through a set of cabinets on the far side of his office. "Went over to his pad lots of times. Sat and listened to records and got high with him and his wife."

"Wife?" Hannibal and Ray exchanged another stunned look. "Camille?"

"Who?" Moon asked. "No, her name was Barbie. Here, check this out." He produced a rolled up poster. When he spread it against the closed cabinet door it revealed a four foot tall photo of "Bobby Newton", now playing at the Moonglow. He looked so happy, so free, Hannibal understood why he chose to leave the life his father provided to make one for himself.

"Barbie was half black, half Latin?" Hannibal asked.

"Yeah, that's the girl," Moon said, laying the poster on his desk. "She really loved him. Never missed a show at the club."

It made sense, Hannibal thought. A guy who would call himself Bobby Newton would call a girl named Barbie by the nickname Dolly. He was getting a picture of this kid as a sharp, rebellious, witty, talented guy. He could go anywhere.

"Did they ever talk about moving on to bigger things?"

"Not seriously," Moon said, pouring the rest of his beer into his glass. "I don't think fame and fortune was his thing. Bobby already had money from somewhere. More than I could pay him, that's for sure. Besides, they were having too much fun here. I tell you, Barbie loved to watch him work on stage. They even hired a maid. The theory was, she would clean and help out while Barbie was pregnant, but after little Angela was born, she took care of her so Barbie could be here at the club when he was on."

Hannibal emptied his glass and leaned forward in his chair to watch Moon's eyes closely. "And where is Mister Bobby Newton now?"

Moon tipped his glass up too, then thumped it down on his desk. "Damned if I know. One night he just didn't show up. The crowd was pretty pissed off, I'll tell you. No call or anything. So I jumped in the jalopy and got on over there. Gone, the whole lot of them. Landlord, neighbors, nobody knew nothing." Moon's cheerful demeanor dipped then, his eyes cast down at the poster's face. "You know, I thought we were friends. I mean, I know it was a tough time for the black white thing, but I thought we were friends. But he never said a word. Just vanished without a trace."

Hannibal stood. "Nobody vanishes without a trace, Mister Moon. Everybody has to be somewhere. Laws of physics. If I can find some old neighbors or the landlord, there's still a chance. Think you can find his old address?"

Moon appeared near tears as he pulled a note pad and pencil from under the traitorous poster. "I don't need to find it. I know it like my own address. Here,

64

and good luck. And if you find him," Moon looked up with reddened eyes, "would you tell him some of his old friends would like to hear from him?"

The afternoon sun stabbed Hannibal's eyes as they drove west down Orleans Street. They had the windows down to take advantage of the Spring breeze. The light wind carried with it the sounds of a series of boom boxes they passed. The effect was like being in a car with a driver who constantly changes the radio station. It also brought the intriguing smells of an endless series of dinners being started. Southern food, soul food, fried food and, once in a while, the tangy scent of barbecue.

"You sure you don't need a map?" Hannibal asked from the back seat.

"Hannibal, I been driving a cab in this area for years. I know Baltimore as well as I know Washington. It ain't far."

"Okay," Hannibal said, clenching his teeth against the thump of a pothole every bit as deep as any in DC. "I guess I expected him to be a bit more upscale."

"Sorry," Ray called from the front, lighting another smoke. "Once you pass Johns Hopkins it's downhill from there. I don't know, makes sense to me. The kid wanted to get as far away from his father's world as he could, right? Join the revolution, get with the real people. He'd go looking for a real neighborhood."

It made sense to Hannibal too. And unless much had changed in eighteen years, Jacob Mortimer had found what he was looking for. Hannibal could almost hear the income level drop as Orleans became Franklin Street. By the time Franklin turned into Edmonson, he felt right at home. This could be Anacostia, his neighborhood. Same people, same buildings, same sparse trees trying to survive at the edge of the sidewalk.

Ray turned a corner, then another, and Hannibal watched a kid exchange money for drugs with an even younger boy. Now every face he saw was darker than his own and the limo was getting hard looks from some of the passersby.

"Uh Oh," Ray said, and Hannibal sat forward, looking around for trouble. He did not see anyone nearby who looked like a threat, so he checked the dashboard. Plenty of gas. No warning lights. But Ray was pulling over to the curb so maybe something was happening to the car.

"What is it?"

"Nothing wrong up here," Ray said, "But I think you got a problem. We're here."

Hannibal checked the street number against the piece of paper he got from Moon. This was Jake Mortimer's last known address. A four-story apartment building in the middle of a block of row houses. He had lived on the first, which was now the only floor completely intact. The place was unoccupied. Large signs on the door and the boards over the front windows declared this building condemned.

-11-

TUESDAY

When a clerk unlocked the door to the Baltimore Hall of Records at eight-thirty Tuesday morning, Hannibal and Ray walked in. Once inside, Hannibal knew which desk he wanted. The woman behind it looked like every librarian in a nineteen fifties film, complete with glasses and her hair with a bun on the back of her head. Before asking for any help, he offered her his private investigator's license and removed his Oakleys. She read it, compared the photo to his face, and returned it to him.

"I'm trying to verify birth records for an estate case," he said. "The girl in question was born in Baltimore seventeen years ago. Are those birth records computerized yet?"

"Afraid not," the clerk replied. "I think they're on microfiche, but they might still just be paper records. We could find that birth certificate for you in ten business days, but since you're a licensed investigator and all, if you're in a real hurry..."

"Yes," he smiled. "If you'll just point me in the right direction, my assistant and I will get started."

Two minutes later Hannibal and Ray were seated at adjoining microfiche readers, poring over poorly organized copies of every birth certificate filed in the state of Maryland.

"I was up too early for this, Chico," Ray said.

"That's why I turned in early," Hannibal said, working to bring his reader into focus. "I knew we'd be fighting rush hour and I wanted to be here when they opened. Don't forget, Kyle's clock is ticking and I want to report some progress to him today."

"Speaking of reporting, did you call Cindy last night? She told me she's involved with the case."

Hannibal never looked up from his search, lapsing into the tunnel vision he knew often led to success. "No, I never got the chance to call."

* * * * *

Cindy paid the cab driver, one of her father's employees, and charged up the stairs in front of Hannibal's building. With his car missing, she had no way of knowing if he was home, but she hoped to catch him before he went out.

She wore her rust colored skirt suit today, because she would be in court and this suit had always been lucky for her. She never heard from Hannibal last night and she did not want to go all day without seeing him. He sometimes had tunnel vision when he was on a case, and he could forget all about their relationship. She hoped they could have breakfast together before they started their respective busy days.

She found the outer door locked. Unusual, but not unheard of this early in the morning. She fished a key out of her small clutch purse and let herself in. Then a walk down the hall on the left brought her to Hannibal's living room door. This time she let herself in through an unlocked door. The living room was empty, but she could hear water running in the kitchen at the back of the house. Good, she was in time. She loved to surprise him.

But her cheerful hello froze in her throat as she walked into the kitchen. A woman stood at the sink, wiping a plate. A tall, slim, beautiful woman with fabulous legs. Cindy could evaluate her body objectively, because she had on a skirt tighter and shorter than anything Cindy would attempt, and the tube top left little to the imagination. She was very dark, with naturally straight black hair. When she turned, her eyes flashed defensively. Possessively?

"What are you doing here?"

"I think that's my question," Cindy said in her courtroom voice. "Who the hell are you?"

"Name's Jewel," the tall woman said, wiping her hands. "Sorry, I wasn't expecting anybody else. Just thought I'd straighten up after breakfast for Hannibal. When he told me I could stay here he didn't mention any other girls." She gave Cindy an appraising look up and down, almost the way a man would. It made Cindy vaguely uncomfortable. "I don't recognize you. You from around here?"

Cindy wanted to sink her fingernails into this woman's deep, alluring eyes, but instead she dug them into her palms. "No, I'm not. And I'm not staying. Looks like you've got everything covered here."

Except the cleavage, she thought as she turned to leave. She always thought Hannibal liked girls with bigger breasts.

"I got it!" Hannibal tapped both fists on the table, grinning like a kid. "This has got to be it."

"Is it the right year?" Ray asked, getting up to look over Hannibal's shoulder.

"Yeah, but even if it wasn't, I'd stick with this," Hannibal said, triggering the printer. "Check out the name. Angela Davis Newton."

"This guy really was a black power freak," Ray said. "Angela Davis was a Black Panther supporter who took a shot at the presidency in nineteen sixty-eight. Just about the only woman of any influence in the movement."

"He really had to dig to find a female name," Hannibal said. "Born to Bobby Newton and Barbara Robinson. He changed his name, but he wasn't going to pretend they were married. Interesting guy."

Ray reflected Hannibal's triumphant smile for a moment, then his face slowly dropped. "This is great and all," he said, "but how does it get us any closer to finding this interesting guy?"

Hannibal pointed, as if Ray could see what he was reading under the microfiche reader. "Just read a little lower. See, the birth certificate includes the hospital, in this case Johns Hopkins, and the doctor's name. Raymond Cummings." Hannibal looked up at Ray's still puzzled face. "The doctor who provided Barbie's prenatal care probably got to know them pretty well. I can find him with a phone call, if he's still practicing, and we can find out what he remembers about our retro couple."

* * * * *

Some white people, Hannibal observed, shrank as they aged. Doctor Raymond Cummings looked like he had a slow leak, and most of the air had escaped his body over the years. His stoop shouldered form supported a head which reminded Hannibal of a dried apple, but his cloud of white hair, beard and mustache

70

gave him a vaguely Mark Twain look. The white lab coat and skeptical expression did not help.

"Sorry I couldn't see you right away, Mister Jones," Cummings said. "I have a rather busy practice and I can't just put these people off to talk to some private eye."

"No problem at all," Hannibal said. Actually it had been four infuriating hours of pacing and watch checking. And there was not a legal parking space within three blocks of the professional building Cummings kept his office in, so Ray stayed downstairs in the car. Hannibal was not sure if this guy was really that busy or if he just did not want to look too available, but he had to make him know this was not a casual visit.

"Doctor, I need your help," Hannibal began, choosing his approach as he went. The waiting room was small and Hannibal knew he could hold the doctor's attention if he placed the words in the right order. "I'm on a missing person's case, and I don't imagine such things usually interest you much. But you need to understand that my client is a seventeen year old boy with chronic myelogenous leukemia. You know how rare that is?"

"Indeed." Cummings sat at the small desk, his knees inches from Hannibal's. "That form usually attacks older people. Is he responding to treatment?"

Hannibal closed his eyes behind his glasses and trotted out all the medical mumbo jumbo he had memorized. "Radiation therapy has proven fruitless. Chemotherapy has helped but that approach has run its course. According to Doctor Lippincott in Washington, my client's only hope, is allogeneic bone marrow transplantation."

Cummings was no stupid man. Hannibal could see in his eyes he was putting the story together for himself. "I know Lippincott. Good man, and better with cancers than this old GP. So, hence the search. The missing person is a close relative, a possible lymphocytic match. An old client of mine I assume, a clue to whose whereabouts may be found in my records. Is that correct?"

Hannibal nodded. "My client's father was known as Bobby Newton. In fact, his name was Jacob Mortimer. Does either of those names mean anything to you, Doctor?"

Cummings stood up, taking such a deep breath, it temporarily inflated him. He nodded a couple of times, then shook his head side to side a few times. He chuckled silently, his shoulders shaking. He said "Oh my" and walked to the wall. Hannibal waited quietly for the payoff.

"Yes, I remember Bobby Newton," Cummings said at last. "He seemed a fine young man when I knew him, loving, attentive to his woman. You've done quite a job of detecting, tracing Bobby to me. But I'm afraid your client has gotten out ahead of you."

"Excuse me?"

Cummings broke into a genuine laugh. "Angela was here two days ago looking for a clue to put her on her father's trail. Of course, she didn't weave as fanciful a story as you have. Quite creative, really, and you did your research well."

While Cummings laughed, Hannibal stood up, trying to take it all in. "Angela? The daughter was here? How did she find you?"

"Oh, I imagine the same way you did. She found my name on her birth certificate."

"Doctor, the laugh here is on you I think," Hannibal said. "Bobby Newton was married before you knew him, to another woman. It's his son by that marriage I'm trying to help."

Cummings sobered somewhat. "Young man, if you're looking for Mister Newton for someone else, I'm really sorry for you. Angela has a right to find her family and I wish her the best. But if you've another motive..."

"You don't believe me." Hannibal made it a simple statement. No problem. He pulled his flip phone and began pushing buttons. "You said you knew Doctor Lippincott. Maybe he can convince you just how serious this is."

It did not take long. Hannibal exchanged a few words with Lippincott, then handed Cummings the telephone. Then he withdrew while the two physicians talked. It seemed unlikely any Mortimers knew about Jacob's extramarital daughter. Would the old man want to see his unknown granddaughter? And how would Camille react? Did he have the right to introduce her to her family? Or to steer her away? This was not what he was hired for, after all.

"I guess I'll have to believe you," Cummings said, interrupting Hannibal's introspection. "Sorry I doubted you, son."

"No problem," Hannibal said, accepting his phone back. "What can you tell me about Bobby Newton?"

"Not much, I'm afraid," Cummings said, sitting again. "I can just confirm much of what you already know. He treated his family well. I know he had money, but it probably wasn't really his. He showed me some collector coins once, but it seemed clear he didn't know what he had. Guess that's why he lived in such a slum. He was good to Barbie, but someone before him had not been. You know about the cigarette burns?"

"Afraid so," Hannibal said. "I know they disappeared together, but I don't have a handle on when."

"Well, let's see." Cummings fished a pipe out of a drawer but never lit it, probably in consideration of future patients. He merely chewed on the stem. "They had a cleaning woman, but she left a couple of weeks after Angela was born. I visited them once a month at the beginning, because Barbie had some problems. So, on my fourth visit, I pulled up and the building had been condemned. Probably should have been when they moved in, but the city is slow."

"You never heard from any of them again?" Hannibal asked.

"Sorry. They all just disappeared. Left owing me for a visit, too. Didn't think I'd ever see any of them again until Angela walked in here couple days ago."

"Guess the trail ends at that apartment," Hannibal said, standing. "Thanks for your time anyway, Doctor."

Cummings followed Hannibal to his outer office, then went to his reception desk. Two very pregnant women sat in plastic chairs, cradling impatient expressions. Hannibal had the door open when Cummings called to him.

"You know, if Angela will talk to you, you might not need to find her father." Hannibal turned, his eyebrows raised. "If all you say is true, she's as likely to be an HLA match as Bobby is."

* * * * *

At first, Sarge thought Jewel was having a heart attack. Her body trembled uncontrollably, her eyes locked straight ahead, and her mouth hung open but no sound came out. He followed her gaze out the front window and realized she was paralyzed with fear. Three black men climbed out of the Coupe deVille parked across the street. Two looked like professional football players in cheap casual clothes. The smallest man, the one with the scar over his left eye wore a leather jacket and handmade Italian loafers, and rolled a toothpick in his mouth. Not hard to guess who was who.

"Get in the kitchen, girl," Sarge said, "and push that button I showed you. I'll deal with this."

After three loud thumps on the outer door Sarge opened it. Floyd stood in the center of the stoop, flanked by his two lieutenants. Sarge smelled alcohol and too much cologne.

"Can I help you?" he asked, holding the door half open, his right hand hidden behind it.

"Hannibal Jones," Floyd said.

"I take it you're Floyd," Sarge said, swinging the door an inch wider. "This must be Joey and Lawrence, or vice versa. Sorry, fellows, Hannibal's not here right now, but whatever you're looking for, I figure I can handle it."

Floyd's expression turned to a scowl, and his followers rolled their shoulders trying to look menacing. Sarge kept his face calm and let his bat slide in his hand until he gripped it almost halfway up. He felt the tension, like when a drunk is about to take his problems out on the bartender.

"You got something in there belongs to me," Floyd said in movie gangster style.

"You need to read the papers," Sarge said, addressing Floyd and ignoring his backup men. "They abolished slavery in this country in eighteen sixty-three." Then he turned to the man on the right. "Hannibal do that to your nose? That's nasty, man."

Joey kicked the door open and stepped in with one smooth motion. Only the bouncer's well developed sixth sense for sucker punches got Sarge back out of the way of the swinging door. Joey was a bit bigger than Sarge, but that only counts in the ring. Sarge brought his bat in and down at an angle. Not a hard blow, but Joey's knee went out and he bellowed as he fell. Lawrence dove in behind him, but Sarge drove the head of his bat forward into his midsection, drawing a loud grunt. Sarge had time to see that Lawrence's face was already twisted in pain just before he smashed a fist across the bodyguard's jaw.

"That's enough," Floyd shouted, stepping inside. His gun was already in his hand. Sarge dropped back onto the center staircase. He noticed how different this one was from the other two. Joey and Lawrence were tough, even nasty, but this one was mean. It showed in his eyes as he waved his pistol in Sarge's face. He would not like using a gun because it was not personal enough, not cruel enough.

"Now," Floyd said, as if he had to get Sarge's attention, "Now you get that narrow-assed bitch out here before I blow your fucking face off. The bitch belongs to me."

"Nuh-uh." A new voice floated down the stairs and Floyd looked up in surprise. Sarge knew what he would see. A tall, white guy with thinning, short cropped hair, an angular face, and a Remington pump scatter-gun sitting on the top step.

"Quaker up there, he won't much mind splattering you all over the hall here," Sarge said, getting slowly to his feet. "Me, I hate to have to clean up a mess like that. So why don't you put that pea shooter away and take your friends and get the hell out of here?"

Hatred flared from Floyd's eyes. "You a dead man," he told Sarge.

"We can end this now," Quaker said, his lanky form bouncing down the stairs in his jerky gait. "You're a trespasser. I could blow all three of you away."

"That would be murder."

Quaker reached the bottom step and pushed the muzzle of his shotgun to within five inches of Floyd's face. "Sucks, don't it?"

Sarge pulled the door wide. "Go, man, before Quaker gets too nervous." Quaker gave a maniacal smile and Floyd signaled his bodyguards. The three backed out the door. Sarge and Quaker watched closely until their car pulled away.

"You know," Sarge said, "When Virgil wanted to put that intercom in between the apartments I thought he was nuts. Not now."

"Yeah," Quaker said, closing the door, "Neat, ain't it?"

* * * * *

Hannibal watched a group of boys playing half a block away as the limousine pulled to the curb. Ray was not happy about returning to Edmundson Village, and Hannibal knew part of his feelings came from concern for his limo. Ray's limousine service and taxi company was new, and like any young business, its profit margin was razor thin. Hannibal shared his concern, since he helped finance the business.

But Hannibal felt he knew those young men playing cops and robbers down the street. They had no reason to attack this car, or any other foreign intruder, as long as it did nothing to disturb them.

"Well, here we are again," Ray said, flicking his cigarette out the window. "The place has been condemned for almost seventeen years. Nobody's been here since that long, including Bobby, or Jake, or whatever he called himself. Everybody says he just disappeared."

Hannibal popped his door open. "I told you, nobody vanishes without a trace. You never know what might give you a clue where somebody is. A matchbook, piece of letterhead paper, even an envelope with a return address. Odds are nobody's cleaned up in there."

Hannibal handed Ray one of the long handled flashlights he picked up on their way and headed for the house. Ornate sandstone banisters climbed up either side of the wide steps leading into Jacob Mortimer's old apartment building. Hannibal thought the building must have been beautiful when it was new, the kind of classy brownstone home that upper class genteel urbanites lived in half a century ago. Long before some enterprising soul figured out there was money to be made by housing a dozen families in what was once a single family dwelling.

The door was nailed shut, but one hard yank wrenched it open. Nails squealed as they pulled loose, and the smell of the tomb belched out at them. Ray stared into the shadows dubiously.

"You know, Chico, what Doctor Cummings said about Jake having another daughter that could make this whole thing pointless."

"Maybe," Hannibal said stepping into the apartment house. "But I don't trust that kind of coincidence. The missing heir routine is one of the oldest and most popular scams, because families in search of long lost relatives want to believe. They don't question things closely."

"But Jacob Mortimer was cut out of his father's will," Ray said, while looking through the kitchen.

"He was," Hannibal said, sweeping bits of paper and dirt from under a ragged couch, "but do you really think a previously unknown granddaughter would be?"

Hannibal and Ray looked under every piece of worn furniture, and opened every drawer and cabinet. They searched the crumbling wallpaper for written notes. Hannibal looked inside the toilet tank and the medicine cabinet. With Ray's help, he dragged the moldy bedroom rug aside.

"Look at that stain," Ray said, shining his light on a shapeless blotch on the linoleum. "It could be blood, eh?"

"Sure," Hannibal said, "or Kool-aid. I don't think there's anything here, Pizo. I'm going to check downstairs."

"Downstairs? What the hell for?"

"Because," Hannibal said on his way, "people hide things in the cellar."

Narrow, street level windows actually made the cellar brighter than the rooms upstairs with their boarded up windows. The sound of scurrying rats made Hannibal move slowly. They would not attack, he knew, but he would hate to surprise one. The space had cement walls and a dirt floor, with an ancient boiler in one corner which was converted from coal to oil in some distant past. Stacks of boxes occupied him for a few minutes, until he realized he was alone.

"Ray?"

"Right here, Hannibal. Top of the stairs."

Hannibal smiled and continued his search. The boxes in the far corner turned out to be empty. The air was so still he could smell cardboard rotting. When he moved the last box he saw the dirt was not as smooth as elsewhere in the cellar. Something had been buried here. Irrational hope swelled his heart. If he left in a great hurry, Bobby Newton might have left something of real value here, planning to return later.

"Ray, I think I got something here."

Something was sticking up out of the ground less than a foot from a partially buried cinderblock. He dropped to his knees to examine his discovery before touching it. It was a straight piece of metal, only two inches showing above the ground. A pipe? No. The handle of a knife. Actually, the tang, with the wooden handle rotted away.

Not wanting to disturb his finding, Hannibal began brushing dirt away from the area, like an archeologist who does not want to disturb whatever artifacts he may find. Only after considerable digging did he begin to see what he was uncovering.

"Oh my God."

Ray went down the stairs to stand behind Hannibal. While Ray held his flashlight, Hannibal brushed dirt away with his hands, revealing rotting cloth over a pair of parallel bones. They were ribs, and the knife was standing between them.

"What have you found?" Ray asked, almost hysterically.

Hannibal considered the cinderblock's placement, right where the head would have been. "Found? I guess I've found a trace."

-12-

Hannibal hated to be in the middle of a scene. Years of training in the Secret Service made low profile his natural mode of operation. Yet he and Ray stood in the middle of the kind of scene that made neighborhoods like Edmundson Village very nervous. A pair of blue and whites sat parked on either side of the street in front of the condemned building, sirens off but bubble lights revolving. Policemen swarmed around the sidewalk and front stoop-like blue yellow jackets at the outhouse door. Two suits leaned against their unmarked car, pretending to direct the investigation. A police forensic van pulled up. Two men and a woman in white lab coats got out, looked around as if to orient themselves, and headed into the house. A few women in mules and housecoats gathered to watch the show, but Hannibal knew most of the people in this area would rather not draw the attention of the police.

The sun hanging directly overhead reminded Hannibal how much he had done before noon. He was tired way too soon and getting hungry besides. He bent to brush dirt off his knees and when he looked up, another unmarked car skidded to a stop in the street. A door popped open and the car disgorged a blob of fatback wrapped in a gray suit. The detective's deep brown skin was stuffed almost to bursting, but he managed to waddle over to Hannibal and glower.

"You Jones? Guy who made the call?"

"Glad to meet you," Hannibal said, watching the light glinting off the man's bald head. "Yes, I'm Hannibal Jones and I'll bet you're the detective in charge."

"Terry Dalton," the detective said, not offering a hand. "Yeah, this is my hassle. Now what the hell were you doing poking around in an abandoned building this morning?"

Hannibal stepped down from the sidewalk to the street to even their heights. While he spoke, he displayed his investigator's license. "Working a missing persons, and I might have found him."

Dalton pulled out a cigarette and touched the flame of a disposable lighter to it. "How nice for you. You any idea how much work this makes. People got to poke through that place, pull in every bit of bone. Then the identification process. Got to bounce this against every disappearance and murder in this area in the last thirty years."

"I might be able to save you some time," Hannibal said. He was walking toward the limo and Ray was already at the wheel. "After I called the cops, I called my client, Gabriel Nieswand. He's a high-powered lawyer. By now he's probably got the paperwork through to get those remains DNA tested. I don't understand it all, but they've got to compare the DNA in these bones to a known reference sample. They found some of the missing man's hair in a comb his widow never got around to throwing out. That ought to pin him down."

"So you're helpful, eh?" Dalton said. "Well, that's good. Drag your ass down to the station. Got a few questions for you, so I can finish my report."

"I'll be down later," Hannibal said, pulling his car door open. "Hot leads to follow up on, and all that." Before Dalton could say another word, Hannibal slammed the door and Ray popped the clutch. The limo's engine gave a deep, throaty roar and it charged down the street.

Two blocks later, Ray stared into his rear view mirror and asked "Where to, Hannibal? I mean, I could see you wanted to get out of there, but I didn't know what was next, you know?"

Hannibal pulled his flip phone out of his jacket. "Next, I need to get hold of Doc Cummings. I want to know where Angela the mystery girl hangs out."

Quentin Moon jumped as if shot when Hannibal burst into his office. As the door slammed the wall behind him, Hannibal marched across the small room and planted his fists on Moon's desk. Moon shrank backward in direct reflection of Hannibal leaning forward.

"I need you to come to a late lunch with me," Hannibal said, a little louder than he meant to. Moon sat silent, as if he thought speaking might somehow drive Hannibal over the edge. His radio played Oldies 100 softly behind him, reminding Hannibal that Moon lived largely in the past. Moving slowly to relax the other man, Hannibal dragged a chair to the front of the desk and sat down.

"Look, Moon, I just left the police," Hannibal said in slow, calming tones. "I think I may have found Bobby Newton. At least what's left of him. He may have been buried in the basement of that building he lived in. They're testing what's left to confirm his identity. But another possibility has appeared and I think you should see it."

The little restaurant was within five blocks of Moon's own club, still well inside the area known as Fells Point. The decor was outdoor olive garden, with murals painted realistically enough to convince urban diners they were in Italy, at least for a little while. It was not very big, but they arrived behind the lunch rush and had no trouble getting a table. The aroma of homemade sauces tugged at Hannibal's stomach. He and Ray flanked Moon at a small table. He had followed reluctantly, numbed by Hannibal's words. Now he was slowly absorbing all of what Hannibal said. "You think Bobby is dead?"

"Right now, all I've got is a stack of bones," Hannibal said. "But I'll bet it's Bobby, or else Bobby's the killer and that's why he ran. The police have the bones, and my client's lawyer, Gabe Nieswand, is getting tests done to find out if it's him."

"Bobby was no killer," Moon said, staring over a menu. "But I'd hate to think he was murdered. In fact, I don't want to think about it at all. Why'd you bring me here?"

"You know a doctor named Cummings?" Hannibal asked, sipping his water.

"Nope."

"He sent me here," Hannibal said, waving a finger at a waitress. "He got a visit from somebody you might know a couple of weeks ago. She works here now and I wanted you to meet her."

The hard part, Hannibal knew, would be to sit quiet and watch. The waitress reached their table and asked for their orders. Hannibal thought Moon's eyes would drop to the table. She was indeed beautiful. A black girl, no darker than Hannibal and not quite out of her teens. Dark brown, wavy hair hung to her shoulders. Her lips were full, and her chin aggressive, but her nose was thin, almost pointed.

"The Alfred special looks awfully good," Hannibal said. "I think we'll all have that. And pick us out a bottle of wine, would you?"

She graced him with a smile. Her eyes were very bright, her teeth very even and very white. When she walked away, Moon blinked and returned to motion, as if waking from a long coma.

"It's the little girl, isn't it?" Moon whispered. "What was her name?"

"Angela," Hannibal said.

On Moon's face, shock wrestled with hysterical joy for dominance. "God, she looks just like Bobby. Well, a little lighter skinned, but the resemblance is amazing. Jones, that has got to be his daughter."

Ray, usually the opposite of the typical talkative cabby, tapped Hannibal's shoulder. "Looks like the girl's the real thing. So what now? You going to hand her to Mortimer?"

"You think they'll want to meet her?" Hannibal asked.

"You think she'll want to meet them?"

Before Hannibal could answer, Angela returned with their meals. She politely placed their plates before them, clearly trying to ignore Moon's stare. Finished serving, she hung beside the table for a moment in apparent indecision. Speaking up might cost her a tip, but Hannibal thought he knew what a person of character would do. To his unexpected pleasure, she did.

"Is there a problem, sir?" Angela's light brown eyes were like lasers, tunneling into Moon's face.

Physically slight, her body language said she was nonetheless ready for trouble.

After a brief pause, Moon's face slid into a crooked smile of reminiscence. "I believe I knew your father, Angela."

"My father?" She took one long step back. "You from Texas? You knew Sam Briggs?" Hannibal had to admit her accent was at least authentic Tex-Mex. Her voice was the surest giveaway to the Latin side of her ancestry.

"Briggs?" Moon repeated. An invisible weight had caved in part of his face. "Texas? No, no your name's not Briggs. I mean your real father. You're Angela Newton from right here in Baltimore."

While Moon talked, Angela took three small steps backward, then moved forward the same distance. Her face reflected shock, hope, disbelief and joy all at once. Hannibal was a natural skeptic, but could anyone be this good an actress?

"What makes you think, I mean, how do you know this?" Her hands moved in small, opposing outward circles, and her vocal pitch was out of control. Her eyes begged for confirmation. Moon leaned forward, working at sounding sincere.

"Your name is Angela Davis Newton. Your father was a soul singer who used to work at my club. Your mother was a beautiful Spanish girl, small and thin like you. I used to visit your folks in an apartment across town. I actually bounced you on my knee. They were a family full of love, your parents and the blond girl they had there to be your nurse."

Hannibal was paying more attention to Angela's face than Moon's babble, but a few words got through. He turned his lenses on Moon, gripping his arm to get his attention.

"Blond? Bobby Newton's cleaning woman was white?"

"I didn't say she was white," Moon said, percolating a chuckle up from his throat. "This was a black woman, but a natural blond, right down to her roots. You don't forget a thing like that."

-13-

Hannibal had seen this police station before, in every old movie he watched growing up. His mother loved Edward G. Robinson, Jimmy Cagney and George Raft, and they always seemed to end up in a place like this. And she was fascinated by the gritty humanism of American policemen, so different from the cold efficiency of the German poletzei. Anything American was exotic to her, partly because she never managed to see America. Hannibal thought it a cruel tragedy that his father did not live long enough to show her his homeland.

A sergeant had seated Hannibal and Ray in a pair of plastic chairs outside Dalton's tiny, glass walled office. Lighting was dim in the room, and what there was got absorbed by dingy once-white walls and dark green floor tiles. Ray waited poorly, fidgeting and grumbling so much Hannibal finally asked him to explore the building to see if there was a snack bar or something.

As Ray stepped out of sight, Terry Dalton lurched up the hall from the other direction. He seemed less aggressive now. Dragging himself along, he looked as old as the building he worked in, and as run down. Continuous use and a lack of maintenance, Hannibal thought, the same as the building. Eventually both would be replaced by a newer model.

As Dalton moved past, he waved Hannibal behind him into his office. Hannibal followed, closing the door behind himself. Dalton got comfortable in his oversized wooden chair and lit a cigarette. The chair opposite the desk was only inches from it, so Hannibal turned it sideways and sat.

"Sorry it took me so long to get here," Hannibal said.

"No big thing," Dalton answered. "I'll be here until eight tonight. You, on the other hand, don't have to be. Your lawyer friend's got the remains. I got nothing. Why don't we do this the easy way and you tell me who the bones were."

Refreshing, Hannibal thought. A man who knows how to come to the point. "Deceased is probably the last resident of the first floor apartment. He disappeared about eighteen years ago. His name was Bobby Newton." Not exactly the truth, but not really a lie either. It was certainly the name on the lease.

"Could be," Dalton said, leaning forward to support himself on his elbows. "Our people said a quick test put those bones at close to twenty years old. That was a pretty rough area back then."

"Then?" Hannibal remarked without thinking. Dalton looked up and nailed him with a hard look, right through his dark glasses.

"Back then, a lot of people come up missing in Edmundson Village," Dalton said in a low, distant voice. "I was just a patrolman then, new, full of piss and vinegar. Every night there was shootings. Stabbings. Fights. Usually over drugs, or gambling, or women. Mostly in that little circle, five or six blocks around Killer's."

Dalton lapsed into silence, staring through Hannibal like a mechanical fortune teller after your

89

quarter runs out. Hannibal did not really want to put in another coin, but it was outside his nature to leave a story unfinished. He had to start the machine again, and he knew the price was to ask a question.

"Okay, so what was Killer's?"

"Just a bar a couple blocks from where you found the bones." Dalton shrugged and took a deep drag from his cigarette. The smoke burned Hannibal's nose and added to the bar room atmosphere in the small office. Then Dalton continued his story in a smoke roughened voice.

"The place was run by Vernon Nilson, a guy everybody called Killer. Like in lady killer, you know, but by the time I met him he'd already earned the nickname for real. Yep, Killer Nilson. Big nigger, must have been six-four or five. He disappeared too." Then Dalton gave a crooked smile. "Maybe that's old Killer you dug up. More likely he killed the John Doe and faded out."

Something tickled the back of Hannibal's mind. It seemed this case was staying within a narrow geographic area. Both cases, actually, the one he was paid to do and the other. He decided to gamble again.

"You ever hear of a tough guy named Pat Louis?"

Dalton's head whipped around in a double take. "You know Louis? He used to hang out with Nilson. In fact, I busted them together. That was a lot of years ago," he said. Did he miss those days? Did he imagine himself one of the latter day untouchables?

Then Dalton sat up and spun to his side, as if he suddenly remembered the reason for Hannibal's visit. He drew a typewriter table toward himself and ran a piece of paper into an ancient IBM Selectric. The typewriter let out a loud click when he turned it on.

"Anyway, I need a statement. Just tell me everything that happened after you got to the building your missing person used to live in. Now, first your full name." Dalton typed quickly with two fingers. He turned the paper up to the address line, but stopped there. "What the hell kind of a name is Hannibal anyway?"

"My folks wanted to name me after a great conquering general," Hannibal grinned. "Alexander was too common, I guess, and Germans don't think much of Napoleon."

"Germans?"

"Long story," Hannibal said.

When Hannibal stepped into the sun, he found Ray in the limo, dozing behind the wheel. He managed to open the door and climb into the back seat without waking his driver. After pulling off his shoes, he stretched his legs out on the white leather and pulled out his flip phone. After getting through a dispatcher, he managed to get Orson Rissik on the phone.

"Hey, I'm glad you called. We found your car."

"Alleluia!" Hannibal snapped a fist into the air. "Where was it?"

"He ran it out of gas on a side street in Pennsylvania. I've already had an officer drive it back here."

"You're a hell of a cop, Orson," Hannibal said. "What about the killer's own car?"

"Stolen too," Rissik said. There was a funny pause which made Hannibal tune in to the phone more closely. "In fact, he stole it from a guy in Baltimore," Rissik continued. "Funny thing, the car was never reported stolen until about half an hour before Paton's murder."

"I got something funnier for you," Hannibal said. "And I want you to remember I was cooperative with you, sharing what I got."

Hannibal could feel Rissik's smile over the phone. "Understood."

Sure was a pleasure dealing with a pro. "Ike Paton was really a hard case named Patrick Louis. Got a record up here and he was in the rackets."

"Thanks," Rissik said, and Hannibal could imagine him examining his own cards to see if he had anything Hannibal might want. When he finally spoke, he said, "You know, I was thinking you might like to meet the shooter again."

"You got that right."

"Well, I was going to ask the Baltimore cops to check out the owner of the getaway vehicle," Rissik said, "but our interagency cooperation isn't always what it could be, you know. Would you consider doing a Virginia cop a favor?"

Hannibal's grin broadened as he swung his feet back to the floor. "I think I've got a couple of hours to kill. If it would help you out, Detective Rissik, I'd be happy to check out the car's owner for you. Just give me his name and address."

Hannibal hit the disconnect button and immediately punched in another number from memory. He had called the offices of Nieswand and Balor earlier but he was not smiling this much when he spoke to the receptionist before. His heart always lifted when he asked to speak to Cynthia Santiago. He was humming an old soul ballad when she came on the line.

"Hello."

"Cindy, it's me," he said. "How's the day going?"

"I'm pretty busy right now."

Hannibal raised an eyebrow. "I see. Well, how about breaking away from all that. The cops tell me they found my car and it's drivable. Why don't you bring it up here and we can have dinner somewhere and you can help out on this case."

Long pause. "Why?"

"Why?" Hannibal was shaken. Did he forget a birthday or something? "Because I don't get to see enough of you when I'm on a case. And because I've got to ask somebody some questions and it would help to have an attorney on the scene." After a few seconds of silence, he said, "Cindy? You there?"

"Yes. Will this help Kyle?"

"I think it will help determine what happened to his father," Hannibal said. "If the DNA tests come out positive, I don't want to have to tell him his dad's dead but nobody knows how or why."

"Okay," she said as if agreeing to scrub the floor. "Tell me where we can meet."

* * * * *

Hannibal had ridden around Baltimore enough to feel he was overdue finding the good side of town. As they approached Wallace Lerner's home, he could see this was not it. Considering the worldwide reputation earned by Johns Hopkins University, he hoped the area around it would be ivy covered and tree laden. No such luck. The neighborhood surrounding the University was better than Edmundson Village, but not by a whole lot. Still, Lerner owned the car Hannibal's skull had been slammed into, so this was where Hannibal had to go. Lerner lived in a large apartment building which, Hannibal guessed, probably housed quite a few students as well. As Ray pulled to the curb, Hannibal leaned over the seat.

"Need to ask you to wait outside on this one, buddy. If the killer's in there and I flush him out, I'll call you on the car phone. I might need you to follow him."

"No sweat, Chico," Ray said. "I ain't exactly inconspicuous in this thing, but who'd expect a limousine to be following them, eh?"

On his way up the stairs, Hannibal felt a brief twinge of guilt. Was he letting Kyle down by taking this detour away from the search for the boy's father? He had to admit he was on a purely selfish mission at the time, chasing a murderer who made the mistake of pounding his own skull, frightening his woman and stealing his car.

Still, most of the normal world would be going home from work in an hour or so. And he had already accomplished a lot. He had certainly earned his fee for this day. Nieswand told him a definitive DNA match on the skeletal remains would take about twenty-four hours. Until then, he had no way of knowing if his job was already done.

The hallway was narrow and dark and filled with a vague scent of mildew and unwashed bodies. At the right door, he positioned himself so his face would show through the tiny security viewer before he knocked.

"Yeah, it's open." The woman's voice carried a sleepy Jamaican twang. Hannibal turned the knob and stepped into a small, narrow apartment decorated in early eclectic. The coffee table displayed racing forms instead of books or newspapers. The old Formica table by the kitchenette was half covered by cans and boxes of groceries no one bothered to put away. A pair of cows held salt and pepper.

"Well, come on," the woman called from the bedroom. The same linoleum covered the entire apartment floor and Hannibal crossed it to the half open bedroom door. The woman on the unmade bed never looked up from her soap opera.

"You looking for Wally?"

"Yes, I need to see him," Hannibal said.

"Well, he ain't here." She stared into a thirteen inch screen on a rolling cart in the corner. She had the type of body women usually pay for these days. Breasts too round to be real almost spilled out the top of the man's shirt she wore. Perfect bronze legs grew out the bottom of the shirt, with no evidence for or against her having anything on underneath. Hannibal figured her for late thirties with a pretty but calculating face and hair too light for auburn but definitely reddish.

"Guess I'll wait." Hannibal's words made her look up. Her smile grew slowly, sincere but crooked.

"Well, hi," she said, sitting up. "I'm Ginger." Yes, Hannibal thought, that was the color.

"Hannibal Jones," he said with a nod. "I'll just have a seat on the couch."

Ginger Lerner stood up, thrusting her chest forward as if she had no choice, and swung toward the bedroom door with the exaggerated sway of a Las Vegas showgirl. "You don't look like any of Wally's other friends. Want a drink?" Without waiting for an answer, she brushed past Hannibal to the kitchenette, where she expertly mixed two gin and tonics.

"I don't know him well," Hannibal said. "I had something I needed to store in a safe place, so..."

"You gave it to Wally?" She gave a melodic laugh and carried the drinks to the table. By sitting behind one, she left Hannibal no reasonable choice but to join her.

"Actually, I put it in the trunk of his car," he said, dropping into the kitchen chair. "I don't really need Wally, just need to know where the car is."

Ginger sipped her drink and sighed provocatively. "That might be tough. Take them cheaters off for a minute, would you?"

"Why tough?" he asked, sliding his glasses off. Ginger made a sound like she was tasting something delicious and the tip of her tongue slowly cleaned her top lip and disappeared. "Why tough?" Hannibal repeated.

"Because Mister Rocket Science loaned the car to his brother Sloan."

"Bad idea?" Hannibal asked.

"Mister, his name's Sloan but most folks call him Slo. Slo Lerner, get it?" She swallowed half her drink, exposing her long neck and most of the rounded treasures beneath it.

"And where can I find Slo?" he asked.

"Who the hell knows?" Her feet found his and started playing games. "He's got a place in town but he's never there. Sure wish we weren't here. We only moved down here from Jersey on account of his boss sent him to work this territory. Wally's too damn loyal." Obviously Wally's wife had no such problem. She leaned in close, using eye contact and a hand on his arm to make sure Hannibal did not miss her message.

"In that case, when's Wally due back?"

"Who knows," she said, but her tone of voice said "who cares" and her breathing deepened as if she had just thought of something quite exhilarating. She stood up, stepped forward and slid one leg between Hannibal's as far as the chair would allow. "You know," she said, placing a hand gently on his neck, "I don't work much these days, but I could be persuaded to make an exception in your case."

The door swung open and all the tenderness drained out of her, but the fire remained.

"Sorry, Ginger," the man at the door said. "You didn't tell me you were having company today."

"Just get the hell out of here, Wally," she snapped, the way an older sister might talk to an intruding baby brother.

"Wait right there, Wally," Hannibal said, standing and moving toward the door in one fluid motion. Wally tried to close the door with himself on the outside, but he was too slow. Hannibal had his sleeve before the door hit his arm. With a hard yank, he pulled Wally Lerner back through the door and flung him onto the imitation leather couch.

Lerner was a little black mouse with marbles for eyes which darted left and right, but never lingered anywhere for long. He was obviously scared, which made Hannibal happy. Frightened people told you what you needed to know.

"Where's your brother, Wally?" Hannibal asked, pushing his glasses back into place. "I want Sloan and I want him now. He's in a lot of trouble and so are you if you don't talk to me."

"Oh God. What's that idiot done now?" Lerner tried to shove himself into a corner of the couch.

"He murdered a man," Hannibal said, using his Treasury Agent voice. Secret Service agents, like FBI agents and U.S. Marshals, learn a speech pattern calculated to make uncooperative people cooperate. When he turned in his badge, Hannibal did not leave anything he learned in federal service behind. "He murdered a man and he used your car to do it. And I know he had it with your permission. If I don't find him in a hell of a hurry, all the shit falls on you."

"Oh God, you got to believe me," Wally whined. "I don't know where Slo is. I been out looking for him all day. Nobody's seen him. I figured he must have gone back up north. You got to tell Zack I got no idea where he went or what he did."

Ginger stalked forward, her anger still focused down on Wally who squirmed on the couch like a moth pinned to a board. "You idiot, look at him. He don't work for Zack. This guy's got too much class to be working for Zack King." Then she turned to Hannibal. "You're not a cop are you, handsome?"

"No, not a cop," Hannibal said. "All a cop could do is ask questions. I, on the other hand, will beat your little husband's ass if he don't tell me what I want to know."

"Jesus, mister, I'm telling you," Wally actually put his hands together, as if praying to Hannibal for understanding. "I can't find him. If he did somebody, he did it for Zack. He's probably back up in Jersey right now, so Zack can hide him out until the heat dies down."

-14-

Coffee shops like the one Hannibal sat in spring up around colleges and universities like dandelions on a well-fed lawn. He wondered why the competition did not kill more of them off. He was lucky to find one which at least served a decent cup of coffee. It was hot and strong and it relaxed him.

At least until Cindy walked in. As expected, she still wore her business suit: a navy skirt a bit shy of knee length, a white blouse under a conservative jacket, and heels. He did not expect her to still be wearing her business smile. A raincoat hung from her arm like a lifeless body. She walked directly to his table but did not sit down. In fact, she hardly looked down.

"Shall we go?" She handed him the car key and turned toward the door in one smooth motion. "Where's Daddy?"

"Staking out a suspect until the cops get there," he said, standing as quickly as he could. "I took a cab here." He hastened to catch up but did not come even with her until they reached his car. Then his attention was diverted.

"Son of a bitch," he muttered, walking slowly around his car in disbelief. The lower half of the Volvo looked like the car was used in a four wheel drive mud bogging contest. Its front left quarter panel was creased almost its entire length. The paint was scratched in five or six places. And the left outside rear view mirror was missing.

Then he opened the door. His white leather upholstery was caked with mud, with dried blood added in the front. The carpets were destroyed. Coffee rings formed the Olympics symbol on his dashboard.

"Can I get in?" Cindy asked. He pushed the button unlocking the other doors, then watched as she spread her coat on the seat to protect her clothes and sat down. Hannibal left his door standing open and went to the trunk. Raised in Germany, he carried a warning triangle, a first aid kit, flares and a flashlight along with his spare tire. From his supplies he plucked his emergency blanket which he carried to the front and spread over his seat. Then he dropped heavily into the seat, slamming his door much harder than necessary. Having his car invaded and mistreated this way made him feel violated. But as he pushed the key into the ignition, he realized he was letting his frustration and anger about an automobile cover up a potentially more serious problem. He leaned back, took a deep breath, and focused his mind.

"I think we need to talk," he said. "Let's find a nice place to get something to eat."

"Ate on the way."

"Cindy," he said, looking straight ahead, "I'll need your legal expertise in a few minutes, but you and me is more important than any case. Tell me what's wrong."

"You've got business to take care of," she said, not looking at him. "Can't we talk about it later?"

Hannibal started the car and turned on the air conditioning. The soft, cool breeze brought his mind into sharp focus. He released the emergency brake. He stepped on the brake pedal and pushed the shifting lever into first. Then he reversed the process, and yanked the emergency brake back on.

"No," he said, turning to face her. "I need to settle this now. Tell me what's going on."

"You tell me what's going on," Cindy snapped. "What's up with us? Who's the bimbo?"

Hannibal's mouth fell open. He first thought of Ginger Lerner, but Cindy had no way to know about her. No one would consider Daisy Sonneville a bimbo. He knew nothing of Angela Briggs' background. He gave up. "What bimbo?"

"What bimbo?" If words had solid substance, Cindy's would have been venom dripping from her mouth. "That bimbo you got stashed at the crib. She looks like a whore but at least she's neat. I found her cleaning up for you after breakfast. Did she make the bed too?"

"Quit shouting at me," he said, keeping his voice low. "Besides, you sound stupid when you try to talk street talk. You must mean Jewel. She's a client. Did you talk to Sarge?"

Cindy's eyes blazed. "Why in hell would I talk to Sarge? He got your alibi set up?" Next she said something in Spanish he could not follow.

"Speak English, girl," he said, putting the Volvo back into gear and pulling out. He crossed the Baltimore beltway headed into the suburbs, where trees cast long shadows across the street to remind him it was getting late. After a few minutes of silence, he said, "Sarge is protecting Jewel. She's staying in the office rooms for a few days."

After venting her initial anger, Cindy lapsed into a moody sulking mode. "She looks like a whore. And she was in your kitchen this morning, cleaning up your breakfast."

"She is a whore," Hannibal said. "At least she was until Saturday night when I told her pimp she quit. That's why she hired me, to get her out of the business. And yes, she came over and made breakfast this morning. But that's all we shared. Burnt bacon and some runny eggs."

"Saturday? She's been there since Saturday?" Cindy looked around at the middle class neighborhood they had coasted into as a new thought occurred to her. "She was there while you were with me Sunday night."

"I was with you," Hannibal said. "What does that tell you?"

"But, Hannibal," Cindy said in a softer tone, "why didn't you tell me?"

He pulled to a stop at the curb on a neat, well paved street. The house across the street had a small but well kept lawn lined with carefully trimmed hedges. Single family, brick with a bay window in front. Flowers lined the front wall and a junior basketball hoop stood guard over the driveway. Hannibal said, "I don't know" into his side window, but he was not sure Cindy heard him.

"That's where we're going and I'm not sure of my legal footing here."

"Lay it out for me," Cindy said, but her tone too was softer.

"Remember you sent me to tell Ike Paton's ex the news?" he asked. "Well, she lives here. I think she knows some things about the Mortimer case, maybe even had a hand in Jacob's death. But I might ask questions I don't have the right to ask, or I might put myself or my clients in a position to be sued."

"I'll make sure that doesn't happen," Cindy said. Then she reached for his hand. "Regardless of the other thing, thanks for making me part of this. I wanted to help Kyle somehow."

"Listen," Hannibal said, squeezing her hand tight, "I'm not good at this relationship thing, all right. Never have been. But I don't want to screw this one up."

"Let's talk more after we get the business done."

The entire neighborhood smelled like it was preparing to barbecue when Hannibal and Cindy crossed the street. The driveway was empty, which was good. Hannibal hoped to finish their business there before he had to explain to another person. He rang the doorbell and within a minute, it swung in. A young girl with cornrowed hair stared up at them with curiosity, but no fear.

"Who you?"

"Is your mom home?" Hannibal asked. Before he finished the sentence, Daisy Sonneville was at the door, dressed as she was in the morning, but covered by an apron. Her eyes grew to silver dollars, but she curled her lips in and swallowed her terror.

"Rose, go over to Mrs. Cole's house and get your homework started so you'll be done when Daddy gets home," she said in a surprisingly calm voice. The girl moved with a discipline seldom seen today. When she was gone, Daisy asked, "What are you doing here?"

"We need to talk, Mrs. Sonneville," Hannibal said. "Please."

Daisy looked at Cindy, then up and down the block as if someone might be watching. Then she waved them in. Once inside, she retreated to the kitchen. The place, Hannibal guessed, she felt safest. It was spotless, and his nose told him there was a roast in the oven. This woman was working hard at living the dream and leaving behind the very things he was forcing back into her life. She leaned against the sink as if she might never move. With a glance at Cindy, he pulled out a photograph.

"This is Cindy Santiago, Mrs. Sonneville," Hannibal began. "She's an attorney, here to make sure I don't abuse your rights or anything. Please take a look at this picture." She did so, then pulled away.

"Who's he?"

"Please, ma'am," Hannibal said with a tired smile. "A reliable witness tells me you knew this man very well. His name is Jacob Mortimer, but you knew him as Bobby Newton."

"I don't know what you're talking about."

"You worked for him," Hannibal persisted, adding power to his voice. "For a while you lived with him. You took care of his baby, right there in that apartment in Edmundson Village. First floor. He was working at the Moonglow."

Each sentence was a hammer blow to Daisy, making her head sag another inch, until she finally said, "All right. I recognized the picture. So what?"

"So what?" Daisy was directly in front of him, with only the kitchen island separating them. Hannibal leaned forward, placing both hands on the island. "I just found that man, or what's left of him, buried in the cellar of that building he lived in."

Somehow, Daisy's eyes grew even wider. "What's that got to do with me?"

"That's what I want to know," Hannibal said.

Cindy stepped to one side, separating herself from Hannibal. "If you don't tell us what you know, Mrs. Sonneville, you could be accused of being an accessory to a murder."

"But I don't know anything," Daisy said, almost in tears.

"You do," Hannibal snapped, slamming a fist down on the island. "Tell me!"

"What the hell is this?" The voice belonged to a short, well dressed man with close cropped hair and a stern expression. He stood behind Hannibal in the adjoining living room, his hands curled into menacing fists.

"Oh, Phil, they think I..." is all Daisy could get out before choking on a sob.

"What are you accusing my wife of?" Phil Sonneville asked through clenched teeth. "You cops? What makes you think you can come busting in here?" His body language said he was well beyond the listening stage. Hannibal dropped his hands but focused his attention entirely on Phil.

"We're not the police, Mister Sonneville," Cindy said in a soothing voice. "We just came here to ask for help. Years ago, your wife was involved in..."

"My wife's not involved in anything," Phil shouted. He swung, but Hannibal dodged the fist and blocked the follow-on left. Phil's face was wide open and Hannibal cocked a fist for it.

"Hannibal, don't," Cindy said, and in his moment of hesitation Phil drove a right into his midsection. Air blew out of Hannibal's mouth, but his hands went up in time to deflect two more punches. Finally he lunged forward, hooking Phil's left arm with his own left. His right hand grabbed Phil's collar. After spinning around behind the smaller man, Hannibal drove him forward, bulldogging him to the carpet. He heard something slide off the coffee table and shatter on the floor. Daisy's scream was sharper, shriller than any breaking glass.

"Stop!" Daisy shouted. "Oh God, stop it, please. Let him go. I'll tell you. I'll tell you." Then her tears broke loose in earnest and her voice dropped to a deep moan. "I can't carry this guilt anymore."

Phil stopped struggling and Hannibal released him. Both men were watching Daisy in the kitchen, her small fists pressed into her eyes. Cindy reached to hold her, but she pushed away.

Phil went to stand beside his wife and she hid her face in his shoulder. Her sobs were buried in his suit coat. Hannibal could smell the roast burning, but no one seemed to care. His stomach knotted at the thought of causing a woman such pain. When Daisy raised her face, she was no longer sobbing, but water still flowed freely from her eyes.

"I don't know how you found me, Mister Jones," she said in her precise voice, "but you were right to. Bobby and Barbie were good to me and in return I killed them."

-15-

Cindy looked at Phil but spoke to Daisy. "I think you should have an attorney of your own present, Mrs. Sonneville."

"This is all a mistake," Phil said. "My wife could never kill anyone."

But as Phil tried to look into his wife's eyes, she backed away from him until she was wedged in a corner, in front of her microwave oven. She was standing straighter, as if a tangible weight was lifted from her. Slowly her shoulders came into the proud position they occupied when Hannibal met her.

"Phil, I never told you any of this," she began, as if Hannibal and Cindy did not exist. "Before I met you, I worked for Bobby Newton and his girl, Barbie Robinson. It was the last time I was separated from my first husband and I was kind of down on my luck. They took me in and I stayed in their spare room. They had money, some rare coins Bobby was trading slowly, one at a time, when he needed cash. I helped Barbie get around, because she was pregnant. When she had the baby, I took care of her so Barbie could get out."

Daisy's story had hit a bump, and she could not drive over it. Cindy said, "You had a weakness for your husband, didn't you? I know what that's like."

Cindy's words shook more tears and the rest of the story loose. "Pat came one day and took me to his place up in Jersey. When I asked about Bobby and Barbie, tried to visit them, he told me they moved away, but I never really believed it. It took me a long time to leave him for good."

"Well, you're not responsible for what might have happened after you left," Cindy said.

"Don't you see?" Daisy held her arms wide, palms out, ready for crucifixion. "I told Pat about the coins and the money Bobby had. I just know he told his friend Killer and he went after them. He'd murdered people before. Everybody knew it."

"Killer?" Hannibal asked. "Killer Nilson? Big guy, like six foot five?"

Three pairs of eyes turned to him in various stages of shock. He seemed to have the floor, so he decided to use it. "From what I've heard, Mrs. Sonneville, this guy didn't need much provocation to do somebody in. And Bobby Newton led a pretty public life as a singer. It was only a matter of time before he attracted the attention of a Killer Nilson, or somebody like that."

Daisy looked hopefully at Hannibal, but she did not look convinced. Phil offered support and, in a moment Hannibal knew he would find funny later, reached over to turn off the oven. Daisy did not quite smile, but the action brought a cool blast of reality to the scene. Hannibal turned to Cindy, thinking she might have the power to relax the other couple.

"Legal liability, Ms. Santiago?"

"None," Cindy said without hesitation. "I see no reason for the authorities to become involved in this. And I think we have all we came for."

For Daisy, the matter was still unresolved in one important way. "Phil, do you hate me?"

"Those people were years ago," Phil smiled, "and what's it all got to do with us?" He held his arms wide and Daisy rushed into them. Holding his wife, Phil turned to his unwelcome guests. He offered no thanks for their kindness, nor did he apologize for defending his turf. Hannibal understood, nodded, and took Cindy's arm as they headed for the door.

Three blocks away from the Sonnevilles' home, Cindy said, "They're very lucky. And you're turning out to be a detective after all. How did you know about this Killer Nilson?"

"Met a cop who's been around here since before Jake ran away," Hannibal said. "Knows a lot, but nobody asks him. In fact, if I can get to him before he goes off duty, I think I'll buy him dinner." As he hit the beltway again, Hannibal reached to touch Cindy's hand. Breathing seemed harder right then. "Look, I'm sorry I didn't tell you about Jewel."

Cindy nodded. "Guess my reaction was just what you expected."

Not an apology, Hannibal thought, but close as he would get to one. And to keep this woman, he would accept it.

Hannibal had never seen anyone eat ribs like Terry Dalton could eat ribs. He looked to Hannibal like an overstuffed sausage, stretching his skin ever tighter with each bite. The place he selected was dark enough to need the candles on the tables, and warm enough to convince Hannibal they really cooked on open pits out back. Even at a corner table, they could not ignore the noise of baseball fans at the bar, cheering for the Orioles on television.

Hannibal had also ordered a rack of ribs, but he did not, nor could he, make the noises Dalton made while eating. It was kind of a slurping sound, but with more air, as if he was literally inhaling his food. Cindy handled her Caesar salad with grilled chicken in a more civilized manner. It was about the only meal on the menu which allowed her to keep her hands clean. Hannibal knew she was happy, despite their company, because he had removed both his gloves and his glasses. She had told him in the past she liked him better without them, as if he was a different person.

"How many men are watching Wally Lerner's place?" Hannibal asked.

"Got three there right now," Dalton said in between licking his lips. "They'll know if he even breathes wrong. Now why don't you tell me about this case you're on? Who was the dead guy?"

Hannibal swallowed a mouthful of rib meat before answering. The sauce was delicious, sweet and spicy and thick enough to stick with the tender meat. "I think he was a guy named Jacob Mortimer from Virginia," Hannibal said. "Actually, he was traveling under the name Bobby Newton."

"That guy?" Dalton gulped his lemonade to clear his mouth. "His daughter was in a few days ago."

Hannibal barely kept his food in his mouth. "You met Angela?"

"Yeah, she wanted to know if there was a missing persons report filed on Bobby Newton. Said it was her father. She showed me a birth certificate, matter of fact."

"That's how she found Doctor Cummings," Cindy said.

"I think her father might have had a run-in with Pat Louis, or Killer Nilson," Hannibal said. "How well did you know those guys?"

Having finished his second rack of ribs, Dalton signaled to a waitress. "I sure knew Nilson. Respected him. Even feared him some, like anybody with sense. Man was a lit stick of dynamite, who might go off at any minute. He and Louis were pals, except when they were fighting. I remember Nilson beating Louis up once, over a girl, of all things."

The waitress arrived and Dalton asked for coffee and pie. Hannibal and Cindy settled for coffee. Steam rising from his cup appeared to make Dalton remember where he was in his story.

"I finally busted them," Dalton said with visible pride. "Nilson, Louis, the whole gang. Got them for fraud. If you're looking for your killer out of that bunch, it was the one with that name. Louis was no killer. He was the sneaky one. Everything he did was underhanded."

It was growing dark by the time Hannibal pointed his car south on I-95. He turned on his CD player and let Joshua Redman's saxophone supply the background music for his ride home. He was pleasantly full and he knew Cindy was too. She leaned her seat back a bit and kicked off her shoes. It had been a long day for them both, he realized. Actually, his was not quite over yet. He pushed a button on the keypad on his visor, autodialing his client's number. He wanted to report in.

"Mister Nieswand? Hannibal Jones. Is it too late to call?" He spoke to the windshield, knowing the microphone would pick his voice up fine.

"Don't worry about disturbing anybody," Nieswand said over the car's speaker phone. "I'm alone. Doctor Lippincott had my wife checked in to a home for observation. He thinks she's had a pretty serious breakdown."

"I'm sorry to hear that," Hannibal said. It suddenly seemed a little darker outside his window. "This guy Paton was using an assumed name. He was born Patrick Louis and he was a born gangster. He lived a life of violence. I'm sorry it caught up to him in your driveway."

"An assumed name?" Nieswand asked. The normally sharp-witted lawyer sounded as if his mind was numb and he was having trouble absorbing information.

"Afraid so. Your place was just a convenient hideout." Hannibal left a respectful silence before going on. "Have you heard anything about the remains I found?"

At the other end, Nieswand seemed to perk up a little. "Larry Lippincott's staying on it all night. Did you know the army has a DNA testing lab right near here? The Armed Forces DNA Identification Laboratory is right up in Rockville, Maryland. Larry's up there working with them. Says he'll have a definitive answer by morning, but he's pretty sure now he's got an exact match. Not only does it look like it's Jacob, but it shows the genetic tendency to cancer, he says."

"If it is, it fits what I got from other witnesses," Hannibal confirmed. "Looks like Jacob was a mob killing, for his father's coins most likely. It could be a friend of Paton's did it too. Poetic justice maybe." He turned to Cindy. "It doesn't help Kyle, but I guess my job's over." She gave him a smile and covered his hand on the wheel.

"I don't know," Nieswand said. "You seem to have found Jacob, but it's not good news for the family. You said something about a girl."

"Angela Briggs," Hannibal said. "Claims to be Jacob's illegitimate daughter."

112

"Jacob's death will be a crushing blow to Harlan," Nieswand said, "but maybe less so if this girl turns out to be his long lost granddaughter. And that would hold out hope for a transplant for Kyle."

"Mister Nieswand, I don't generally believe in coincidences," Hannibal said. "Now, I'll admit I interviewed witnesses who claimed Angela looked very much like Jacob, and I can see a resemblance to the photo I have, but her appearance is just too convenient for my tastes. I don't want to raise anybody's hopes."

Broken lines rushed past while Nieswand considered Hannibal's words. When he spoke, it was with the first genuine emotion Hannibal had heard in his voice. "I think we have to know. Please stay on the job a bit longer. Go with me to Baltimore tomorrow, introduce me to your sources and then to the girl. If there's even a chance..."

After a moment of quiet, Hannibal said, "I understand. All right, I'll stay with it until we have the truth."

After exchanging goodnights with Nieswand, Hannibal pushed the button to hang up. Cindy sat straighter and turned in her bucket seat to face him.

"He's a good man and a good lawyer, Hannibal. My mentor more than anyone else. He cares. But you're not optimistic, are you?"

"I'm afraid not," he said. "I want to believe, because I want to think I can help Kyle, but I suppose I'm too cynical."

"No, just realistic. Anyway, I think you'd better call Sarge now."

"Yeah. Let him know I'm on the way in," Hannibal said, reaching again for the telephone controls.

"No, to tell him you won't be back tonight. You're not spending another night in that apartment as long as that woman is there."

Hannibal smiled and stretched his right hand toward her thigh. "For a while there I wasn't sure..."

Cindy intercepted his hand, holding it tightly on the seat between them. "Don't jump to any conclusions. That doesn't mean anything's going to happen tonight. For now, we need to talk some, and then you sleep in the guest room. We can maybe work on making it right between us this way. I know we can't if you go back there to her. So you stay with me if it's worth it and take your chances."

Hannibal nodded and squeezed her hand back. "Your place," he said. "No promises. No rules."

"You understand?"

"No," he admitted. "But I understand enough to know that going home tonight could push you away. And I won't risk losing you."

Cindy released his hand to rub his arm lightly. In the dark, he could see the ghost of a smile starting on her face. "That's a good start," she said.

-16-

WEDNESDAY

The little examining room felt even smaller with three men in it. The room smelled of antiseptic, as all doctor's offices do, but somehow with an extra strength, which stung Hannibal's nose. He stood to the side, in his usual black suit, gloves and sunglasses, watching the two men. He was fascinated by their reactions to each other.

The stoop-shouldered Doctor Cummings invited them in pleasantly enough, but his discomfort with Nieswand was palpable. The lawyer was nattily attired in a custom-made gray pinstriped suit, his toupee almost undetectable. Hannibal was impressed by his presentation, his style, his ability to communicate with and relate to his audience. However, the old family doctor was unimpressed. Hannibal was not sure if the years had given him a distrust of lawyers, Jews, or men with money. In any case, while he listened politely to the story, it was clear he considered Nieswand the enemy.

"So you see, the man you knew as Bobby Newton was, in reality, Jacob Mortimer," Nieswand said. "And we have definite proof, thanks to DNA analysis, of that man's death. Jacob Mortimer was the only child of a very wealthy man. Any progeny of his would be heirs in line for part of the sizable Mortimer estate.

Under those circumstances, you can surely see why we must be very careful to verify such a person's identity."

Cummings glanced around as if he was looking for a good place to spit. When his eyes finally lit on Nieswand they narrowed to slits only wide enough for daggers to fly out of them. "You smile too much. I like him better," he said, jerking a thumb toward Hannibal. "He only smiles when something's funny. I can tell you I delivered Angela Newton eighteen or so years ago. She came here to see me because she found my name on her birth certificate. But all I can verify for sure is this girl's a sweet kid and if she isn't heir to a fortune, she ought to be. Any family would be better off with her than without her."

"I'm sure that's true," Nieswand said, "but I'll have to talk to her myself before I introduce her to the family I'm sworn to serve. I'd hate to embarrass her by walking in on her at her place of work, but so far, it's the only place we know to find her."

Cummings looked at Nieswand for a moment before turning to Hannibal. "Who talks to her?"

"Just the two of us," Hannibal said. "No crowd, no police, no hassles. I'll guarantee it."

After another long pause, Cummings pulled an address book from a cabinet drawer and scribbled on a pad. Another pause, a long sigh, and he tore the top sheet off the pad, handing it to Nieswand.

"I don't want her rousted at her job," Cummings snarled. "Here's her address. She doesn't start work until ten, so if you hurry you can catch her at home. But if there's any trouble," Cummings pushed his dried features and cloud of white hair into Nieswand's face, "you'll answer to me, shyster."

Angela's apartment was not very far from, nor any nicer than, Wally Lerner's. Nieswand was nervous about leaving his Mercedes parked behind Hannibal's Volvo on the street.

Nieswand continued his complaints inside. They faced a three-story walkup in a stairway someone had used for a bathroom not too long ago. The hallway leading to Angela's apartment was claustrophobic, with bare bulbs casting harsh shadows around it. They passed one young man on the way whose eyes advertised his drug use. And when they reached the right door, someone had spray painted a crude word across it. Hannibal knocked, then stood back as far as the hall allowed. There was no answering call asking who it was, but he knew he was being inspected through the tiny viewport such doors have. Then he heard two locks disengage and the door swung inward to the length of a small chain. Angela's face peeked through, and Nieswand whistled almost too low to be heard. Her eyes went from him to Hannibal. She neither smiled nor frowned, looking way too world-weary for her age.

"You, I know," she told Hannibal. "Him, I don't."

"I'm Gabe Nieswand," the lawyer said, turning on his courtroom smile. "I represent the family of the man who might be your father. They're very interested in clearing up all this uncertainty, as I'm sure you are as well. We'd like to talk to you for a minute. May we come in?"

The face disappeared. The door closed. The chain rattled. Then the door swung open. Angela was walking back into the studio apartment before either of her guests moved. Hannibal entered first, taking the room in quickly before waving Nieswand in behind him. The living room hardly looked lived in. True, the sofa and chair were worn, the table old, the walls dingy from going years unpainted. But the furniture and even the worn linoleum were clean. There was no clutter, no mess. No curtains at the windows. No pictures hanging. No knick knacks, books or magazines. No television.

"So talk," Angela said. She was taking clothes from a laundry basket on the table at the kitchenette end of the room, folding each piece with machine-like precision and placing them neatly on the table. Her clothes were stacked by category, socks here, underwear there, skirts, blouses, pants, all neatly folded.

"You told Doctor Cummings you were Bobby Newton's daughter," Nieswand said, standing at the other end of the table. "How does your name come to be Briggs."

"My last foster father," she said, never looking up from her careful folding. "All I can remember of childhood is a series of foster parents. Then, in junior high, I got picked up by Samuel Briggs. He was a sweet old man. I didn't like school but he turned me on to books and, you know, learning because you want to know."

"And this was in?"

Angela glared at Nieswand, bristling at his apparent skepticism. "We lived in Corpus Christi. I went through high school there. Graduated third in my class."

Near the door, Hannibal watched the hard look on Nieswand's face. A few questions had turned into an interrogation. Nieswand's face was cold and Hannibal suddenly realized this man could do anything he thought necessary. He must be vicious in court, Hannibal thought.

"He was obviously a kind, loving man," Nieswand said, stepping a bit closer. "I'll bet he considered you his own daughter in every way. I'm rather surprised he told you about your birth parents."

"Mister Briggs died right after I graduated," she said. There was no emotion in the statement, but the empty space it left implied the pain and sorrow had simply dried up. "He didn't leave much money, but he did leave me a note and a birth certificate. He thought I should know who I really was. I'm still looking."

She turned empty eyes toward Nieswand and he smiled in return. But Hannibal knew it was not the genuine smile he had seen before. This was his game face. So his next words surprised Hannibal.

"Angela, Bobby Newton was a stage name for Jacob Mortimer. The Mortimer family has been searching for Jacob for years without success. Now, you might be their only link to him. Would you be willing to come with me to meet them?"

Life sprang into Angela's face, and she put a tee shirt down without folding it. "Meet them? If they might be related to me, of course I'll meet them. When can we go?"

Angela grabbed a small purse and headed toward her door. As Hannibal turned to open it for her, his phone rang. He answered it on the way down the hall.

"Jones? This is Dalton. Got some news for you."

He sounded tired to Hannibal, but then he always sounded tired. "You going to tell me where Wally Lerner went when he finally left his place?"

"I'm going to tell you my guys screwed up," Dalton said. "Somehow, they lost him. He got out without them seeing him. I'm afraid he's gone."

"Damn. Well, will you keep the place under surveillance? Never know. He might be stupid enough to come back."

Hannibal reached the bottom of the stairs and went out into the sunlight, but behind his lenses it was still dark. He barely heard Nieswand saying good-bye as he and Angela climbed into the Mercedes. He did notice an annoying lack of surprise on Angela's face. When he was her age, boarding a Mercedes would have been an electric experience. But he said nothing, because his mind was on other matters.

"Dalton, do you have any leads on Lerner? You know his brother's the prime suspect in a Virginia murder now. Aside from that, I owe him a beating, and I owe him for taking my car and driving it like a demolition derby."

"Look, son, I'm doing what I can," Dalton said, "but I don't give a rat's ass about your personal revenge. I'll chase him like any other murder suspect and no snot-nosed P.I. is going to tell me how. Hey. What's that noise?"

Damn! "Got another call coming in," Hannibal said. "I'll talk to you later." He cut the connection with Dalton while getting into his own car. Frustrated, he let his forehead drop to the steering wheel. "What the hell else can happen?" he asked aloud, then answered the phone.

"Hannibal, this is Sarge."

"Sarge, how's it going?" Hannibal asked, turning the key to nudge the Volvo's smooth engine into life. "Is our guest getting restless?"

"Not exactly, Hannibal." The tension in Sarge's voice drew Hannibal's close attention. "We had a little action here."

"Floyd's boys come back to play?" Hannibal asked.

"Not like the last time, no, but I think it was them. This was a drive by. Five nine millimeter bullets through your front windows."

-17-

Two matched pairs of BF Goodrich Comp T/A tires locked up and screeched to a halt in front of Hannibal's building. His car vibrated when he slammed the door. He stared for a few seconds at his front office windows, largely missing. He stared up and down the street, looking for a good target for his anger before crossing the sidewalk. His shoes tapped up the outside steps like machine gun fire. He burst into his office, to find Sarge in the visitor's chair pointing a shotgun his way.

"It's good to see you're all right, man," Hannibal said. Sarge nodded. Then rapid-fire footsteps approached from the back of the building. Hannibal could smell Jewel's fear before she came into view. She threw her arms around him, less like a lover than like a drowning man clutching a life preserver.

"Oh, thank God you're here. God, there were bullets everywhere and I was sure I was dead. He's crazy. He's crazy and he wants to kill me and I know only you can save me. I'll pay anything, anything."

Hannibal kept his eyes on Sarge while he pulled Jewel's arms down from his neck. "Tell me what happened."

"Not much to tell," Sarge replied. "I'm sitting in here, Jewel's at the desk, starting to get the hang of surfing the net, you know. Black Cadillac cruises by, three or four brothers inside. An arm comes out the window and fires five shots at us. I kind of land on top of Jewel, all the shots go over our heads. Mother Washington was in the kitchen but you know the Lord looks out for her. When I gets up, the car's gone. I sent Mother Washington on home. Only casualty's your machine."

As Sarge talked, Hannibal's breathing deepened and his lips curled in, revealing his teeth. He walked slowly behind his desk. Window glass still littered the floor five feet out from the windows. Sunlight sent painful reflections up into Hannibal's eyes. His computer's monitor was now a hollow box and one of the bullets had smashed his keyboard.

"Okay," he said, finally looking at Jewel, "where does the son of a bitch live?"

The man on the stoop was obviously a guard, broad and squat, his bald head shining like a bowling ball. Floyd's chosen guard type. He was more alert than the men Hannibal met before, but by the time he figured out how to react, Hannibal figured it would be too late. He set his emergency brake, got out of the car, and stalked directly toward the man. Momentarily flustered, the guard braced himself like a linebacker, his right hand moving slowly toward his waistband. Hannibal stopped three steps from the top of the stoop.

"You know who I am?"

The guard nodded, pulled a stiletto and stepped back two paces. Aside from jeans and sneakers, he wore a black tee shirt and a ball cap with the letter X on the front.

"You really want those to be the clothes they bury you in?" Hannibal asked. "Put that down before you piss me off."

"You get out of here, Jones," the muscular man said. "You supposed to be tough but your rep don't mean shit to me."

Hannibal nodded. Another mouth-powered idiot, probably on drugs. He turned his head, as if checking on something over his right shoulder. Then his left hand whipped past the guard and his right foot spun around him. His right heel whipped back, around and up, cracking like a flail against the guard's right elbow. With a strangled cry, the guard dropped the knife and fell to his knees. Hannibal stepped past him into the building.

Inside, the smell of musk and malt liquor hung in the air. Hannibal burst up the narrow stairs to the second floor where he knew his target was busy gambling, or drinking, or doing drugs or getting laid. Not that it mattered. Whatever he was doing, he was about to be interrupted.

Bass-heavy music rattled Floyd's door on its way out. Idiots. A platoon of police could storm the hall unanticipated. If they cared to. Disgusted, Hannibal drew his Sig Sauer P229 from its holster, took a deep breath and executed a front stamp kick. Floyd had installed a good lock, but the door sill was thin wood which splintered easily. The door flew open and slammed against the wall on the inside.

"Just don't," Hannibal said as he stepped in. Through his dark lenses and a thick cloud of marijuana smoke, he saw Floyd playing cards with his two lieutenants and three fairly attractive girls. The girls all appeared to be on the losing end of a game of strip poker. He had seldom seen such an impressive collection of dilated pupils.

He was surprised, first, that all the furniture, and even the stereo, were high-end items, the most expensive things available, but poorly cared for. His second surprise was Lawrence's ability to react, almost like a professional. He dropped the joint from his left hand and the cards from his right and produced a gun from his waistband in a fraction of a second. Hannibal sent a forty caliber hollow point slug through his right biceps. The impact drove Lawrence to the floor. The women screamed and slapped hands over their ears against the gun blast. The raised arms made three pairs of nipples jump humorously.

"Girls out, men freeze," Hannibal snapped. The women scrambled and stumbled through the door without a backward glance.

"You a dead man," Floyd muttered, the scar over his left eye flaring red.

Hannibal stepped within arm's reach and spoke what sounded like three harsh words: "Shut! The fuck! Up!" After which he backhanded Joey with his gun. The big man dropped to the floor and did not move. Hannibal then slid his pistol back under his right arm and snatched Floyd up by his collar. The player's face twisted into a snarl and he started to resist, so Hannibal slammed him into the wall. That brought the widened eyes he was looking for. He jammed his knee up between Floyd's legs to hold him in place and put his face so close to Floyd's they almost touched. Close enough to finally smell fear.

"Did you think you could threaten my friends and just go about your business? Did you think you could shoot up my office and I'd just ignore it? Huh?" Hannibal slammed his right fist into Floyd's stomach. Once. Twice. Three times and Floyd began coughing like he was about to retch. Hannibal stopped him with a forearm across his throat.

"What do you want?" Floyd gasped. "What is it with you?"

"Me?" Hannibal's throat, restricted by rage, only allowed his voice out in a strained growl. "Well I ain't no hooker. Hookers are all scared of you. And I ain't no cop. Cops play by rules. And I ain't another pimp or gangster. They all hide behind a gang of muscle men. See, I take care of trouble up close and personal. You ain't never met a nigger like me."

While Hannibal stared into Floyd's cruel but terrified eyes, he saw realization dawn. Under the threat of physical damage, Floyd suddenly appeared to have a light bulb moment.

"Look, why don't I just forget Jewel ever existed?" Floyd croaked. "If she can go straight, good for her. She can go anywhere she wants. She can go on back up to Jersey where I picked her up last year."

Hannibal eased the pressure on Floyd's throat as those words sifted down into his brain. "You hang out in Atlantic City?"

"Sometimes," Floyd stammered, as if he was not sure if admitting it was a mistake. "Lot of girls up there, working independent. I can usually find seasoned girls like Jewel up there."

"You might just come out of this with a whole skin, pimp," Hannibal said, spinning Floyd around and tossing him onto the dirty leather couch across the room. Hannibal spun a chair away from the table, faced its back toward Floyd, and dropped onto it. He again drew his automatic and aimed it casually at Floyd's nose.

"I was thinking of breaking your arm," Hannibal said, "or maybe blowing out one your knees. That would be fair for shooting at my client and ruining my computer. But maybe I won't if you turn out to be of some use. So, give me the 411 on Zack King."

Floyd screwed his forehead up into a puzzled expression. "Who?"

Hannibal squeezed his trigger, and a hole opened up in the front of the sofa, less than two inches below Floyd's crotch. The pimp drew a sharp breath. He controlled his voice, avoiding a scream, but he could not stop drops of moisture from welling up on his forehead and dripping down his face.

"You mean Zack King in Jersey," he said, as if the original question had somehow confused him. "White guy, runs a club up there. Has prize fights there, and takes bets on his fighters."

"His fighters?"

"Well, yeah," Floyd leaned forward, as if confiding in a friend. "He runs a gym downtown where most of the fighters train. I think he's skimming a pretty good amount off the gambling, because he knows the fighters so well."

Hannibal heard Joey stirring behind him, but he put his gun away and continued talking to Floyd. "You know, Floyd my man, if you tell me exactly where this place is, and stay away from my client, you might not get your ass kicked today." Then he stood to face Joey. "You, on the other hand, just need to sit down and shut up." Joey hesitated, fists curled but face blank.

"Look man, I been kickboxing since I was sixteen," Hannibal said. "You're nothing like fast enough, or skillful enough to take me. If you got any sense, you'll get your buddy there to a doctor before he bleeds to death."

Joey continued to stand, facing Hannibal. He never looked at Floyd, but his eyes wandered from Hannibal's face to his hands and back again.

"What's it going to be?" Hannibal asked. His anger had passed, leaving him with the weariness that comes when adrenaline stops pumping and the rational mind reminds us how little violence solves. Perhaps Joey saw all that on Hannibal's face, because he raised his fists into a defensive stance and stepped forward.

"All right," Hannibal said, his mouth pulled to one side. His stance shifted subtly and his hands rose to chest height. When Joey leaned in with his first punch, Hannibal ignored it and unleashed a burst of left-right combinations. When Joey staggered back, he switched to three-way combos: left, right, left crescent kick to the ribs. When Joey hit the wall, Hannibal delivered a single side stamp to his midsection, putting Joey on his knees. Hannibal did not have the heart to finish it. He turned back to Floyd.

"That's you if you give me bad dope, or if you ever come within a mile of hurting Jewel," Hannibal said. "In fact, if you ever come down to my hood again I'll break your knees. You reading me, you slimy pimp?"

Floyd nodded, but his eyes were on Joey and Lawrence. Hannibal wondered what might happen to him when others on the street got the word his main protectors were out of business for a while.

When Hannibal got home, the broken glass was cleaned up. Sarge was perched on the desk, shotgun in hand. Cindy sat in his desk chair reading Cosmopolitan. Jewel was nowhere in sight.

"So, did you kill her while I was gone?" he asked her.

Sarge grinned and dropped to his feet. "Jewel's in the back. She's been keeping a pretty low profile since Cindy got here."

"I didn't say a word to her," Cindy said, rising. "I think she just figured out who I was."

"So what brings you down here?"

She stood so she could rub her hands up his chest. He was instantly less tired. "I called to find out what happened in Baltimore," she said. "Sarge told me there were shots fired and you took off after the guilty party. I just wanted to know you were okay."

"I'm fine, and the guy who did this won't do it again," Hannibal said. He held her hands in his. They reminded him of commitment, dedication, and responsibility. In such a short time, this woman had become his anchor, his tether line to reality. He could not say what was in his heart, but he hoped she guessed how important she was to him. He leaned in and kissed her lips gently.

"Babe, I need a break from all this. Can you get the rest of the day off? We can maybe put together a picnic and go over to Riverside Park and just sit."

"I think I can arrange that," Cindy smiled. "Want to go right away?"

"Not quite. I've got to go take care of one responsibility first, and I'm hoping you'll come with me."

* * * * *

When Hannibal walked in, Kyle Mortimer was sitting up straight in bed playing a video game. On the television screen, a dinosaur screamed like a swooping eagle while battling a sword wielding skeleton. He hoped Kyle was the dinosaur, because its tail was pounding the skeleton. Kyle looked stronger than when Hannibal met him, and his eyes were more alive. His windows were open, and the room filled with the scent of newly mown lawn.

With a whoop of triumph, Kyle watched the dinosaur eat the skeletal warrior. Then he turned toward the door, his smile as bright as the sun coming in his window.

"Hi, Mister Jones. Come on in. It's good to see you."

Hannibal gripped Cindy's hand hard and walked over to Kyle's bed. The boy continued his game, his dinosaur now facing some sort of ice being.

"Kyle, I said I'd report in to you," Hannibal said, "so I wanted you to know everything I've found out so far. I actually made a lot of progress in finding your father."

"Oh, yeah. Grandpa told me my dad's dead. You sure work fast." Kyle never looked away from the screen and his smile never wavered.

"He told you?"

"Sure," Kyle said. "He said he died a long time ago."

"Kyle, I'm sorry," Hannibal began.

"Not your fault. I'm glad to have an answer." Kyle turned to Hannibal. "See, all these years I've thought my father was somewhere hiding from us, that he didn't want to know how I was or what I was doing. Now I know he died soon after he ran out on us. I mean, sure he left us, but he never really had a chance to change his mind."

The boy's optimism was bottomless and Hannibal's throat thickened thinking about it. He heard Cindy sniff, then rummage in her purse for a tissue. "Still,"

Hannibal said, "I'm sorry I didn't bring better news. Your best shot at a transplant just evaporated."

Kyle took Hannibal's empty hand, and Hannibal could feel the electricity of his courage. "Not really. There is still my half sister."

"They told you about Angela?"

"She came up here," Kyle said. "She only stayed for a few minutes, though. Some people just..." he looked down at his covers, "they just can't, you know?"

Hannibal did know. "You think she might be your donor?"

"Well, the odds aren't quite as good as with a true sibling," Kyle said, in his clinical way. "But even half brothers and sisters often provide compatible bone marrow. Trouble is, the HLA test takes a few days, and I've only got a few days. But hey, that's the way it always works, isn't it? Just before the deadline, a miracle happens."

"Yes, and I believe you could make a miracle happen," Hannibal said, shaking Kyle by his shoulders. "If there's anything I can do to make this all any easier..."

"There is one thing," Kyle said. A shadow crossed his face as if he suddenly realized how short his time might be. "Just in case things don't work out. I know it's a lot to ask, but do you suppose there's any way you could find out how my father died, and why? I'd hate to leave without knowing that."

Hannibal considered for a moment. "I found out about one man who probably knew, but he was murdered. Then I found out the murderer might know. Today I think I found out how to find the murderer. I was planning to give that information to the police and let it go at that, but this is different. Gabe Nieswand

131

asked me to stay on the payroll for a couple more days, and you are the client, after all. I'll see what I can turn up and get back to you. I promise to be here before..." Hannibal choked and had to clear his throat, "before you have to leave."

-18-

THURSDAY

Now, this is a gym. That was Hannibal's first thought when he walked into Farley's Gymnasium in Atlantic City. You could tell by the smell of sweat and leather. He could name a dozen health clubs and fitness centers in the Washington area, but real gyms were becoming rare. He was really more comfortable here, among the heavy bags and speed bags, jump ropes and sparring rings.

Funny how this scene brought him back to the inner city, the real neighborhoods. Not at all the scene he associated with previous visits to Atlantic City. Leaving the boardwalk was like stepping behind the set of a western movie and discovering that the buildings have no back wall. Two blocks away from the shore, bright lights gave way to deep shadows, and ultramodern casinos and shops were replaced by sagging, rundown, dirty buildings on dingy, cluttered streets.

This was no situation for suit, gloves and glasses. But he fit right in wearing gray sweats and sneakers. A quick scan of the busy area led his eyes to a short, dumpy man dressed as he was. He was the kind of beefy athletes become when they stop working out. Standing beside the ring at the center of the room, he was shouting to one of the boxers inside. A trainer, Hannibal thought. Good place to start.

"Hey, Pop, got a minute?" he asked.

The older man looked at Hannibal, reacted quietly to his eyes, scanned down his six-foot frame, and turned back to the ring. "Okay, Roberto, that's it. Hit the showers." Then he turned back to Hannibal. "Roberto's fighting tomorrow night. Think he's ready?"

"Drops his right too much after the combination," Hannibal said. "First good counter puncher who survives that right cross is going to tear him up."

The trainer smiled and offered his hand. "Been telling him that for two weeks. I'm Connie Allen. You looking for a sparring partner?"

"Hank Jones, and actually I'm looking to book some fights," Hannibal said. "Got into kick boxing while I was stationed in Korea. Now I'm out of the Army, I thought I'd try it for money."

Connie crossed his arms, tilting his head to one side. "So you'll need a trainer, is that it? Well, let's see what you got under the sweat suit."

Hannibal peeled off his outer layer. Bare chested in boxing shorts, he felt like a slave on the block as Connie walked slowly around him, mumbling as he went.

"Good muscle. Abs. Shoulders. Legs. Pretty good definition. What do you go, around one eighty? Kind of light for a heavyweight. Have to lose a few, fight you as a light heavyweight. Hold out that arm. Um-hum, good reach. Show me a jab. Again. All right, quick enough. Yeah, I think I could do something with you if you're willing to work."

"Great," Hannibal said. "I heard this was the place to start from a guy I knew years ago down in

Baltimore. Name's Sloan Lerner. We called him Slo back then. Know him?"

Connie rubbed the sagging skin of his jaw. "Lerner? That name does kind of ring a bell. He a fighter?"

Was he? All Hannibal knew for sure about Slo Lerner was his appearance. He mentally flipped a coin. "No, I don't think so. He said he worked for a guy named Zack King."

"Don't know if I know him," Connie said. "Why don't you check with some of the guys in the locker room?"

Hannibal thanked Connie, gathered up his sweats and headed for the back of the gym. As he passed shadow boxers and one fighter checking his footwork in a full length mirror, he remembered how close he came to making a career out of getting beaten up. Police work had turned out to be more satisfying than boxing could ever be, but once in a while he felt the drive to prove himself in the ring against another warrior.

Hannibal signed for a lock and a towel at the door. The locker room was small, with columns of lockers pushed so close together they barely left enough space for the rows of obligatory benches. He chose one in a far corner. After tossing his sweats in, he sat on the bench to consider his next move. If nobody knew Lerner, or would admit to it, he figured he would play out the masquerade, maybe do some sparring. He could at least get a decent workout.

"You the guy looking for Slo?" It was Roberto, the heavyweight who was sparring when Hannibal walked in. He stood to face the Latin boxer.

"That's me. You seen him?"

"No," Roberto said, "I just wanted to make sure I had the right guy." The straight left came out of

135

nowhere, spinning Hannibal's head and dropping him to the floor, his back against the wall. Blue floaters clouded the space in front of his eyes. Roberto stood behind them, his fists raised.

"You must have a hard head, hombre. That shot should have put you out."

Hannibal eased to his feet, his own hands raised. "What the hell did I do to you?"

"Nothing personal, Chico, but it's fifty bucks to bring in anybody asking about Slo."

"Really?" Hannibal said, before digging his left into Roberto's stomach and adding a right uppercut. Roberto landed flat on the bench behind him. "Well, you're going to have to earn it."

Roberto was up faster than Hannibal expected and two other boxers appeared behind him, cutting off any hope of escape. Roberto floated in closer and Hannibal, his back to the wall, raised his guard. Roberto served up a blistering one-two which nearly, but not quite, knocked Hannibal down. His arms were already sore from deflecting two hard punches. Roberto moved in again, his left smashing into Hannibal's eyebrow, his right glancing off Hannibal's forearms. And with the last punch he dropped his left.

Hannibal drove his own right cross through Roberto's guard and across his jaw. He followed with a jarring left uppercut. His fist screamed and he wondered if he broke a knuckle, but Roberto spilled onto the concrete floor and did not rise. The two fighters who had joined him moved forward. Hannibal spun to deliver a stamp kick to the knee of the man on his left. The man on the right blocked Hannibal's overhand right but had no defense for the stamp kick which smashed into his chest. He flew backward, but three more boxers joined them, all looking unhappy to interrupt their training. Outnumbered and outmaneuvered, Hannibal decided to change the location of the fight. He jumped to his right, high enough to grasp the top of the lockers. His momentum was enough to spill the column over into the next aisle. It landed with a loud hollow clatter, with him on top of it. With a little luck, he could escape the locker room and from there get to his car.

Stomping across the gray sheet metal of the lockers, Hannibal made it to the end of his aisle before another fist swooped at him. He dodged, then snapped a foot into the fighter's groin. But even as one man groaned and went down, another swung in from Hannibal's left. A hard fist bounced off his head, sending him staggering. He blocked the next punch and dodged another, but a third caught him in the mouth. This guy was directly in front of Hannibal, but he went down under a sweeping roundhouse kick.

Hannibal ran as hard as he could but a rough shoulder check shoved him into the shower stalls. He slipped on the tiles trying to get out, and a vicious right hook smashed his ribs hard enough to push him back into a steel control lever. It stabbed painfully into his back, and started a rush of cold water down on his shoulders.

The cold burst cleared the cobwebs from his mind as it cleared the sweaty locker room smell from his nostrils. He tasted blood and wondered if any teeth were loosened. Fire fighters rushed toward him, their footsteps echoing in the narrow shower area. He certainly couldn't beat them all. So he picked out the biggest one and swung a wide crescent kick to the side of his head. The boxer's head made a hollow sound against the wall when he fell, but then the crowd was too close to swing in. Two men managed to gather Hannibal's arms behind him while another went to work on his face and body until his mind stopped accepting the pain messages and then his mind simply stopped.

After a long internal debate about the wisdom of taking any action at all, Hannibal finally opened his eyes a crack. Incoming light from an overhead fixture set off a series of explosions in his brain, building to a throbbing pain which threatened to burst his skull before easing down to a dull ache. Raising a hand, he found a small bandage over his right eye but no moistness from blood. His nose was intact and his jaw, while sore, worked normally. A deep breath brought him the pain of muscle soreness but not the sharp stab of a broken rib.

"They must have stopped soon after I passed out," he mumbled to himself. Then, to check his brain function, he decided to go over the five W's. He knew who he was, a good sign. And he remembered what happened. A quick check of his watch told him when. It was still Thursday. He was only out for three hours. He could not know where he was beyond the fact that he was on top of the covers on a single bed with worn springs. As to why, he would have to investigate to find out. Then a familiar voice cut through his headache.

"Tell the boss Sleeping Beauty is awake."

"I know that voice," Hannibal said, pushing himself into a seated position. He was in an office of some sort, on a bed at the opposite end from the big oak desk. The man behind the desk stood up, revealing a sling supporting his right arm. The hand hanging from it bore the faint mark of an old, horseshoe-shaped tattoo. He stood a couple of inches taller than

Hannibal, and he was much wider. He wore an ill fitted, cheap brown suit.

"I know you," Hannibal repeated, rubbing the back of his head. "You're Sloan Lerner, aren't you? You killed Paton. Then you stole my car when I tried to help you."

"Sorry about that," the big man said. "I kind of had to get away. The cops were after me. And I don't know no Paton."

Hannibal looked more closely. The resemblance to his brother was there, but the mouse-like features were morphed by the shift in proportions usually associated with slow wittedness. His eyes were too close together, his brow too low. And in place of his brother's low cunning, a blank look covered his face. His movements and words were not childish, but rather childlike. A very real difference, it seemed to Hannibal.

He swung his feet to the bare wooden floor and was about to stand when the door opened. A short, round, well dressed man with an old world Jewish face and slicked back hair strolled in with an air of control. A huge, six-dollar cigar poked out of the right corner of his mouth. He was followed by three white men whose shoulders barely fit through the door. He stopped facing Hannibal, his three followers moving in so he was cloaked in their shadows. He drew on his cigar, took it out of his mouth, and blew a long tube of smoke before he spoke.

"Don't stand up," the short man said in a low, smooth voice. "These guys get nervous."

Hannibal put his hands behind his head and leaned back against the wall. He lifted his left ankle to his right knee. "Zack King, right?" he asked.

"That would be me. And you are in fact Hannibal Jones, yes?" Hannibal nodded. "You help people in trouble, get involved in other peoples' problems. Admirable. Don't always help the cops. Even more admirable."

"Glad you approve," Hannibal said, wrinkling his nose at the smoke. "Mind telling me why I'm here?"

"Slo's on the run. I put the word out I wanted to see anybody who came looking for him. Now your turn. Why are you looking for him?"

"Handful of reasons," Hannibal said. "For one, he banged my head and stole my car. Can't let people go around doing things like that in my business."

Zack looked around at Slo Lerner and puffed on his cigar again. "Yeah, he told me about that. He might not have gotten away if you hadn't come along. He damage the car much?"

"Insurance will cover that," Hannibal said, "except for the deductible of course." The mundane nature of the conversation disturbed him a little.

"Good. Now, tell me about this murder thing. You put that story in the street?"

"Your boy was running from the crime scene," Hannibal said. "Apparently he shot Ike Paton in the head."

Slo moved over to Zack, his face twisted in confusion. "I don't know no Ike Paton, Mister King."

"You know him as Patrick Louis," Hannibal told Zack. "He used to work for you. Look, I don't care much about that. The guy was a low-life. Much like yourself. I just want to know why you had him killed. Did it have to do with something he did years ago? Did he kill Jake Mortimer?"

Zack was staring at Slo sternly, as a teacher who caught her star pupil cheating might. For all his bulk,

Slo was cowed by the icy stare. Zack finally removed his cigar again and pointed with it. He spoke slowly and quietly.

"You kill Pat Louis, Slo?"

"I swear, Zack," Slo said, pleading with his good hand. "I went to get the money, just like you said. He must have thought that lawyer's house was a good hiding place. He was sure surprised to see me again, I'll tell you. And he must have thought I was after him or something because he just went crazy. He threatened me and, I don't know, I guess it turned into a fight. I don't mind a good fight. But when he started losing, he pulled a knife on me. After he cut me, I clocked him. I clocked him good, knocked him out. But I didn't hit him hard enough to kill him."

"He was shot in the head," Hannibal said, putting both feet on the floor and watching Slo squirm.

"Shut up," Zack told Hannibal.

"I didn't shoot nobody," Slo told Zack. Then he actually started to pout. "I didn't shoot nobody," he said again.

Slo wandered back to the desk and sat down. The room was very quiet for a minute. Then Zack released a bored sigh and shoved a pudgy hand into his pocket. His hand came out wrapped around a roll of hundred dollar bills. He talked to the bills as he flipped them upright, one at a time.

"Okay. One, two, three, four, five. That ought to cover the deductible for the damaged Volvo. Two hundred for the lumps you got from Slo. Couple more for the little punch up at the gym. And let's say one more to keep quiet and get off my back. See, I believe Slo. He's never lied to me before, and I don't think he could anyway. So you and me, we're square, right?"

Hannibal slowly leaned forward so his elbows rested on his thighs and dropped his chin onto his fists. He was not sure what was most offensive. Being handled so casually? His bruises and lumps being reduced to money? Or Zack thinking his silence could be bought so cheaply. It was degrading to be brushed aside this way. He felt the anger beginning to boil in his belly again. He must learn to control that. Perspective, he told himself. Aloud, all he said was, "I thought you knew me. You found out some, but you missed some important points."

Zack had a big laugh, and it bubbled up from deep inside him like tar from the LaBrea Pits. "What, like you can't be bought? Face it, little man, everybody has a price. Only difference is, when you get to be where I am, you set the price." Grinning arrogantly, Zack flipped the stack of bills into Hannibal's face.

Hannibal did not move until all the bills had fluttered to the floor. Then he dropped his hands to his legs and turned his face slowly downward and to one side. Perspective, he told himself. There was that anger again, like a knot pulled tight in his stomach. He must learn to control that. Someday.

He uncoiled like a steel spring, his right fist flying upward to smash into Zack's jaw with all the strength of his arm, stomach, back, legs and heart. The impact was loud as a shot in the small room. Zack lifted off the floor, flew backward a few feet, and crashed down on his desk. And like the Dallas Cowboys' front line, Zack's three followers guaranteed Hannibal would not gain one more inch.

-19-

FRIDAY

First sound...an alarm clock near his right ear. First smell...antiseptic. Alcohol? Probably. First taste...blood, probably old. First sight...Cindy's beautiful face in profile, aglow in a soft wash of dawn sunshine. First thought...sure would love a hot cup of coffee right now.

A nurse stood beside his bed, fussing with an intravenous drip bag. The alarm he heard was not a clock, but the electronic monitoring device on the IV pole which buzzes when a bag runs empty. He followed the path of the colorless liquid down into the crook of his own right elbow. Probably saline or glucose, maybe with a painkiller and a mild sedative. The best patients are those who stay asleep.

The scratchy sheets meant a public hospital. A private room meant they knew who he was and somebody had sent money. He was Hannibal Jones and a trio of sadists had beaten him rather badly because he got stupid and made a statement by knocking their mobster boss across the room in a fit of anger. He must learn to control that. The when and where he would have to investigate. Cindy sat in a chair six feet away, against the far wall. She faced the door, which was not far beyond his feet. She wore jeans and the green sweatshirt she brought back from her vacation in Barcelona. Her makeup was almost gone. Her hair and clothes looked like she spent the night in that chair. He lifted his head from the flat spongy pillow and tried to whistle to her. That was how he found out about his split lip.

"Hannibal!" Cindy sprang from her chair and threw an arm around him. She smelled of jasmine and honey and her soft, pliant flesh pressed into his chest made him want to do things he probably was not up to.

"Okay, I'm healed," he said. "Let's go home." He hoped his words were not as slurred as they sounded to him.

"Not until a lot of paperwork's done," she said, carefully kissing his forehead. "God, you had me worried this time."

"You too, huh?" Hannibal smiled as best he could. "Look, Babe, I'm a little fuzzy on the chain of events here. How long have I been here, and just where is here, anyway?"

Cindy stood back and put on her stern mother face. "Here is the hospital, where people go when they do very risky things without any backup. The Jersey Shore Medical Center, to be exact, in the sleepy little town of Neptune, New Jersey. Which, by the way, is a good sixty-five miles farther up the coast than you told me you'd be. It's where you've been lying since late last evening. God, they could have killed you."

"But they didn't," Hannibal said. "I hurt everywhere I can think of, which probably means these guys were very good and very careful. Any real injuries?"

"Your doctor says no," she said. "A lot of bruises and lumps, you're black and blue from head to toe, but no broken bones and no damaged organs. Said he's seen it before. Says they must have worked on you for quite a while, and what you needed most was rest. They patched what they could and kept you asleep. Hannibal, I was here for hours, waiting while they did x-rays, ultrasounds, even an MRI."

"Whoa. Who authorized all that?"

She put her hand on his forearm and stared seriously into his eyes. "Now listen closely, all right? I got a phone call last night. All the guy said was you were here and the bill is paid, including every reasonable test. Then he said something really funny. He said, no hard feelings. Hannibal, when they brought you in here, they found a thousand dollars in one of your tennis shoes. I don't know all of what went on, but I think this time you ought to take the hint. Whoever you were messing with, back off."

Cindy's lecture trailed off into a plea at the end. And this time, he considered, she may be right. This beating was Zack King's way of saying back off. But if he was guilty of anything serious, Hannibal would have simply disappeared. So Zack was also telling Hannibal he was on the wrong trail. Was Zack concerned about Hannibal's condition being traced to him? It would explain why they took him so far away. No, the long ride was probably Zack's way of saying get out of town and stay out.

Still, he was more certain than ever that things were not as they appeared. And while he rolled in a drug induced stupor, his mind had been pushing the parts of the Angela puzzle around. They would not fit together, but the pattern he saw said they would fit into the Paton/Louis puzzle. He was about to sit up when the door eased open.

"So, he's alive I see." Ray's face revealed genuine concern his voice tried to cover up. "I leave for a minute to grab a little breakfast and he recovers."

"You here too?" Hannibal asked, lifting his head. The pain came in a burst, then faded back.

"You okay, Paco?" Ray asked, moving in until he stood beside his daughter. "You still don't look too good."

"You were worried, eh?"

"About you?" Ray asked, with a wave of his palm. "Hell, no. You harder to kill than crabgrass, man. But Cynthia wanted to get up here right away and it was easiest just to drive her on up, you know?"

"Yeah, Ray," Hannibal said, grasping his friend's hand. "I do know. Now, it's time I checked myself out of this place." Using Ray's hand for balance, he pulled himself up and swung his feet around toward the floor. His green hospital gown almost choked him, until he shifted so he was not sitting on it.

"You loco, Paco?" Ray asked. "What's the rush?"

Hannibal looked around the room for anything that might be his. "I guess my mind's been running while I was asleep. But I'm surer than ever that this Angela is a fake. And if Doctor Lippincott stops looking for a donor because of her, it only cuts Kyle's chances. Where the hell are my clothes?"

"What can you do about it?" Cindy asked, pulling Hannibal's sweat clothes out of the room's locker.

"Well, that depends," Hannibal said. He took his sweatpants from Cindy and squirmed into them under the covers. "Am I still on the payroll at Nieswand and Balor?"

"Yes, until Mister Nieswand specifically says you're not. I expect that will be soon, but not until he's sure Mister Mortimer is satisfied."

Hannibal disappeared for a second, then his head popped through the neck of his sweat shirt. "Then I don't have much time. Ray, are you willing to be on my payroll again?"

"Sure," Ray said, rubbing the back of his neck, "long as I don't end up looking like you, Paco."

Leaning forward to pull on socks set off the pressure charges in Hannibal's head again. He opened his mouth and screwed his eyes shut until this latest blast of pain subsided. "Okay, first I need you to get me to my car. Then we'll drop you at the airport. I need you to do a little research for me and your language skills might come in handy."

"Somewhere out of town?" Ray asked, handing Hannibal his Nikes. "I'm no detective, you know. Why you not doing it yourself?"

Hannibal pulled his shoes on and fumbled with the laces. He tried not to show it was taking all his concentration to form the simple knot. "Cindy and I will be back in Baltimore. If I'm right, we can do a little digging of our own."

-20-

This time, when Hannibal knocked on the door, Ginger Lerner opened it herself. She wore different clothes, but the basics were the same. Her wary eyes went from Hannibal to Cindy and back. Her face asked who the woman was, but her mouth simply said, "Wally's not here."

"I know," Hannibal said.

"I don't know where he is," Ginger offered, flipping her golden hair, as if that might end this awkward conversation.

"That's okay," Hannibal said. "You're the one I want to talk to anyway."

Ginger stuck the tip of her tongue through her lips as her eyes cast down. Hannibal took this to be her look of deep thought.

"Please," Hannibal said. "We've been on the road almost seven hours." Then, knowing he had taken it as far as he could, Hannibal shut up. Ginger's eyes went back to Cindy, who smiled as reassuringly as she could. Eventually, in the face of their silence, Ginger opened the door and waved them in.

Hannibal walked in toward the table with Cindy close behind him. He seated Cindy, then pulled a chair out for Ginger, but she walked past the table. She paced back and forth nervously, but Hannibal did not think he was the cause of her edginess.

"So, what do you want?" Ginger asked, picking up a pack of cigarettes and fumbling one out of the pack.

"Just to chat about some things," Hannibal said. "Like about your old friend Ike Paton."

Ginger lit her cigarette with a long shaky drag and released a plume of smoke. "Don't know him."

"Maybe you do," Hannibal said, sitting opposite Cindy. He hoped he was less threatening this way. "Maybe you know him as Pat Louis."

"Oh, that bum." Ginger patrolled the perimeter of the apartment's main room, which allowed her to check the door's peephole, the little window over the sink and the bedroom window on each circuit. "Yeah, I know him. Actually, Wally does. Actually, he's one of Slo's friends. One of those creeps that's always getting my Wally in trouble. Even stayed with us a few years ago, before he got that job in Atlantic City. What about him?"

"He's dead," Hannibal said. Ginger stopped her pacing, her eyes widening briefly. "And that might be why Wally's on the run."

"No, no, no." Ginger swung her head back and forth, turning her hair into a reddish fan around her face. "Not my Wally. He wants to be a tough guy, but he's not. Not really. He couldn't kill anybody, not even that lowlife."

Watching her inhale fear and nicotine, he could hardly believe this was the same woman who made a pass at him a couple of days ago. The relaxed confidence he saw then had deserted her. He thought he knew why, but knowing did not mean he understood.

"He's left you behind, hasn't he?"

Hannibal's words hit her like a slap, but she recovered quickly, almost stilling her quivering lower lip. "He's gone. Out of the country. He said he'd send for me, but I know he's afraid the police would follow me. Why do I need him so?"

Hannibal could not guess. "You know, I don't think Wally hurt anyone. I thought Slo might have killed Pat Louis, but if they were friends..."

"That louse ain't loyal to anybody but Zack King," Ginger said, dragging on her cigarette until the glowing embers almost touched the filter. "If Zack said kill Pat, he'd kill Pat. Not like his brother. Wally's been taking care of that retard all his life."

"Louis stayed with you because he was Slo's friend," Hannibal said.

"Right. And Wally's gone now because of his stupid brother. They're on the run together. They're on the run and I'm..." she hesitated to state such a simple truth, "I'm here."

"Are you all right here?" Hannibal asked before he realized he was talking.

"Oh, sure," Ginger said, smashing her cigarette into an ashtray as if it was someone's face. "I'll be fine. Maybe I'll just go back to what I was doing before I met him. After all, I've stayed in shape. Any man would be happy to..." Tears washed her last few words away. Wiping the tears from her face with the back of her hand, Ginger smeared her pancake, lipstick and eye makeup together into a collage on the side of her face. Then she stood in the middle of the floor, fists clenched, racked by silent sobs until Cindy went to her, put her arms around this stranger and held her while she cried.

An hour later, Hannibal eased his Volvo up the gentle grade into Harlan Mortimer's driveway. The day had become bright and sunny somewhere in Pennsylvania, and stayed that way into the afternoon.

As he opened the car door he heard distant laughter from the deep porch on the left side of the stately, two story house. Standing beside his car, he relaxed for a moment, watching the Potomac River roll past behind Mortimer's house. Cindy stretched when she stood up, filling her lungs with the sweet smelling air surrounding the house. Hannibal wished the roses and hyacinths could lift his spirits as easily as they clearly buoyed hers.

"Smile, you old grump," she told him as they headed for the door. "It's almost over."

"Not until I hear from your father."

Hannibal had not imagined Mortimer a party animal, but there was quite a gala going on. Soft jazz sounds embraced the house, dodging in and out between the laughter. As they approached the house the scent of flowers gave way to the aroma of burning barbecue sauce. Then one form broke from the group on the porch. A figure which even ran with perfect posture. Camille Mortimer was careening toward Hannibal, arms outstretched. On impact, her arms wrapped around Hannibal and squeezed him hard. From the corner of his eye he saw Cindy's face harden.

"Thank you, thank you, thank you," Camille said. "Thank you for finding her. Now at least my Kyle has a fighting chance."

"Slow down," Hannibal said, gently prying her arms loose. "I can't take credit for this. I ran into this girl who claims to be your husband's daughter, but I can't guarantee..."

"I know nothing's certain," Camille said, "But at least now my Kyle's got a fighting chance. Doctor Lippincott says the test results could take more than a week after they get a blood sample from her, but even today she's had an effect. Kyle has more hope than ever." Then her voice dropped, and she changed gears into a less comfortable subject. "And thank you also for doing the job Daddy H hired you for. Jake's remains have been positively identified. I can't tell you what it means to bring that story to closure. After all the years of wondering where he was, what he was doing." One second later life flowed back into her voice and she took Hannibal's arm. "Daddy H is cooking out on the deck. Come on out so he can thank you personally."

But Hannibal and Cindy did not reach the deck at the back of the house. Kyle, Angela and Malcolm Lippincott were inside the French doors leading to it. At sight of Hannibal, Kyle turned his chair and wheeled toward the newcomers. Within inches of Hannibal, Kyle locked his brakes. His smile was as broad as ever, but emotion clogged his throat.

"I won't forget this," Kyle said. "I may not have a dad, but thanks to you I've got a sister. And she's terrific. Doctor Lippincott's not as optimistic as I am, but even he admits she might turn out to be the perfect donor for me."

Hannibal knelt and looked into Kyle's innocent eyes. His face was gaunt from weight loss, and as pale and dry as desert sand. His skeletal arms, bared by the tee shirt he wore, displayed bruises which were signs of the disease eating his body up. Did it make sense to impair his optimism?

"Son, things aren't always the way they look," he said, "but a lot of people are working to make sure it all comes out right for you."

"You're too modest." Malcolm Lippincott moved in, slapped Hannibal on the back and held out a hand. "I owe you an apology and I'm glad you came back to get it. When you first came here, I thought you were just going to stir up a lot of trouble."

"It's not too late," Hannibal said, accepting the shorter man's hand but returning only half his smile.

"I guess I have to thank you too," Angela said, taking Hannibal's hand. After Malcolm's grip, her hand felt cold, bloodless. "If not for you, I might never have found my family."

"Yes," Hannibal said, his mouth now a tense line, "I'll have to take responsibility for that, won't I?" Despite Hannibal's Oakleys, something passed between their eyes and even he was not sure what. But he was sure more than gratitude lurked behind the girl's smile. She smoothed her wavy, shoulder length hair and backed away a step. Then Malcolm put an arm around Angela, and Camille guided Hannibal through the doors to the deck. Hannibal looked around to make sure Cindy was with him. She looked at him the way women do when they are trying to send a message to their man, but he did not know what she was trying to point out to him.

Bright sunshine bathed him, and Hannibal was suddenly part of a milling throng. He did not know decks came this big, or held this many. At one end, two big electric grills poured thick smoke into the sky, smoke carrying the mouth watering smell of mesquite. The other end of the deck held two kegs, which guests were emptying as quickly as they could. He spotted Gabriel Nieswand nursing a beer in one corner and started toward him, but Camille used his elbow to turn him.

"All right," Harlan Mortimer bellowed from in front of one of the grills. "I was wondering if you'd get by here today." He wore a chef's hat, and a "kiss the cook" apron was wrapped around his barrel of a body.

Pulling thick pot holders off his hands, Harlan headed toward Hannibal. Guests parted like the Red Sea before his oncoming bulk. Hannibal smiled and held out a hand, but Harlan brushed it aside and wrapped an arm around Hannibal's shoulders.

"You're a remarkable young man behind those cheaters," Harlan said, his rumbling voice vibrating Hannibal's body. "I want you to know you've lightened an old man's soul. I've thought all these years my son was out there somewhere avoiding us."

"Yeah, well, you never really looked for him, did you?"

"And this treasure you've brought us," Harlan went on, as if Hannibal had not spoken at all. "She's beautiful, and the spitting image of my boy Jacob. After we get the tests run, I'm betting she can save Kyle's life with a bone marrow transplant. I know that's not a guarantee but, even if it fails, I've still got a granddaughter I never knew about. One last remnant of Jacob. And I owe it all to you for being so good at your job."

Harlan's crinkled eyes and broad smile should have made Hannibal happy and proud, but instead he was chilled. "Look, Mister Mortimer, about finding this girl,"

"Yes," Harlan said, shaking Hannibal's frame, "I haven't forgotten the business end of this deal. Here comes Gabe now. He'll take care of you." Then the French doors opened out and Angela stepped onto the deck. The crowd of well wishers swarmed around as if she were the victim saved from some rare disease. Hannibal and Cindy were pushed out to the perimeter of the action. She smiled helplessly at him. While they stared, amazed at the family's reaction,

Nieswand managed to reach them. He pressed something into Hannibal's hand while shaking it.

"Mister Mortimer is very happy with your results," Nieswand said. "This will enhance your reputation at our office, I assure you." He turned to Cindy with a fatherly smile. "Yours too, my dear. Your star is definitely rising at Nieswand and Balor. I think it's time to talk partnership."

Hannibal looked at the piece of paper in his hand and blinked in surprise. "Hold up. This is almost twice what it should be," Hannibal said. "And don't you want a report of my actions and expenses?"

"Sure, when you get around to it," Nieswand said. "Meantime, enjoy. This little cookout's as much for you as anyone. And as for the payment, Harlan decided the amount. That's what he thinks you're worth, and I for one agree with him."

Hannibal nodded his thanks and pulled away to a bench near the steps leading down to well-kept gardens. Cindy snuggled close to him, holding his arm. Her smile was so pure, so open, it almost made him forget the crosscut currents of meaning and intentions he suspected of everyone he had spoken to since arriving at Mortimer's place.

"So it's over," she said. "You're unemployed again."

"Not really," Hannibal said. "I do have another job in progress, remember? Even though Sarge and Quaker seem to be handling that one fine. But this check says I'm off Harlan Mortimer's payroll. Problem is, I don't feel like I'm finished, if you know what I mean."

"So, how do you feel?"

"Babe, I'm sore, I'm tired, and right now I'm a little confused. What I really want to do is just go home, have a nice quiet evening and go to bed." Hannibal stared down at the redwood planks beneath his feet. They reminded him that nothing in nature is a straight line. Including human nature.

"Mind if I join you?" Doctor Lippincott's Harvard accent asked. Hannibal shrugged, and Lippincott settled onto the bench beside him. Sipping a tall drink, he did not look as impressed as many others. He spoke to Hannibal, but his gaze seldom strayed from his son's back.

"So now you're off Harlan's payroll," Lippincott said.

"Afraid so," Hannibal answered.

"In that case, perhaps you could do me a favor."

Hannibal looked at Lippincott with renewed interest. He seemed to have been pushed to the perimeter of the case. Which might explain why he did not share his friends' festival mood. Or he might have unrelated troubles of his own. Hannibal was no psychic, but he had developed the ability to recognize people with problems. Despite so much going through his mind, all he said was, "Perhaps."

"Good." Lippincott leaned toward him the way amateurs do when they want to share something confidential. "I'll be working down at the clinic tomorrow. I know it's the weekend and all, but do you suppose you could stop in and have lunch with me? I'll gladly pay for your time. I need your professional opinion about something."

"I can do that," Hannibal said, standing. Lippincott had unintentionally reminded him he was not really part of this party. With his job done, he felt he did not belong here. "Right now, I've got to be going. I'll meet you at the clinic at noon."

"That will be fine," Lippincott said as Hannibal worked toward the door back into the house. "Please come alone."

"Guess he doesn't trust me," Cindy said as they climbed into Hannibal's car.

Hannibal gunned the engine and punched on the CD player. Foreplay filled the car and he instantly felt better. "Don't take it personally. People often talk to me about things that are real private."

"Bet it's his son," she said as they eased out of the cul-de-sac and into traffic.

"What makes you say that?"

"Surely you noticed," she said in her teasing tone. "The way he was looking at Angela. The whole dynamic has changed."

"What are you talking about?" Hannibal asked. "Everybody's treating Angela like the second coming. She's got them all conned."

Cindy let a beat of silence pass. "Don't like her do you? Well, Malcolm Lippincott sure does. When we first met him, he only had eyes for Camille, Jacob's widow. But his puppy dog infatuation has switched over to the new kid in town."

"You could tell that the two minutes we saw them," he said, his lip curled sarcastically.

"You'd have to be blind not to see it. So, my place? I'll make pasta."

"No," Hannibal said, raising Cindy's eyebrows. "I'll drop you if you want, but I want to be home."

He worked at not looking at her, but it did not work. From the corner of his eye he saw Cindy stare out the window, heard her take a deep breath and let it out as quietly as she could. Then she straightened her smile and turned to him. "Okay. Your place. And I'll make pasta."

He held his smile to a reasonable level. "Jewel's still there you know."

"I know. She's a client. I'll be good, as long as she doesn't get too close."

-21-

SATURDAY

Hannibal shoved his face into the hot water and let the tensions of the week flow down the drain. He loved a hot shower, but hated washing Cindy's scent off himself. They had shared a perfect evening. Candlelight and soft jazz, wine and cheese, back rubs and foot massages. And Cindy used her body to prove he was irrefutably, exclusively hers, at the same time demonstrating why he should want it that way.

He could still feel the warmth of the night while drying himself. He planned a do nothing, robe and slippers morning. Maybe they would sit around and watch cartoons. Or maybe, they would stage an encore of last evening. Wrapped in his navy blue terry cloth robe, Hannibal stepped out into his living room. The pleasing aroma of frying bacon started his mouth watering.

"Cindy?"

"In the kitchen," she answered, and he reached the kitchen doorway before he heard "and we have company." Cindy was at the stove, flipping silver dollar pancakes in a large skillet. Bacon crackled in a second pan. Over by the door to the backyard Jewel stood with her hands behind her. She wore a too small tee shirt and jeans which must have interfered with her circulation from the waist down. She offered him a tentative smile, but she looked for all the world like a child sent to the corner by her teacher.

"She came to the door and offered to help with breakfast," Cindy said, focused exclusively on her pancakes. "Honey, you want to get the juice and the syrup out?"

Jewel moved as if her mother, or a drill sergeant, had snapped out an order. Without a word she got orange juice and syrup out of the refrigerator, and without being told went back for the butter. The small table was already set for three. Hannibal dropped into a chair at one end and waved Jewel to another, but she did not move. Cindy, wearing nightgown and sheer robe, her fuzzy slippers and her Stepford Wives smile, delivered the food to the table on two platters. After she sat, Jewel sat.

"Papa called while you were in the shower," Cindy told Hannibal. "He said he'll be at National Airport at two o'clock."

"Good, I'll pick him up," Hannibal said, picking up his fork and knife.

"Oh dear," Cindy said in mock surprise, "I've forgotten the coffee." Jewel was up before Hannibal could brace to stand. She retrieved the pot, poured three cups, and replaced it. When she returned to her place, Cindy said "Thank you, dear."

Hannibal buttered a stack of pancakes and gathered bacon onto his plate. "So. You two seem to be getting along."

"Well, once I got a chance to talk to Jewel," Cindy said over her coffee mug, "she turns out to be a nice young lady who's just made some bad choices in life."

"Miss Santiago says she'll help me find my family back in Jersey," Jewel said, flashing her bright teeth.

"She says I can stay here, I mean across the hall, until then."

"Does she?" Hannibal asked, smiling through a mouthful of food. Cindy knew how to handle pancakes. And competition.

"I tried to call home before," Jewel said, "but no luck. I guess Mama moved and had the phone turned off. I'm scared to go back, but I got nowhere else to go, you know? Besides, I miss my Mama."

"Did you know Jewel's the same age as the girl you introduced to the Mortimers?" Cindy asked. "Another child trying to survive on the streets."

Hannibal hoped his eyebrows did not go up too high. If Cindy was right, he had misjudged Jewel's age by a decade. Now he looked at her again, racing through her breakfast, and thought about her actions since he had known her. Yes, beneath the signs of abuse was a girl not quite out of her teens, but with a lifetime of experience and wear. It made her hiring him and breaking with the street life an even greater act of courage than he originally thought.

"Miss Santiago told me a little about that girl from the other case you were on," Jewel said. "Her father ran away, just like mine did. But I guess you found out her dad's dead. I know you're off the case now, but any idea who killed him?"

Hannibal leaned back, sipped his orange juice. "Jewel, it could be almost anybody I've met in the last week. But there's this mob boss named Zack King. From the sound of things, he found out the victim was sitting on some rare and valuable coins he stole from his old man. He might have sent his man Slo Lerner to kill him."

"Didn't Daisy Sonneville say Pat Louis knew about the coins?" Cindy asked. "Instead of involving King, he might have done it himself and kept the coins."

"Or told his buddy Killer Nilson," Hannibal added. "Baltimore cops say he was a known murderer at the time and we know he and Pat Louis were pals."

Cindy turned to Hannibal, a twinkle in her eye. "If this was a mystery movie, I'd finger Malcolm Lippincott. When we met him, I could see he was mad in love with Camille."

"Who?" Jewel asked.

"The dead man's widow," Cindy said. "He's been around the family all his life. He might have bumped Jacob off to clear the field, so to speak. How could he know she'd be loyal to her dead husband?"

"Loyal, or keeping a deep secret of her own?" Hannibal asked, playing into her game. "He ran out on her, remember? And she was pregnant. What if she found him up in Baltimore? Suppose she walked in on him with the Barbie doll? Don't you think she's got the stuff to stab a man?" Hannibal ended his question with an evil chuckle.

"Well, what about the father?" Jewel asked in a quiet voice. Hannibal and Cindy both turned to face her. She swallowed, but went on. "You said he stole from his father. Couldn't he have found his son first? It's hard to believe he didn't even look for him. If they argued, he might have done it himself."

Hannibal grinned as he crunched up his last strip of bacon. "Got a point there, girl."

"Yes," Cindy said. "Too bad it's not your job to solve this mystery. And considering the interest we saw yesterday, probably nobody will."

"Maybe not," Hannibal said. "I have to move on to my next case, which might well start this afternoon in the district."

* * * * *

Less than half an hour after dropping Cindy at her home in Old Town Alexandria, Hannibal pulled up in front of the Northeast Free Clinic. Doctor Lawrence Lippincott's clinic was neither bright nor shining, but it was remarkably clean. When Hannibal parked his Volvo behind Dr. Lippincott's Mercedes, there was a man with the look of the homeless sweeping the sidewalk in front of the clinic. Another was washing the windows. Inside, the cramped reception room appeared recently scrubbed and sanitized, except for the plastic chairs, and the people waiting in most of them. The floor was industrial tile, the walls painted stark white. Each wall held a framed painting, the kind usually found in hotel rooms. The waiting patients carried their own offensive odors, but none of them could overpower the smell of iodine, or whatever antiseptic was in use these days. Two of the people waiting coughed with the kind of congestion Hannibal associated with tuberculosis. Without meaning to, he shrank away from them.

"Can I help you?" the receptionist asked in an icy voice. "You don't look like our usual client." The woman was rail thin, ink black in a white uniform, and very definitely in charge. Hannibal nodded.

"I have a lunch appointment with Doctor Lippincott."

"He's upstairs in the cafeteria," she said, raising a frail arm, pointing to the stairway on her right.

Two flights of stairs later, Hannibal found himself in a small, clean lunch room. The choices offered at the counter were limited, but the food looked and smelled good. Hannibal spotted Dr. Lippincott in the corner, sitting behind a tray, talking to another man in a white coat. He looked up and smiled in recognition.

"Get your lunch," Lippincott called. "We'll be done by the time you get here."

Hannibal picked up a tray and selected the pot roast and a piece of corn bread. He drew a lemonade from the machine and stopped at the cashier. The man at the register, in Rastafarian braids, looked surprised to see someone in front of him.

"How much?" Hannibal asked.

"Donations accepted," the man replied in a strong West Indian accent. Hannibal fished a ten dollar bill out of his wallet and handed it to the man, who rang it up with a look of shock.

When Hannibal reached Lippincott's table, he pulled off his gloves, but not his glasses. Lippincott was starting a plate of spaghetti. He smiled at Hannibal, with the kind of superiority saints always beam from their paintings.

"I see you found us," Lippincott said. "I don't suppose a fellow like you spends a lot of time here in Northeast, eh?"

Hannibal kept his smile from sliding into a sneer. "Actually, just about every Tuesday I volunteer at the homeless shelter three blocks from here. But I'm glad your Georgetown clientele pays you well enough that you can keep this place running for those who can't afford health care through the normal channels. Is it all free?"

"Oh, I collect from Medicare or Medicaid from those who qualify," Lippincott said. "But otherwise I don't charge for the care we give here. My doctors are all volunteers from George Washington University

Hospital, or the military hospitals: Walter Reed and Bethesda. They each give up a few hours, just like you do, to try to help those less fortunate."

Hannibal chewed a mouthful of his salt free but otherwise tasty lunch. "You understand that this visit is not part of my volunteer work. I'm on the clock here."

"Yes, as agreed," Lippincott said. "But before I tell you why I want to hire you, tell me what you know about Jacob Mortimer's death."

"Not much, really. I believe his murder was gang related. I believe Ike Paton, alias Pat Louis was involved somehow, and I think his death is related to Jacob's. But it's no longer my concern, officially."

"And the girl, Angela?" Lippincott asked, sipping from a tall glass of milk.

Hannibal looked up, feeling a trap closing in. "Look, I never said she was Jacob's daughter. She says she is, and I've got no evidence to the contrary."

"Whoa," Lippincott said, raising his hands in mock defense. "I know that, and I think you're still interested. Which is good. Because that's why I want to hire you. To prove her story false."

Hannibal put his fork down slowly and took a long drink. This was an unexpected gift. "You have a theory?"

"Well, yes," Lippincott said, dropping his own silverware. "I like your idea that Jacob was killed by gangsters. I think Angela's a fake hired by the mob to get Mortimer's money. They knew he'd want to find his long lost illegitimate granddaughter. The old boy's told me to stop looking for any other bone marrow donor for Kyle until she's been properly tested. Mister Jones that could waste a week to ten days. That's time Kyle does not have to waste. But I've seen you

165

can get results in short order, when you're put on the right scent."

"I see," Hannibal said. His body was very still for a moment, except for the middle finger of his left hand, which tapped up and down on the arm of his chair. "You may be right about Angela, but the motive is murky. Won't it blow the whole thing when she doesn't turn out to be a bone marrow match?"

"That won't prove she's not Jacob's daughter," Lippincott said, scratching at the ring of gray hair which circled his head from ear to ear. "You know DNA evidence isn't held in very high esteem by the general public. She'll still be accepted into the family. She already has been. Harlan sent her to get her things and bring them to his house. When he found out she didn't have a car, he gave her one."

"Wait a minute. He gave her a car?"

"Just like that," Lippincott almost raved. "A shiny new yellow Porsche. Called the dealer this morning and told him to give her what she wants. And he's told Gabriel to put her in his will."

Hannibal pushed his plate away. "He told you that?"

"He had to," Lippincott said. "I'm the executor of Harlan's estate. There's no reversing these things unless you can prove she's not who she says she is."

The bottom had dropped out of his case, and Hannibal could see it was deeper than he thought. Perhaps Lippincott was an ally, but even if he was not, he was a convenient excuse to continue his investigation.

"Doctor, you should know that I've already taken steps, on my own hook, to look more closely into Angela's past."

"Good!" Lippincott smiled warmly, and slapped Hannibal's shoulder. "Charge any expenses to me, son. Together, we'll get to the bottom of this evil deception."

"Uh-oh, another conspiracy theory." Malcolm walked toward them with Angela in tow. He looked less stiff in a flannel shirt and jeans. She looked a lot less vulnerable in a black silk blouse and a leather skirt. Malcolm leaned on the table between his father and Hannibal. "What are you rattling on about, Pop? Medicare? Or is it Social Security this time?"

Doctor Lippincott's mustache puffed in and out with his ragged breath as he stood. "It's that girl," he snorted. "She's evil, son. Evil and twisted and she'll drag you down with her."

"What's the matter old man?" Malcolm asked. "Jealous?"

Hannibal stood so quickly his chair flipped over behind him. Doctor Lippincott swung an open hand at his son's face. Malcolm snapped back, and the hand cut through empty air. When Malcolm swung, it was a with a closed fist, aimed at his father's jaw. Hannibal's gloved hand stopped it in midair.

"I think that's a little extreme," Hannibal said, his voice tight. "He is your father." Then Hannibal turned his hand, twisting Malcolm's arm around and down. Malcolm stared into Hannibal's lenses for a moment, until he realized he could not win this contest and yanked his hand away. As he turned to go, Hannibal caught a final view of Angela's face. For a brief instant, he saw a flash of terrible hatred, a hate that struck out like venom from a spitting viper. Then it disappeared so quickly a man could doubt if he really saw it at all.

* * * * *

Horns blared from all directions, making them virtually pointless. Hannibal pulled his car onto what he hoped was the correct ramp and stopped at the end of the line. Ray Santiago was flying in on USAir, but the pick up area in front of the building was only a distant mirage. To reach his friend, Hannibal would have to fight his way through a mob of taxis, all flowing toward the same point like a school of demented fish.

Hannibal considered newly renamed Ronald Reagan Washington National Airport a thinly disguised welfare program for the construction industry. For seven years he had watched the traffic pattern in and around the airport continually shifting, transforming, and morphing more often than the political winds around Washington. A low flying jet roared overhead, raising the tension level of a long line of frustrated drivers. Hannibal reached down and cranked up his CD player.

The public Hannibal Jones listened to jazz, blues and older R & B. Alone in his Volvo, especially at times of high tension, he would indulge in one of his guilty pleasures. Growing up where English was spoken only on the American Forces Network, he had been raised on rock-and-roll. Right then, Eric Clapton's jamming guitar licks were helping to keep him sane.

Inch by creeping inch, Hannibal approached the curb. When he could see Ray clearly, he switched the player to an old CD of Roberta Flack and Donny Hathaway. Eventually he came within reach, and Ray swung into the seat beside him, tossing his overnight bag into the back seat. Now Hannibal faced the equally intimidating task of getting out of Ronald Reagan Washington National Airport.

"Welcome back, Ray," Hannibal said, showing none of his frustration. "How'd you like Corpus Christi?"

"It's a lovely city, Hannibal." Ray leaned back and yawned contentedly. He was not used to having people drive him around, and he was going to enjoy it. "A lovely city filled with lovely people. Clean. Quiet. And the most amazing Mexican food, Chico. The city has everything, except maybe what you sent me to find. "

Hannibal saw his break, downshifted, and powered up the ramp onto I-395. From there, home was a snap. "You mean Angela's adoption papers? Hey, I'm not sure I wanted you to find them."

Ray looked puzzled. "Long, expensive trip for something you don't want."

"I'm just not sure Angela's who she says she is," Hannibal said. "If you found adoption records at the local orphanage, or a name change at City Hall, it would support her story. Since you didn't it throws a certain amount of suspicion on her."

"Maybe," Ray said as Hannibal cut across three lanes of traffic to reach the eastward extension of I-395, headed toward Anacostia. "The lady at city hall, she said people change their names all the time without going through the legal motions."

"True," Hannibal said, "but what about the orphanage?"

"Burned to the ground two years ago."

"What?" Hannibal slowed and pulled into the right lane. "Everything?"

"All the records were destroyed," Ray said. He pulled out his cigarettes, but reconsidered lighting up in Hannibal's car.

"Damn. Can't even prove whether she was ever in Corpus Christi."

"Oh, she was there all right," Ray said. Pride shone from his sly, round face.

"And just how do you know this?"

"Because, Chico, I went to the library." Ray puffed up at the look of surprise on Hannibal's face. "Know what they had there? All the high school year books. I found Angela Briggs in last year's graduating class, and it's this girl's picture."

"I'm impressed," Hannibal said. "You're a better detective than I am."

"She was also in the two years before," Ray went on, his face beaming, "but that's all, so I figure she was somewhere else her freshman year. So. What does that prove?"

"Not much," Hannibal said. "We just know she was there. But did her adoption records burn, or does a convenient fire allow her to make up this story. And what about the guy she claims adopted her?"

"Dead," Ray said, "two years ago."

Hannibal looked at his friend with new respect. "You looked for Briggs?"

"I figured Sam Briggs could tell us for sure if this girl was his daughter," Ray said. "But I couldn't find him in the phone book, so I tried the obits. There he was."

"At least, there was a Sam Briggs," Hannibal said. "Any mention of Angela?"

Ray closed his eyes to prompt his memory. "He is survived by his sister Edwina Briggs, and an adopted daughter. That's all it said. No name."

Hannibal was quietly thoughtful for the rest of the drive. In a few minutes he was off the highway and onto the narrow streets of his part of the District, the area surrounding the Washington Navy Yard. Traffic was light, and a few minutes later he pulled up in front of his building and set the emergency brake. He turned in his seat to face Ray.

"Where you going?"

Hannibal looked like he was about to swallow something bitter. "I hate to say it, but I think I ought to take my suspicions to the police."

-22-

The Fairfax City Municipal Center was a clean, modern facility on Old Lee Highway, two miles south of Gabriel Nieswand's house. Hannibal called ahead, prepared to give a report to whatever policeman was on duty. He was surprised to find Orson Rissik in the office on Saturday, and even more surprised to hear the duty officer say Detective Rissik was anxious to speak with him.

Hannibal parked in the nearly empty lot and pushed through the glass doors, following the directions he was given to Rissik's office. It was medium sized, but very clean and brightly lit. Rissik was talking on the phone when Hannibal arrived, so he sat in the visitor's chair and looked around. Rissik wore a conservative blue suit, but his Structure tie was pulled down from his throat and the top button of his crisply starched shirt hung open.

His desk was fanatically orderly, every sheet of paper in one of the neat stacks, or in an OUT box, or one marked Hold. His IN box was empty. Three framed citations clung to the walls left and right of the desk. Behind Rissik's head hung the only other picture of any kind in the room. It was a poster of a pelican trying to eat a frog. His head already in the bird's mouth, the frog had reached out and wrapped a hand around the pelican's throat, preventing it from swallowing him. A caption under the picture said "Never Give Up".

When Rissik hung up, he took three deep breaths. Then he stood, fixing his dangerous blue eyes on Hannibal. "So? What are you doing here?"

"Looking for a cop," Hannibal shot back. "You got a problem?" Rissik was polite, friendly and respectful during their last meeting. His change of attitude caught Hannibal off guard.

"Problem?" Rissik repeated, leaning on his fists on his desk. "Problems line up to come visit me. Want to know why I'm in here, working on a Saturday? I got a murder investigation going on. I got a prime suspect too. Got a name. Know where he usually hangs out. Only thing is, some P.I. trying to solve his own case chased my prime suspect underground, along with his nearest known relative. The Lerner brothers have disappeared."

Hannibal's eyes flared wide behind his shades, but he held his tongue long enough to stand, turn, and close the half glass door to Rissik's office. When he turned, his teeth were bared, his hands curled into fists.

"You got a lot of damned nerve, Chief," he shouted, pacing toward the desk. "First of all, you sent me looking for Wally Lerner, hoping for a lead to his brother. Second, you wouldn't have had a suspect if I didn't hand you a description. And one more thing, pal." Hannibal leaned on his own fists on Rissik's desk, leaning in until they were nose to nose. "Your junior G men would have had the perp under wraps minutes after the murder if they had asked me a couple of questions before they slapped the cuffs on me and hauled me away." They stood there, face to face for nearly a full minute. Finally, Hannibal said

"Now, are you interested in a shot at maybe finding this guy?"

Rissik stood straight, then motioned for Hannibal to have a seat. When Hannibal was in a chair, Rissik walked to his side table. He refilled his coffee cup, poured another and handed it to Hannibal. Then he sat down, took a long sip, and leaned back. His chair squeaked in the silence.

"All right. Those knuckleheads were faulty on procedure. And so was I, asking you to do what should have been police work. Now, what you got?"

"Apology accepted," Hannibal said, tasting his coffee. At least this cop could do one thing right. "Actually, we can help each other. Can your case extend to Great Falls?"

Rissik rubbed his chin with thumb and forefinger, like a real old-fashioned detective. "It can if I have a good reason. Is that where the Lerners are?"

"Not likely," Hannibal said. "But there's a connection. Bear with me for a minute here. You know who Harlan Mortimer is?"

"The black real estate wheeler dealer?" Rissik asked. "I've heard of him. I don't think he's got any mob connections, though. You saying he does?"

Hannibal held up a gloved palm. "Not like that. But he's got a granddaughter he never knew he had, by his son who's dead now. She just turned up, and it looks like he's ready to put her in his will."

Hannibal could see Rissik's mind clicking as he did the arithmetic. He knew exactly how this equation added up. "You figure she's not legit."

"Bingo. In fact, I'm pretty sure she's the bait in a mob plot to get the old man's money. Now, I'm not going to give you details, because there's a question of confidentiality here, but I think maybe the old man's son, the girls supposed father, was killed by Sloan Lerner and his friends. So it makes sense..."

"They're the bad boys who put the girl in," Rissik said, finishing Hannibal's sentence. Both men were smiling now. "And that probably means Zack King. So what do you want, Mister Jones?"

Hannibal leaned back and put his right ankle on his left knee. "Well, I thought you could put some men on watching the Mortimer house. If the bad guys come sniffing around to see how the girl's doing, you can nab them. And if anybody tries any violence, your boys can be on the spot to stop it. Now, how do you know about Zack King?"

"I do my homework," Rissik said. "Ike Paton used to be Pat Louis. I take it you know that already. You probably also know he was working for King a year ago in Atlantic City. Did you know he was in Killer Nilson's gang years ago? It was Nilson's bunch who called themselves Omega and got those tattoos."

"Sure," Hannibal vamped. "Sloan Lerner was in that old gang with him. Maybe they set this scam up a long time ago, eh? With Louis, as Paton, as the inside man. Then maybe Louis had second thoughts."

Rissik nodded and waved a finger at Hannibal. "Sure. That makes a dandy motive for murder. And it raises the possibility one of them might come back to check on the girl. Okay, I'll have the house watched."

Hannibal emptied his cup. "Just wish I knew where they're hiding now."

"Well, I've got warrants out in Baltimore and New Jersey, but I figure it's too hot in those places for these guys," Rissik said, heading for his coffee pot. "I sent e-mail to the boys in Texas too."

"Texas?" Hannibal sat up very straight. "Why?" Rissik made an odd face and turned to fill his cup again. When he returned to his desk he stared down into the cup. Hannibal said "Come on chief. You owe me."

Rissik seemed to mull it over before deciding to open up. "Louis' last bust was in Texas," he said. "They caught him driving in from Mexico with a truck load of illegals. Most of his cargo got away but he went up. That was four years ago, and he only did a couple of years. But he might have had something going on down there. What do you think?"

Hannibal froze while his mind processed this new information. This case was littered with thin connections that looked important, and now it had one more. Patrick Louis, AKA Ike Paton was coming across the Mexican border into Texas four years ago, which was when Angela Briggs, AKA Angela Mortimer, first appeared in Corpus Christi.

-23-

Sometimes, Hannibal wished he could simply walk away. He drove back to Washington in a fog of uncertainty. The case seemed as twisted and dirty as the narrow streets he was driving on. The Rolling Stones in the CD player could not blast the confusion out of his brain. He wished he had not agreed to prove Angela Mortimer a fake. He wished he did not care who killed Pat Louis, or why.

But he did care, and he had agreed. And while he had no interest in following the trail of these two dovetailed mysteries to the Mexican border, he figured he knew where he might get a lead closer to home. Floyd had spoken to Hannibal once under threat of violence. He might be more informative about the New Jersey mob with cash as his incentive. But Hannibal began to have doubts when he pulled up across the street from Floyd's building.

Hannibal did not believe in extra sensory perception. But he knew experienced policemen and bodyguards developed a clear picture of how things should be, and became sensitive to situations when things were not. He thought all the senses must be involved, which explained why various people sometimes said they felt, smelled, or sensed trouble.

The first thing he noticed was the absence of a guard on the stoop. Of course, it might be the case whenever Floyd was away from home, but it did not feel right. Then there was the green Ford Explorer parked in front of the door. It might not have anything to do with Floyd, but Hannibal sensed it did. And the outside door to the building was an inch or two ajar. No one who lived in this neighborhood would purposely leave the door open. It might mean no more than the presence of a careless child. But Hannibal smelled trouble.

The sound of breaking glass drew his attention to the second floor. Bits of a window flashed and glittered as they fell slowly toward the ground. He rolled his window down, trying to stare into the now open portal to Floyd's apartment. He heard the unmistakable thump of a rubber coated baton against human flesh repeated five times. Then he saw Floyd himself. He emerged from the window head first, chasing his own blood curdling scream. Catapulted into space, he seemed to be trying to swim to the other side of the street. In fact, he covered the distance to the gutter in front of his building. He neither flashed nor glittered. Nor did he fall slowly. His head hit the street first, and he was surely dead by the time his feet bounced off the concrete. Not much splatter, but Hannibal's stomach lurched.

In the next ten seconds, three onlookers wandered slowly toward the body, unable to resist the lure of death, but not wanting to get too close. Then the door at the top of the stoop slammed open and three huge men ran down the stairs much more quickly than he would have expected. One jumped behind the wheel of the Explorer and fired up the engine while the other two hopped into the back seat. The license plates were caked with mud, making them unreadable. The vehicle laid rubber as it darted away. Hannibal watched it disappear in his rear view mirror.

Hannibal may have been inclined to help even scum like Floyd. But Floyd was beyond help now. And Hannibal knew it was pointless to mess with those three unless he was prepared to do anything to win. This was surely Zack King's revenge for talking to Hannibal. How he knew it was Floyd who led Hannibal to him was a mystery not worth puzzling over. Mobsters had ways of learning things. However he found out, King took action to make sure it would not happen again.

Hannibal swallowed his frustration, slipped his car into gear and pulled away. Zack had sealed the only leak Hannibal knew about. The Jersey mob was a closed book to him again. It might have to do with keeping him away from the secret behind Angela's appearance. Or it could be Zack's way of telling people not to talk about him.

* * * * *

A cloud bank moved in, making Hannibal's neighborhood seem darker than usual. The few trees on the block were sickly and weak. Hardly anything thrived in this environment and he wondered for the millionth time why he chose to stay here. He shuffled into his hallway, feeling defeated. He closed the door behind himself, turned left toward his apartment, and froze. New energy seemed to flood into him as he realized he did have another option. He sprinted to his office, shoving the door open.

"Whoa!" Hannibal froze, his heart missing one beat then bursting into triplets. Sarge's finger spasmed on the shotgun's trigger, barely avoiding dropping the hammer. They stared at each other for a minute, then Sarge let out a long breath and lowered the barrel.

"Man, you could get yourself killed like that," Sarge said. "It's been a long, hairy week."

"Yeah, and you've done a great job," Hannibal said, pulling his sports coat off, "but now it's over. Jewel's in no more danger."

A face afraid to show hope peeked out from the next room. "Are you sure?" Jewel asked in her high pitched voice. "How can you be sure?"

"Because somebody a lot bigger than Floyd just tossed him out of his apartment," Hannibal said, plopping into the chair behind his desk. "In fact, they were in such a hurry, they had him take the elevator down."

"But his building doesn't have an...oh." Hannibal saw the light come on in Jewel's head, and heard Sarge chuckling. Then Jewel's expression changed, as she realized all that this news implied.

"He's gone," she said slowly, smiling at the sky outside Hannibal's office windows. "He's gone. I'm free." Then she rushed across the floor to fling her arms around Hannibal's neck. "How can I ever thank you enough for what you've done?"

"Well, there is my fee," Hannibal answered, easing out of her embrace and leading her to his visitor's chair. "But you can also help me with this case I'm working on. Floyd told me you were working in Atlantic City when he found you. What do you know about Zack King?"

Jewel looked at the ceiling and rubbed the back of her head, which apparently was how she engaged the memory of her internal computer. "Isn't that the name of a promoter in Atlantic City?"

"You've never met him?"

"Not that I knew," Jewel said

Hannibal walked slowly around her. "How about Wally Lerner, or his brother Sloan?"

Jewel swiveled in her chair, trying to keep Hannibal in view. "Never heard of them guys, I'm afraid."

"Okay, then how about Ike Paton?"

She shook her head left to right. "Sorry."

Hannibal's frustration was mounting. He leaned toward her, his hands on the arms of her chair. "You might have known him as Pat Louis. Big black guy, tattoo of the Greek letter omega on his hand."

"Don't know that name either," Jewel said. "And I don't think I know anybody with a tattoo on their hand. Sorry."

Hannibal turned and banged his desk. He hoped Floyd shared his knowledge of the underworld when he was drunk, or being intimate. But he could see Jewel had never gotten involved with the mob connections, in DC or New Jersey. She no more knew where the Lerners might hide than he did. He was sure the Lerner brothers held the secret to Angela's scam, if it was a scam. But now he had no way to find them.

"How am I going to prove to Nieswand that the girl's a fake?" he asked the desk.

"Nieswand?" Jewel asked in a shaky voice. "I know that name."

Hannibal felt a jolt of electricity flash up his spine. It was too much to hope for, but the name was so uncommon he had to believe Jewel recognizing it was significant. He breathed deeply, trying to contain his optimism. Forcing a smile, trying not to intimidate the girl, he turned and leaned back against his desk.

"Jewel, are you sure you know that name from Atlantic City?"

181

"Of course," she said with a nervous laugh. "You don't forget a name like that."

"True," he said. "What was he doing up there?"

Jewel's confidence fell, and she began rubbing her hands together. "He? Sorry, this was a girl."

He knew he should not have gotten overconfident. He gritted his teeth against the frustration rising in his gut. "A girl." he repeated.

"Yeah," Jewel said. "Another hooker, I think. Abby Nieswand. I'm sure that was the name."

"Abby?" Hannibal felt another jolt, strong enough to lift him from the desk. Resisting his drive to hug Jewel, he probed deeper. "What did she look like, this Abby Nieswand? And what was she doing there? When was this, anyway?"

Sarge stepped in and put a hand on Hannibal's shoulder. "Easy, man. This ain't no interrogation. She's trying to help." Hannibal nodded to Sarge, then to Jewel to continue.

Jewel took a deep breath, gathered her thoughts, and went on. "This is like a year ago, maybe a little more. Not long before I left Jersey with Floyd. For a while she was in the hotel room next door to the one I used for," Jewel hesitated for a second, "for business, you know. I don't think she was doing street work. She had to be pushing forty pretty hard. Bottle blonde I think. I mean, she was a white girl, but her complexion was kind of dark for a blonde, you know? Dark eyes like Jewish girls have a lot of times. Pretty nice figure. And I guess the guy she was with liked real bright red nail polish."

"The guy she was with," Hannibal said, waving his hand to encourage her to continue.

"She stayed in that one room most of the time." Jewel was again following Hannibal as he paced around her. "When she came out she would talk, and she seemed pretty nice. And pretty lonely. She was, what do you call that? A kept woman, right? The guy was black and pretty big, and he was paying the bills. But he only came back to the room to, you know, for service." Hannibal's face must have shown his distaste because she added, "That's the way some guys are." Hannibal nodded and pulled his jacket back on.

"Where to?" Sarge asked. "Trouble?"

"Not your kind," Hannibal said, his voice hard. "I feel the need to talk to Mister Nieswand about his wife's extracurricular activities. Who knows? Maybe she can give me a lead to the Jersey mob."

* * * * *

When Hannibal pulled into Nieswand's driveway, he was thinking about how much territory he had covered on what should have been a quiet Saturday. Lunch in a clinic meant to be a bright spot in the lowest of slum neighborhoods. Then to a police station in the supposedly higher class suburbs. Back to the inner city in time to see a pimp take a header. And now, back to Oakton, probably to see one of its upper class citizens hit rock bottom himself, figuratively if not literally.

Walking up the flagstone path toward the door of Nieswand's huge brick colonial house, he considered how much its owner's life had changed in the last week. Today, no trusted chauffeur would hassle visitors about where they parked. And for now, he had no drug dependent wife to hide away. Despite the brochures, Hannibal decided, sometimes gracious country living sucks.

The doorbell was a cheerful series of chimes. A minute later, Gabriel Nieswand pulled the door open. His hairpiece was slightly askew and he did not appear to care. He looked somehow unnatural in a knit golf shirt and Dockers. Bags under his eyes and the glass in his hand explained his condition better than a painted sign would.

"Hello. Didn't expect to see you again."

"Thought I should give you a final report concerning the case," Hannibal said. For lawyers, keep it formal. It usually worked. "May I come in for a moment?"

"Glad to have the company," Nieswand said, swinging the door fully open. Hannibal closed it behind himself and followed his host across the marble floor through his two story foyer, then down three steps into a plush den. Classical music was coming from somewhere. Nieswand dropped onto a love seat and motioned Hannibal to the overstuffed chair by the antique globe.

"Help yourself to a drink," Nieswand said, waving his own glass toward the bar. "I'm having scotch myself. There's quite a variety. I've probably sampled it all sometime in the past week."

Pain leaked out of Nieswand's eyes, and Hannibal felt a little guilty taking advantage of it. But his need to know overrode any other feelings he had. "No drinks for me, thanks. I'm driving. But how have you been? How's your wife doing?"

Nieswand stared into his half empty glass as if it were a crystal ball. "I'm doing about as well as expected with my wife twenty miles away in a private hospital. She has a substance abuse problem, Mister Jones. Finding a corpse in our garage seems to have pushed her over the edge into actual schizophrenia.

Her grip on reality has weakened, or so Lawrence Lippincott says."

"I see." Hannibal sat forward on the edge of his chair, hands folded, elbows on knees, the picture of sincere concern. "I think you're bearing up well. You know, a friend of mine thinks he might have met your wife. Were you vacationing in Atlantic City last year, by any chance?"

Nieswand's eyes narrowed as he searched his memory. "We avoid places like that Mister Jones. Too much of a temptation, what with all the liquor and drugs about."

"That's funny," Hannibal said, "my friend is sure he saw her up there. Described her well, and you do have a fairly uncommon name."

"Last year?" Nieswand leaned back with his eyes closed. A closer inspection of his memory, Hannibal assumed. "My wife disappeared for a few days last year. God knows where she went. Maybe up to that sinful place. They say the seventh year of marriage is tough for men, but for my Abby it was, I don't know, maybe she just felt too restricted. Anyway, she came back and I didn't ask a whole lot of questions. I was just glad to have her back. I love my wife very much, Mister Jones."

Nieswand gulped the last of his drink, and Hannibal gulped too. His throat was dry with self hatred. It was wrong, cruel, unfair for him to continue. But Hannibal's religion was the truth and he would not betray his idol. "Does your wife have friends in New Jersey, Mister Nieswand?"

Nieswand's answer was almost too low to hear. "I don't know." Then he turned to Hannibal and the alcohol forced confessional words out his mouth. "I don't know, really. Abby was married before, you see.

I don't know much about her life before me. I know her past wasn't too pretty, though, so I tried to give her everything in the present. I guess it wasn't enough. Maybe you can't outrun the past, eh?" Then a brief wave of clarity crossed Nieswand's face and he stood, stepping purposefully to the bar. As he twisted a Chivas Regal bottle open, he said "I appreciate the ear, but you didn't come by to hear my hard luck story. What was it you wanted to talk about?"

"Angela Briggs," Hannibal said, a part of him glad to have the subject changed. "I'm not convinced she's the genuine article, and I'm not alone. I hear Harlan Mortimer has already written her into his will. I think that's premature, and I guess I thought I should tell you that."

When Nieswand sat down he was the canny attorney again, his clear mind peeling away the layers of what Hannibal said. "You got that from Larry didn't you? You working for him now?"

It took Hannibal a moment to realize Larry was Doctor Lippincott. He remembered now they were introduced to him as friends. "Yes, he's very concerned about the Mortimer family."

"Really," Nieswand said, gulping from his drink. "Well you can tell him nothing's been changed in the will, at least not yet. Angela Mortimer, or Briggs if you prefer, is not the recipient of any inheritance. He still gets his money." Hannibal didn't move but Nieswand went on. "He didn't tell you that, did he? Oh, you've got a good poker face, son, but don't forget I read people for a living. And yes, Larry and his son Mal are both mentioned in the will. More importantly, there's a big lump of funding for Larry's downtown clinic. I think it represents the sum of Harlan's social conscience. So I don't think Larry qualifies as an objective source."

"Maybe not," Hannibal said, "but I don't have any vested interest in this and I personally am not convinced she's the real thing."

"Look, I'm not saying I can prove who Angela is in a court of law, but the evidence is certainly with her. And besides, the girl's brought the first real joy into that house since Kyle was born."

Hannibal's hands opened, accenting his plea. "If you don't temper their acceptance of her with some common sense, they could be in for a real crash if she turns out to be a phony."

Nieswand climbed slowly to his feet. "Let me make this clear, Mister Jones. It makes Harlan Mortimer happy to believe this girl is his long lost granddaughter, his only connection to a son he lost years before he disappeared. If he learns that isn't true, he won't hear it from me."

* * * * *

Camille Mortimer answered the door in a black gown, diamond earrings and subtle but complete makeup. Her face was warm, aglow with hope. She was transformed from the cool, worried woman he met days ago at this very door.

"Hi," Camille said, flashing white, even teeth. "We were just heading out. The Kennedy Center and dinner. Were you looking for Angela? I'm so glad you found her. She's like a daughter to me already."

"Actually, I was hoping to have a word with Harlan," Hannibal said. Camille waved him inside and left him at the door while she went to fetch her father-in-law. Hannibal looked around, registering again the hugeness of the house and considering what a daunting job it would be to have to paint the interior of this cavern. As his head slowly panned around he found Angela walking toward him. Her gown was a match for Camille's. Her dark brown hair cascaded down onto her shoulders in natural waves, and high heels showed off sturdy legs. She looked up at Hannibal with a reluctant smile, ready to turn to a frown at a moment's notice.

"Can I talk to you for a minute?" Hannibal nodded, and followed her through the French doors onto the now deserted deck. When she turned he almost gasped at the change. Gone was any hint of hesitation, or lack of confidence. Her eyes were now diamond hard, her aggressive chin stabbing at him defiantly.

"I don't know why you're after me, but I want you to leave me alone," she said. "So what's the price to make you back off?"

"The truth," Hannibal said. "I back off when these people know the truth. Money is important, but it won't take the place of the truth."

Angela shook her head, her hair fanning out around her as if to blur Hannibal's view. She looked at him with disbelief. "Why are you doing this? I'm not here to hurt anybody. Can't you see I've brought some happiness to this dreary place?"

"Why are you doing this?" Hannibal countered, now sure his suspicions were correct. "Is it really all about money?"

"What do you know?" Angela asked. "You don't know what it's like. Being raised a half-breed. An orphan. To survive, you do what you have to do."

"I don't know?" Hannibal said in a low voice. He pulled his glasses off and pushed his face into Angela's. "Take a good look."

Angela stared deep into his hazel eyes, mostly green with his anger right then. "I didn't see before," she said. "You're like me, aren't you?"

"My father was a black soldier, a military policeman," Hannibal said, his voice still low but hard now. "My mother was a German girl he met while stationed in Berlin. He left me there when they sent him to Vietnam. But he never came back. My mother raised me in Berlin, among the American military community, at a time when mixed marriages weren't really accepted. Children of those marriages even less so. I think that qualifies me to say I know exactly what you're about. But that don't make me think it's okay for you to commit fraud."

"What's this about fraud?" Harlan Mortimer stepped onto the deck, looking even bigger than he really was in a navy blue suit and maroon tie. In the time it took Hannibal to get his Oakleys back on his face, Angela went from aggressive to conciliatory, her remarkably facile eyes softened and damp.

"That Doctor Lippincott sent him," she said, barely avoiding an actual whine. "They think I'm a, a, I don't know what they think I am."

With one last glance at Hannibal she ran into the house. He was impressed. Her eyes were actually starting to water before she left. How many Hollywood actresses could turn on the tears so fast?

"Well?" Harlan stood with his fists on his ample hips. "Is this true?"

Angela had removed the option of easing into the conversation. "Yes, I am working for Doctor Lippincott now," Hannibal said. "And I share his doubts about

Angela's background. I just wanted to ask you for a little time to verify her story. And for you to not pin all your hopes for Kyle on this girl until I could."

Storm clouds gathered on Mortimer's dark face and the top of his ears tinged red. "Now you listen to me young man. Anybody with eyes, who talked to her for more than a few minutes could have no doubt Angela's a Mortimer. And I won't have a member of my family doubted, not even by Larry. You tell that pompous windbag I know what he's up to and it's too late. You understand? Tell that quack he's out of my will as soon as I can get the paperwork done. And tell him I'll get Kyle's medical care from somebody who can be a little more objective from now on. And now I'll thank you to get out of my house before I forget all the good you've done up to now."

Hannibal stalked through the house away from Mortimer as quickly as he could without running. His rage may have bubbled out of him if he had not met Kyle in his wheelchair at the door. A tie and dinner jacket wrapped the boy's skeletal frame, his head almost bald but not shining because the same chemotherapy which killed the roots of his hair drained the oils from his skin.

"Mister Jones," Kyle called. "I was afraid I might not ever see you again. But I want to make sure you're around after the transplant, when I'm up and around."

Hannibal stopped to take Kyle's hand. "Don't worry. You're not rid of me. My job for your grandfather is over, but you're still my client, and my job for you isn't done."

As he climbed into his car, Hannibal realized how contracted his time schedule had become. Harlan could begin legal action Monday morning to change his will, maybe even to adopt Angela. Certainly he

190

would move to legally change her last name. And since Nieswand was his lawyer, Hannibal could lose his most valuable ally to a conflict of interest by then. So Sunday would have to be a work day. He hit an autodial button on his phone while be pulled out of Mortimer's driveway. The phone rang twice before it was answered.

"Hello, this is Cindy."

"Hi babe. I need some help, a legal overwatch, but it'll mean working tomorrow."

"For you, lover?" Cindy said. "Anything. What's up?"

"A long flight," he answered. "Ever been to Texas?"

-24-

SUNDAY

Stepping out of Corpus Christi International Airport, Hannibal was grateful to Cindy for convincing him not to wear his traditional work clothes. She said he might intimidate people who were used to a more casual, relaxed, Southwest style. Whether or not she was right, he now agreed a black suit and tie were inappropriate dress for springtime in east Texas.

By twelve-thirty, when they arrived, the temperature had already crossed the ninety degree mark on its way to beyond one hundred. The sun looked twice as bright to him here and, despite Corpus Christi sitting on the coast, he detected not the slightest breeze. Yes, he would have died in his black suit and tie. Not that he strayed far from his personal norm. He walked into Texas in a short sleeved white dress shirt and neatly pressed navy blue walking shorts. The biggest change for him was having to carry his backup Colt Mustang in an overnight case, instead of his full size Sig Sauer in a holster.

Cindy was dressed as Hannibal was but somehow it looked so much better on her, partly because while he left his top shirt button open, she left three. She wore the Oakley sunglasses he gave her and a ruby pendant nestled snugly into her cleavage, an unnecessary draw for any passerby's attention.

Once in his rented Lincoln Town Car, Hannibal set the air conditioner at the maximum setting and handed Cindy a map of the city he picked up at the rental counter.

"See if you can find the library on that thing, babe," Hannibal said. "On Sunday, it's our best shot at finding a phone book. And that's our best chance of finding Edwina Briggs."

Corpus Christi was a pleasant surprise to Hannibal. He was expecting bowlegged cowpokes in ten gallon hats with guns on their hips. In fact, he found a civilized urban community not unlike what he was accustomed to, except somehow these people managed to keep their city fairly clean.

The ride through town reminded him of a fact he did not like to dwell on. In his teens he saved his money, bought a Europass, and explored the continent with a handful of adventurous friends. Since landing in the United States, he had worked hard at building a law enforcement career first in New York, then in Washington. When that soured, he worked at building a business of his own. As a result, he belatedly realized, he knew Europe much better than he knew his own country outside the narrow strip between New York City and northern Virginia.

The white pages at the library led them to a small cottage near the Gulf. They parked half a block away and got out of their car to look around before knocking on the door. Hannibal could swear the temperature was fifteen degrees lower on the coast, and a gentle breeze did bring the tang of salt air. Between cottages, he could see the island across the Laguna Madres.

"I've read the Padre Island out there has one of the ten best beaches in the country," Hannibal said. "Fishing. Wind surfing. What would you think of this for a vacation?"

"Looks like a gorgeous vacation spot," Cindy agreed. "I've spotted a dozen restaurants I'd love to try, and the shopping looks fabulous."

Hannibal chose to say nothing more, but went to the house and rang the doorbell. After a moment, a bell clear voice said, "out back." After the slightest hesitation, Hannibal took Cindy's hand and followed the flagstone path around the house. In back they found three long rows of bushes. Cindy gasped at the beauty, and Hannibal had to admit it was a sight to move the hardest heart. A rainbow of roses glowed on the bushes: red, white, pink, yellow, orange, even some with black trimmed edges. Near the far end of the center row, a woman in white awaited them. Her hat brim hid her face from visitors, but when she stood, Hannibal caught sight of parchment skin and bright blue eyes. She was small boned, but her posture was dramatically erect. A proud woman, he thought, aging gracefully in her garden by the sea.

"Well here are a couple of new faces," she said in a gentle drawl.

"Are you Edwina Briggs?" Hannibal asked, trying not to be hypnotized by the unbelievable sweetness of the garden's perfume.

"Probably. Why?"

Cindy stepped forward, letting her eyes wander to the roses on her right. "These are so beautiful. Miss Briggs, my name is Cynthia Santiago. I'm an attorney. This is Hannibal Jones. We've come a long way to talk to you about your late brother, Sam."

Edwina seemed to consider this, then she sat on a small stool and began pruning a rose bush. She moved the small shears with great care, nipping the bushes as if they might scream if she cut too close. "Did you know my brother?"

Cindy looked at Hannibal. He indicated she should continue. She squatted next to the older woman. "No, ma'am, neither of us knew him, but we've met a young woman who claims to be his adopted daughter. Did you know her?"

"Could be," Edwina said, sparing no attention from her roses. The sound of each snip carried a grim finality. "What's her name?"

"Angela," Cindy said. "Black and Latin, thin pointed nose, full lips, quite beautiful."

"Even teeth and real bright eyes," Edwina added. "Refused to wear glasses, even though she needed them. Yes, I knew her."

Hannibal and Cindy exchanged a glance, then Cindy asked "Did she stay with you after your brother passed away?"

"She was only what, sixteen, seventeen when Sam died?" Edwina said. "No, she went and got herself a room in town. Rented from Shawn Boyd, boy I went to high school with." She flashed a nostalgic smile, then went on pruning her roses.

"I think I'd like to talk to him," Hannibal said, almost to himself. Edwina never looked at him, but now he noticed she was watching Cindy, whose eye had been attracted to a particular rose. It was a blood red cup, yet the edges of its petals paled almost to translucence. She stretched a finger toward it, but appeared afraid to touch a thing of such delicacy.

"Go on," Edwina said. "Take it. Your beauty will complement it."

Cindy plucked the stem from its limb and lifted the flower to her nose. "Miss Briggs, why wasn't Angela's name mentioned in your brother's obituary?"

Without missing a beat, Edwina said "Because I wrote it."

"Didn't you like Angela?" Hannibal asked.

Edwina stood up and took three or four steps down the row. Hannibal lifted her stool and placed it where she wanted to sit. She smiled a thank you.

"There was something about that child," Edwina said. "Something cold. Dead inside. What's she doing now?"

"As it turns out," Cindy said, peering into her new rose, "she appears to be related to a rather wealthy family in Virginia. We're just checking her background, but it looks as though she's coming up roses."

Edwina lowered her pruning shears and looked up, first at Cindy, then to address Hannibal. "Know why these roses smell so sweet? Eh? It's because of all the manure down around their roots. They grow up in manure, and they smell so sweet and climb so far because they're trying to get away from those roots. Let me give you Shawn Boyd's address."

Like any city, Corpus Christi has its high rent districts, its slums, and its in between places, populated by older people trying to survive. Homes there are older, smaller, less modern, but well kept up. Over the years, some of the larger older homes get recast as boarding houses. Like Shawn Boyd's house. It reminded Hannibal of Wayne Manor in old Batman comic books, except this place was crouching behind a wall of perfectly manicured hedges. As he parked across the street, Hannibal saw he and Cindy could again avoid going inside. The white haired gentleman rocking on the front porch had to be the owner.

"You must be the two strangers Edwina called about," the older man said as they approached.

"And you're Mister Boyd?" Cindy asked.

"Nope, I'm Shawn," he said, leaning forward in his chair and extending a hand. "My father is Mister Boyd. Now, what can I do for you folks?" Shawn did not look frail exactly, just tired. He wore overalls despite the heat, and heavy work shoes. Hannibal found his handshake firm, even though he could feel every bone in the man's hand.

"We're trying to find out about Angela Briggs," Cindy said, dropping into a green wicker chair. "Do you remember her?"

"Angela? Of course. Stayed right up there in number four."

"Did she have visitors," Cindy asked. "Was she traveling with anybody?"

"She'd have a boy up now and again," Shawn said. "Can't say I ever saw any of them twice."

"Miss Briggs didn't seem to know her very well," Hannibal said, leaning against a porch support beam. "Did you ever talk with her?"

"Of course," Shawn said. "I always chat with my boarders. It's funny how willing people always seem to sit and talk to an old man. Or else they're just real polite."

Shawn gave a little chuckle, then focused on Hannibal. He seemed to be waiting for more questions, so Hannibal tossed one. "Did she ever give any indication she might be from the East Coast?"

Shawn's chuckle almost burst into a guffaw. "East Coast? Mister, that little girl come from due south of here, right over the Mexican border. Little town called

Esmeralda. She didn't cross over but a couple months before she hooked up with old Sam Briggs."

"What?" Cindy lurched forward to the edge of her chair. "She tell you that herself?"

"Told me when she first got here." Shawn knew he had something good, and he held it for a moment, purposely creating suspense. "Angela stayed here a couple of months while she got herself together. Mighty young to be traveling alone, but she was tough enough to make it."

Hannibal stood still, but his left middle finger began slowly drumming against the pillar. He thought he may finally have turned over the right rock. He was almost afraid to ask what he wanted to know, for fear Shawn would know how important the answers would be to him. He asked anyway, speaking as softly as he could.

"So you knew her before she was Angela Briggs."

"Heck, yeah," Shawn said, clearly pleased he was being of such value. "When I met her she was Patty Johnson."

"Johnson?" Cindy asked. "That's an awfully American name for a Mexican girl."

"Do y'all know her?" Shawn asked. His eyes narrowed with disbelief. "Anybody can see the girl's not all Mexican. Some black blood in there somewhere. I figure an American give her life, then give her that name. Besides, all you had to do was look at her."

"Meaning?" Hannibal asked.

Shawn rubbed the back of his neck and shook his head at his visitor's ignorance. "Look around you boy. How many faces like yours you seen today?"

Hannibal's brow wrinkled as he considered the old man's words. Maybe half the people he had seen since he arrived in Corpus Christi were Hispanic. Almost all the rest were white. How unusual Angela's appearance must have been here. How much more south of the border, he wondered. Did it make her enough of an outcast to be willing to do anything to change her life? Even to abandoning her family? He looked at Cindy and shrugged with his whole body. Pursue this to the end of the trail?

She smiled and shook her head, cocked to one side. I suppose so. Then she reached to touch the old man's arm.

"Shawn, do you suppose there's any chance we might find Angela's real parents?"

"I suppose," he said. For the first time he avoided her eyes, trying to make contact with Hannibal. "Esmeralda's a pretty small town, just south of Rio Bravo, not twenty miles into Mexico. You can just ask for the black couple. Any man you see can tell you where they are, because Angela's mother runs the, eh," Shawn was stuck for words for a moment. His voice became low. "You know, the local bordello. The cat house."

-25-

In calling Esmeralda a pretty small town, Shawn Boyd had understated the case by half. After four hours on roads designed to torture the American luxury automobile, Hannibal pushed his rented Town Car down an unpaved street which was dry and flat as a stale tortilla. Eyes followed him down the street, mostly children's eyes. Houses here were adobe. Only businesses lived in brick or stucco buildings. The few vehicles he saw were four wheel drive or ancient pickup trucks with huge steel bodies.

The almost empty streets and the overall quiet testified to the time of day. Hannibal guessed by four o'clock most of the day's activity was over, the night time action not yet begun. Beside him, Cindy was half asleep, bouncing easily with the gentle vibrations of the car's motion. She was clearly more relaxed, more comfortable in this situation than he was.

Hannibal eased to a stop in front of what looked like a small grocery store. A chair outside the door held a man in canvas pants, tee shirt and thong sandals. The chair rested on its two hind legs, pressing the man's head back against the wall. He was a bit jowly, with the straight black hair and swarthy complexion Hannibal expected. He shook Cindy gently, rolled down the window and waved to the man on the chair. The only response he got was a cold stare. Cindy leaned across him to push her head out his window. Her face was enough to bring a smile to the seated man's face.

"Donde esta el casa del Johnsons?" she asked. Then she exchanged a torrent of verbiage which, to Hannibal, was almost complete gibberish. With what looked like a great effort, the man raised his arm far enough to point a couple of times. He and Cindy chattered on for a moment, then she ended the conversation with "Gracias" and sat back down.

"Straight ahead about two miles," Cindy said. "Then hang a right and drive until we cross a wooden bridge. Then go left. There's a huge tree at a four corners. The Johnson's place is about a hundred meters before that."

"Uh-huh," Hannibal muttered under his breath. "You can't get there from here." He pressed the accelerator and rolled his window up. It had been down long enough for him to taste the road dust. The town smelled to him like a musty closet, and the smell had gotten into the car.

"I didn't understand much of what you were just talking about," Hannibal said, "but I know the word negros. What was he saying about me?"

"Not you," Cindy said. "After he gave me the directions, he said we should go down there with the other blacks."

Hannibal's stomach had begun to gnaw at him when they arrived. The Johnson house may well have been fancy at one time, although at present peeling paint and missing shingles gave it an unwanted, abandoned appearance. Its design was more Georgian than Spanish. The wide, two-story building had a deep porch which wrapped around it on three sides. The lathe turned spindles supporting the porch railing reminded Hannibal of a row of decaying teeth. A deep balcony wound around the second floor, matching the porch in every way. A variety of chairs were spread around both, all empty except for one occupied by a tall Mexican woman on the balcony, sunning herself on a lounger. She lay with her face to the sun, wearing nothing but a secret smile any normal man would want to unlock.

"Down boy," Cindy said as they got out of the car.

"Don't worry. Only thing I want in this place is some answers."

Hannibal and Cindy crossed the narrow road and mounted the stairs to the front porch. Before they reached the door, a creaking board made Hannibal spin to his right. A man had walked around the corner from the side of the house, and he was plainly as surprised to see Hannibal as Hannibal was to see him.

The first black man Hannibal saw in Mexico was four or five inches taller than he was, but not at all threatening. If he was at all frightening, it was the way a zombie or a corpse might be. The man was bent and sallow, his head covered by a short layer of kinky white hair. He carried a hatchet, which he raised defensively, but the arms growing out of his work gloves were little more than bony frames wrapped in acorn colored skin. Hannibal suspected his ribs would show if he took off his frayed work shirt. A smear of scar tissue started under his jaw on the left and continued down under his collar. His eyes shifted suspiciously, as if seeing a stranger was the same as seeing an enemy.

Hannibal straightened and willed himself to relax. He did not want to present a threatening appearance. "How you doing?" he asked. "You Johnson?"

"Who wants to know?"

Cindy stepped forward. "Sir, I'm an attorney. I'm trying to get some information about a young woman I believe to be your daughter."

"Ain't got no daughter," Johnson snorted, but his face denied his words. On closer inspection, Hannibal saw the blotchy scar on his neck was in fact the result of a badly healed burn.

"Are you saying Patty Johnson isn't your daughter?" Cindy asked. The older man turned his head and spit over the railing. He braced his feet defiantly and stepped closer to Hannibal. He opened his mouth to speak, but they never got to hear what he had to say. Johnson froze in place when the front door swung open. Hannibal turned to see a very dark Mexican woman filling the doorway. Her body was a series of rolls. First her chin, which rolled down onto her chest. Then her bosom, grotesque inside the simple cotton dress, flowing down onto her waist, which then rolled onto vast hips which only fit into the door because she turned to one side. Even her hair was rolled up in a bun on top of her head. She rolled big, watery cow eyes toward the tall man.

"What you blubbering about, old fool?" she snapped. "Get on back to your work." Johnson, nearly a foot taller than the woman, still shrank back from her voice, the way whipped dogs do from their masters. The low growl was there, but it had no power to frighten when you could see the dog's tail between his legs.

Then the woman turned to the newcomers and flashed a syrupy smile which chilled Hannibal more than her appearance. "Won't you come in?"

Hannibal and Cindy followed her into a wide front room almost choked with love seats, sofas and chaise lounges. Four of the seats were occupied by scantily dressed Mexican girls whose condition Hannibal rated as fair to good, on a scale where Cindy would be near mint. Lighting was low, supplied mostly by red bulbs glaring from standing lamps, adding to the general atmosphere of cheap warmth. The furniture, all chintz and chenille, showed signs of continuous repair. The room carried an oddly attractive scent. The weird combination of baking fruit pies and musk should have been disgusting but wasn't. In the background, Spanish guitar music played very low. At the far end of the room was a counter which projected from the left side wall about six feet. Their hostess walked past it and turned to face them, leaning on it. Her eyes wandered up and down Cindy's body, the way a man's might.

"Are you the owner? Mrs. Johnson?" Hannibal asked

"I'm Mrs. Johnson," the woman replied in clear English. "The customers call me Scooter. But you don't look like my usual customers."

"We haven't come here for what you sell," Cindy said.

"I see. Are you here to audition for a job, then?" Scooter leered at Cindy's chest.

"We're here about your daughter," Hannibal said.

"Patty?" The smile dropped from Scooter's face. "What about her? Is she all right?"

"If she's the girl we know," Cindy said, "she's fine."

"Couldn't miss Patty," Scooter said. She waddled into the next room and returned a few seconds later with an old photograph. Cindy took it, stared at it for a moment, then passed it to Hannibal. There was no mistaking those cheekbones or jaw line, even in a four year old photo. It was clearly Angela.

"Is my baby in any trouble?"

Hannibal looked around, noticing how the other girls ignored them. "Not at all, Ma'am. She's just applied for a job and we're doing the standard background check." He saw Cindy turn her face to the floor and prayed she had not given him away. "Can you tell us how long she lived here, and when she left?"

A deep sorrow crossed Scooter's face, or it might have been the wash from the red lights. "Patty lived here all her life until..." a deep sigh, almost a sob. "She left about four years ago. She was so smart. She was reading all the time, reading about this and that. And she sure didn't get that from me, no sir. She was just starting high school, you know. She was just a child, too young to be on her own."

"What made her leave?" Cindy asked. Hannibal did not see why it mattered.

"She had a big fight with her father," Scooter said. "Almost killed him. They never got along very well. One day he said something to her, and she walked into that kitchen and carried the coffee pot back out here and threw a whole pot of hot coffee at his face. That scar you see on his neck? That's from her. She probably figured he'd kill her behind that, so she ran away. Haven't seen or heard from her since." Then she looked up to Cindy's face, searching for sympathy. "How is she doing?"

Hannibal figured he had her. It all fit. Young runaway, gets across the border, hooks up with the first bad dudes she meets. One of them notices the resemblance to the dead man, Jake Mortimer, and senses a good scam. But who down here would know about a murder in Baltimore years before. Then Hannibal thought he saw his chance to climb aboard the clue bus. He could be within reach of the linchpin connecting one train of events with another. He had nothing to lose by asking.

"Ma'am, do you happen to know anything about the man your daughter's hanging around with? His name's Pat Louis."

Scooter's expression did not really change so much as deepen. Her concern for her daughter was clearly quite real. One hand went to her face, pressing her jowls together. Her eyes squeezed together and she spoke through her hand. "Dear God don't be so cruel. Please don't tell me my little girl is with that low life scum." Her eyes opened, looking too small, set too deep in her round face. "He's my age. Why would she be with him?"

Cindy moved forward to rest a comforting hand on Scooter's shoulder. "Don't worry," she said, turning dagger eyes on Hannibal, "They've gone their separate ways now. He can't hurt her anymore."

Hannibal was unmoved. "How did you know Pat Louis? He's from way up in Maryland isn't he?"

Scooter gave herself three deep breaths before she answered. "They come down here to hide out, when the law's after them. I rent rooms upstairs in the back. I hate them, but it's cold hard American cash and that stuff's scarce around here."

"When did you see him last?" Hannibal stepped in closer, and Cindy eased an arm around Scooter, as if to protect her.

"Does it really matter?" Cindy asked.

"He was here back then," Scooter said. "They was staying here when my little girl ran off. He probably left a few days after. God I hoped I'd never hear that name again."

"Who are they, Mrs. Johnson?" Hannibal asked. "Gangsters from up north?"

She nodded. "He usually travels with them Lerner brothers, but I guess they split up."

"What?" Good luck can be as intoxicating as the finest liquor. Hannibal's trip to Mexico was a gamble, taken with the hope of getting to the bottom of the mystery of Angela's secret past. But now, the prize at the bottom of the box turned out to be much bigger than he could have hoped. He grabbed Scooter's arm so hard she yelped, more in surprise than pain. "You talking about little Wally and a big guy they call Slo? How do you know them?"

"Known them for years," Scooter said. "I told you, they always come down here to hide out when it gets too hot in the States. I rent them a room upstairs until..."

Cindy pulled Hannibal's hand away from Scooter, then actually stepped between them. "Ma'am, we have reason to believe those men are a threat to your daughter. Can you tell me where they are now?"

Scooter looked from Cindy to Hannibal and back. Her eyes were calculating, perhaps measuring the possible trouble involved with talking as opposed to keeping quiet. Or maybe she was concerned about violence in her little business. Hannibal knew he had to stay quiet. Anything he said now would push her away from the decision he needed her to make. Ultimately, an outside force influenced her choice.

Her husband bent his head to come in the front door, sweat soaking through his shirt, work gloves making his hands look like hammer heads at the ends of his arms. Her eyes glowed and Hannibal could see she associated this man with all the trouble she had ever seen. Maybe she could not get rid of him, but some other troubles, maybe they could be shoved away. Her face hardened in resolve as she turned back to Hannibal.

"They right here mister," Scooter said. "Right upstairs in room two oh three."

-26-

"Hannibal wait!"

Cindy's cries bounced off Hannibal's ears unheard. He bolted up the winding staircase, taking the steps three at a time. Angela's con game, Jacob Mortimer's murder, and the more recent killing of Pat Louis were all forgotten. This was about getting his skull battered by a man he was trying to help. This was about his car being stolen, his being accused of murder, the hammering he took at the hands of a locker room full of fighters. This was about payback.

His feet stamped across the carpet runner covering the hall. At room 203 he grabbed the door knob and twisted. Locked. His fist slammed against the door three, four, five times, threatening to punch it down.

"All right, all right, hold your water." A latch clicked and Wally Lerner swung the door open. He shouted "Whoa" as Hannibal's face came into view, and tried to slam the door shut. But Hannibal's shoulder was in the way. The door bounced back open and Hannibal lunged in. Wally had a gun, a thirty-eight, and he nearly got it pointed in the right direction before Hannibal grabbed his wrist and twisted hard. Wally squealed and the gun flew across the room. Hannibal's right hand arced around and jarred Wally with an open hand blow across his face. Then

Hannibal released Wally's arm, using both hands to gather up the front of his shirt.

"Where is he, you little weasel?" Hannibal screamed into Wally's face. His breathing came in short gasps now, his nostrils flared, and his teeth showed in a death's head grimace. Wally's oil spot eyes darted back and forth and his voice deserted him for a second.

"Out back," Wally said. "He's out there trying to fix the car."

Hannibal thrust Wally out the door like passing a basketball. Wally crashed hard into the wall, sliding down the repeating flower print to the floor. Hannibal jerked up on his collar, half carrying, half dragging him to the stairs. They went down them together, Hannibal in control all the time. He imagined they got some odd stares from the girls in the front room, but he looked neither right nor left. Steering Wally by the back of his collar, Hannibal got him through the door and down the porch steps to the ground.

Hannibal was shoving Wally ahead of himself as he rounded the corner of the house. They almost walked into Sloan Lerner, on his way to the front of the house. Sloan's hands were covered with grease, and he shone with sweat from working in a full set of coveralls. And he was even bigger than Hannibal remembered him.

"Hey!" Sloan shouted as he realized the situation. His right fist swept up, missing his brother by inches, and thwacked into Hannibal's jaw. For Hannibal the world went black for a moment. He staggered back three or four steps before dropping onto his back. The hard ground sent the impact of his landing throughout his frame. He lifted an arm and one leg in a ground defensive posture.

It was unnecessary. Sloan was easing Wally into a seated position. "You leave my brother alone," he shouted at Hannibal.

Hannibal rolled a little farther away and got to his feet. His tailbone hurt from his landing. Still his anger drove him to continue. "That's okay, Slo," he said, raising his fists. "It's you I want anyway."

Sloan grinned, the way a man does when he first realizes the girl he is with is about to say yes. He drew to his full height and rubbed his greasy hands together before putting up his own fists. His massive shoulders rolled forward as he loosened up, and his feet shifted into a strong fighting stance. Hannibal shuffled forward and snapped off a couple of jabs which smacked solidly into Sloan's forearms with no apparent effect. Sloan tossed a few punches which Hannibal easily avoided, despite the bigger man's reach advantage. Frustrated, Sloan took a couple of charging steps forward and got in a left which scraped across Hannibal's left ear.

"See, I spent some time in the ring," Sloan said. "I knocked out more fighters than you've met in your life."

Hannibal's ears were ringing and his head had settled into a dull ache. His knuckles pulsed too, reminding him how he hated to do this without gloves on. Still, he was not going to be intimidated by this guy's size. Instead, he put more energy into his footwork, dancing out of reach.

"You've probably done this with a lot of boxers," Hannibal said from behind his raised fists. Then he planted a stamp kick into Sloan's belly. "But how many kickboxers?"

Sloan drove forward again, and Hannibal met him with two left jabs, a right cross and a right crescent kick to the ribs. "I learned kickboxing as a teenager in Germany," he said. "I was in a lot of fights in school before that, but after a few kick boxing lessons, I stopped losing all the time. Now I don't lose at all."

"Yeah, well I got tired of the kids laughing at me," Sloan said. "That's why I stopped losing fights." He stomped forward again, ignoring Hannibal's stiff left to his mouth, brushing past a kick to his right thigh, and sank his right fist deep into Hannibal's gut. Hannibal doubled over, but quickly unwound, his fist sweeping up and back around, across Sloan's jaw.

He could not let this fight become a close battle. Trading punches with Sloan was a losing proposition. Nor could it become a long battle. Each time he got hit, Hannibal's body reminded him of all the abuse it had taken earlier, including the beating that put him in the hospital. His ribs ached and hot knives slid invisibly into his stomach muscles. He needed to end the fight now.

Hannibal took a deep breath, watching Sloan stand easy, waiting for the next attack. Fine. Hannibal slid forward, ducked, bobbed, and brought an uppercut up through Sloan's guard, snapping his head back. Then Hannibal tried a combination: left jab, right hook, right kick to the outer thigh. Sloan grunted so Hannibal tried it again, this time moving the kick up to the big man's ribs. A trained boxer, Sloan had no defense for the kicks.

Panting against his own pain, Hannibal repeated the pattern. Left, right, kick. Left, right, kick. When Sloan tried to attack, Hannibal slipped past his punch and repeated the combination. After the fifth time, Sloan's left knee buckled. Hannibal snapped his left foot up into Sloan's stomach. The air went out of Sloan in a rush, and with it, his will. His hands dropped and Hannibal dived forward with a right cross that bloodied his nose.

The streak of red on the ground in front of him was a victory flag for Hannibal. He grabbed the front of Sloan's shirt with his left. Sloan wrapped his huge left hand around Hannibal's arm, giving Hannibal a clear field of fire. He smashed his right fist down across Sloan's face. The bigger man made no sound, which for some reason infuriated Hannibal. Instead, it was Hannibal who grunted with each blow. Like a piston, his fist pumped down that same path again, and again, and again. Each time Sloan's face snapped away, then slowly turned back toward him, only to be smashed away again.

"Stop it!" Wally Lerner stood six feet behind his brother, too scared to physically interfere, trembling with his own helplessness. "Please," he said. "Please, please, please stop hitting my brother. Please."

Hannibal realized Sloan probably protected Wally all his life. Wally's loyalty to his brother, so resented by his wife, was very strong. He probably protected Sloan from the world when he could, but he had no idea how to defend him from a physical assault.

Then Hannibal shifted his gaze to Sloan. He was defeated, on his knees, staring dumbly up. Blood covered his face from his nose down. It was on his neck, too, and his shirt and, Hannibal noticed belatedly, on his own fists.

And Sloan's eyes were clear. There was no rage there, no shame of being beaten, not even sadness. Just a puzzled expression which had been hidden from Hannibal by his own anger. His own anger. He must learn to control that. Now, looking past his anger he could see the obvious.

"You really are slow, aren't you?" Hannibal asked, suddenly ashamed of his actions. He let go of Sloan's shirt, but neither of them moved, except for their heaving chests trying to bring in enough air to flush out the adrenaline of battle. Wally took one step forward and opened his mouth to speak.

"All right, stop it right now!" Cindy's voice. Hannibal turned to find her walking toward him, his Colt Mustang automatic held forward with both hands. A mere twelve and a half ounces of weight, the little gun holding six rounds of .380 ACP fit her hand perfectly. When he ran upstairs to grab Wally, she must have searched through his luggage for his gun. Maybe she knew Wally and Sloan had guns and she wanted to even things up a bit. Or maybe she simply wanted to control the situation. In any case, his pistol was now irrelevant. The fight was over.

Hannibal put a hand on Sloan's shoulder, giving them both balance to stay upright, and thought about Pat Louis' execution. One bullet, neatly placed in the back of his head. He saw no evidence of this man being capable of such precision. He pulled his sunglasses off, making eye contact with Sloan, realizing for the first time how little depth he encountered there.

"You didn't kill Pat Louis, did you?"

Sloan shook his head. "I didn't kill nobody mister."

"But you went there that day," Hannibal said. "To Nieswand's house."

Sloan nodded. "Sure. I went to get the money. Zack sent me to get the money." Then he smiled. His swollen, bloody face was forgotten. He seemed pleased Hannibal was listening to him, giving him a chance to explain. Hannibal glanced back at Cindy who now stood close behind him, his gun hanging in her small hand at her side, pointing toward the ground.

"To get the money Pat owed Zack from years ago," Hannibal said.

Sloan closed his eyes and shook his head. His open hands shook beside his face, as if he was trying to erase something in the air. "No, no, no, no. Not Pat. I didn't even know Pat was there. It was Abby."

"Abby? Abby Nieswand?" Cindy asked, placing a hand on Hannibal's shoulder.

"Oh my God," Hannibal muttered, helping Sloan to his feet. This case, so confusing to him up to this point, was beginning to streamline. He had forgotten his own advice about never trusting coincidences, and now his mind was tying loose ends together. "Jewel said she met Abby in Jersey last year."

"Wait a minute," Wally stepped forward now, talking to his brother, ignoring the others. "This the same Abby that Pat was boffing in Atlantic City a year ago? They both borrowed money from Zack. I think she gave hers to Pat. But then they just disappeared. Zack couldn't find Pat, but I guess he found her."

Cindy produced a handkerchief and started to clean off Sloan's face. He stood like a child and let her rub blood off his face, although Hannibal knew it must hurt. Not wanting to watch that, he started pacing around the others. "So Pat Louis owed Zack King money too," he said. "When he saw his old pal Sloan, he must have thought he was after him."

Sloan's eyes widened, and he gently pushed Cindy's hand away. "I get it. That's why he pulled a knife on me. He thought I was after him."

"And he cut you," Hannibal said. "I saw the blood on your arm when I found you in the car. Just before you bashed my head into the car roof."

"I'm sorry about that," Sloan said. "I had to get away. I figured Pat was shacking at a pretty classy place. Whoever's house that was, they'd be the type that calls the cops on account of I knocked Pat out cold. But then the rain got real bad and I kind of lost it."

"And put my car in a ditch," Wally snapped. "Meanwhile they find Pat dead. How hard you hit him, anyway?"

"No, that doesn't fit," Cindy said. "The police said they found the man we now know as Patrick Louis face down on the Nieswand's garage floor, with a single twenty-two caliber bullet hole in the back of his head."

"Come on, lady," Wally said. "Look at my brother, would you? He ain't no hit man. Do you really think this dimwit could pull off a neat, tidy mob style killing? Whoever smoked old Pat had it together a whole lot better than Slo."

Hannibal looked at the backs of his hands and suddenly felt very dirty. "I think you're right. I believe Sloan's story. It makes too much sense not to be true. And I'm sorry I jumped to the wrong conclusions. And since he's innocent, you guys need to come back with me and tell the police what you know."

"No way, brother," Wally said. "Cops ain't good listeners, and they still got Slo figured for the hitter. They can't touch us down here."

"Sorry fellows," Hannibal said, "but I made a deal with a detective to bring you in if I found you."

"Look, you can kick both our asses all day, but we ain't going back to the States. There's still cops in Maryland that remember me and Slo from the old days. They're looking for a chance to lock us up and throw away the key."

"We'll do this in Virginia, where the murder took place, not Maryland," Cindy said. The men looked at her, and she glanced down at the apparently forgotten gun. Hannibal held his hand out and she quickly handed the pistol to him. "If you're telling the truth, you've got nothing to fear."

"Right," Wally said, "I've heard that one before."

"Maybe," Cindy went on, "but you've never had me as an attorney. Believe me, I don't let innocent clients go to jail."

"You're a lawyer?" Wally's surprise was echoed on Sloan's face.

Hannibal's eyes flared and his jaw literally dropped. He shoved his glasses into his shirt pocket, grabbed Cindy's arm roughly and pulled her to the side. "You think this is a good idea?"

"I already do most of the firm's pro bono work," she said. "Besides, this case can be good publicity for the firm. They'll like that."

"Even when it comes out where your boss' alcoholic wife was hiding out when she ran off last year?" Hannibal asked. "Even if all the evidence points to a very young con artist that one of his clients is crazy about? Think about this."

"Mister Nieswand is one of the finest attorneys I know," Cindy answered. "His first loyalty is to the truth, no matter what. Besides, you would have told them all about it anyway. We can't let Angela get away with defrauding the Mortimers. And the way things look, she might be getting away with murder, too." She must have sensed Hannibal was weakening, because she pointed to Sloan for her closing argument. "Besides, look at him. He'll never get a fair shake unless I do this."

217

Hannibal and Cindy turned toward the brothers, which Wally clearly took as an invitation to join them. "You really one of them high class Washington lawyers?"

"Yes I am," Cindy said. "So what do you think? Will you come with us?"

Wally turned to face his brother, skeptical and encouraging at the same time. "It's your ass, Slo. They ain't after me this time. But you're getting kind of old for doing federal time."

Sloan nodded. He was working hard at thinking, but managed to keep the concepts pretty simple. "You and Zack took good care of me most of the time, Wally. But I can't keep running forever. And I don't want to stay down here. I miss home, Wally. And..." there seemed to be more, something important. For some reason, he had a hard time getting it out but when he did, Hannibal understood entirely. It made his decision crystal clear.

"It's just, I didn't do it this time."

Wally turned and nodded. Cindy smiled and squeezed Hannibal's hand, and Hannibal considered what a long flight he was in for.

-27-

MONDAY

Hannibal could see it was not easy, but Rissik stood up, held out his hand, looked Hannibal squarely in the face and said "Thanks. I owe you one."

That unpleasant duty out of the way, Rissik offered Cindy his guest chair, and asked a uniformed officer to bring another into the office. Hannibal was more comfortable now, in suit, gloves and dark glasses. Rissik looked happy to start his day in Hannibal's company, his dangerous blue eyes softened a bit. He did not even seem unhappy about working late the night before, which made sense considering what it allowed him to tell his bosses Monday morning.

"I know it's not over," Hannibal said as his chair arrived, "but at least you can say you've got the fugitive your men were chasing. At the very least, he's a material witness."

"Yes," Rissik said. With hand signals he directed the officer through creating three cups of coffee and getting them to the right people. "Believe me that saves me a great deal of embarrassment. I assume you're here to find out where we are in our little murder case, and how it relates to your situation with the long lost granddaughter."

"My first interest is with Sloan Lerner," Cindy said. "I do want to keep this friendly, detective, but I feel I must remind you before you start talking that I am Mister Lerner's attorney of record." She was a little nervous, but Hannibal figured he was the only one who could see it. He knew her decision not to mention their most recent discoveries to Nieswand was a tough one for her. She felt a great deal of loyalty to the partners who took a chance on her right out of law school. As she explained it to Rissik, she wanted to make sure she did not put her boss into a conflict of interest situation. She needed to know where the police case was going before she laid it all out to Nieswand.

Rissik leaned back in his chair and crossed his legs. "I got no secrets to keep, ma'am. You were present when he gave his statement and he hasn't said anything since. I don't think the county attorney's going to drag the Jersey boys into this unless they have to. We're not really interested in the extortion angle, only the murder on our turf. And without a weapon or a decent motive, I don't think Sloan's got anything to worry about."

"So how do you see the big picture?" Hannibal asked. He sipped from his cup and thought he would spend more time conferring with the police if they all knew how to brew a cup of coffee this good.

"I don't think this is all that much of a mystery," Rissik said. "I figure this Pat Louis was a professional criminal who knew Jacob Mortimer, the guy you originally went looking for. Maybe he even had something to do with his death, but we might never know that for sure. Anyway, he apparently went to Mexico frequently to avoid capture. At the bordello you told me about, he spotted the girl and noticed her resemblance to Mortimer. When she ran away from home, he followed her and offered her a deal. She could pretend to be Mortimer's daughter, become part of the family, and inherit a fortune. Naturally, since it was his idea, she would have to share the fortune with him."

"Well that's pretty sound so far," Cindy said, "but why the long delay?"

Rissik opened a notebook on his desk and consulted its pages. "As it turns out, Sloan Lerner was involved in a smuggling operation with Pat Louis. They did some time together just about four years ago."

Hannibal snapped his fingers. "That's right. Dalton, the cop up in Baltimore, told me Louis was arrested four years ago, but the sentence was light."

"So the girl was adrift in a strange place with no friends," Cindy added.

"Check," Rissik said. "So she finds herself a sugar daddy, settles down, goes to school. For all we know, she might have gone straight from there on in."

"Except her adoptive father died," Hannibal said. "She was on her own for a while, long enough to finish school, and to learn how hard it is for a young girl to make it on her own."

"That's my picture," Rissik said. "Louis gets out of stir and finds her again. She's ready to try the con but he wants to be close to the action, just in case. So he checks out the Mortimer family, looking for a way to be where he can watch the whole situation."

Cindy leaned forward and slowly put her cup down on the desk. Her eyes were focused on a point on the side of the cup, almost as if she was reading the truth there. "And he finds out who their attorney is. And he spots Abby Nieswand. So weak. So vulnerable. And he seduces her. Then he makes her get him hired as the family chauffeur just so he can watch the Mortimer situation. The bastard. I'm glad he's dead."

The room was very quiet for a moment. Hannibal heard the air rushing out of the air conditioning vent overhead, but the sweat drying on his forehead was not the cause of the chill he felt. He had seen Cindy's fiery Latin anger many times, but never this cold hate. It shook him far more than any tantrum ever could.

"Obviously you're not the only one glad," Rissik said after a moment. "I've got to think the girl was watching him. Maybe she had a prearranged meeting with him that day. Anyway, I figure Angela saw Louis' tussle with Sloan Lerner and saw an opportunity to get the albatross off her neck. If he was already unconscious it was no trick to get up behind him and pop him."

"Makes sense to me," Hannibal said. "So what happens now? You go pick her up?"

Rissik chuckled into his cup. "Not likely."

"All we have here is supposition," Cindy added. "And most of that based on the testimony of a lifelong felon who, until recently, was the prime suspect in this murder. There isn't even enough evidence to take her in for questioning. If I was the county attorney, I wouldn't even consider it."

"We have kept her under surveillance," Rissik said. "It's pretty easy with her tooling around in that brand new canary yellow Porsche 911. This morning she was heading off toward Baltimore."

"Where she can fill in holes in her story," Hannibal said.

Cindy looked from him to the police detective and back again. "This isn't right. There must be something we can do."

Rissik tilted his head at her naiveté. "Like for instance?"

"Like for instance," Hannibal said, "we can go question the only eyewitness."

* * * * *

Hannibal did not get many chances to surprise or impress Cindy, but standing at the reception desk of the Charter Behavioral Health System Facility at Potomac Ridge, he got to do both. The nurse was pleasant and so soft-spoken, he wondered if she thought he was a patient. Or maybe she could not tell patients from visitors, so she treated everyone the same. Looking around, he thought this much white could drive anybody over the edge.

The nurse looked up from her computer screen with the same frozen solicitous smile she wore when they walked in. "Why, yes sir, Mrs. Nieswand is one of our recent admissions. She checked in voluntarily, as many of our patients do. If you'll step into that waiting room, I'll see if she can come down for a brief visit."

He was aware of Cindy's eyes on him on their way to the wide, antiseptic waiting room. The room was empty and painfully quiet, with a smell of vanilla he figured someone sprayed on some regular schedule. Cindy never said a word until they were seated side by side on a green, plastic covered couch.

"All right, Sherlock. How did you know she was here?"

"Real detective work," he said, "not like they do it on TV. When I went to see Nieswand he said his wife was twenty miles away in a private hospital. She has a substance abuse problem, and according to him, finding a corpse in their garage pushed her over the edge into schizophrenia. Well, while you were snoozing last night, I got out a map and I drew a circle around his house about twenty miles out. Then I got out the phone book. There aren't very many places around here that can take care of somebody with that set of problems. I figured Lippincott would go for the best. Rockville, Maryland was the right distance from his house and this place was the right hospital."

"Very impressive," a man's voice said from the doorway. Hannibal turned to see Lawrence Lippincott march into the room. He leaned forward as he walked, light glinting off his bald brown scalp, hands thrust deep into his pockets. "I told Gabe the day I met you, you looked like a man who got things done. This time, though, I'm not sure what you're trying to accomplish."

"Just trying to get next to the truth," Hannibal said, standing. "I know the guy who was arrested didn't kill Pat Louis, AKA Ike Paton. At first I thought it was a mob hit, but now I think maybe Angela pulled the trigger. In any case, Abby Nieswand's got the best chance of knowing something that can help me prove that."

Lippincott sighed. "You may have a point there. Unfortunately, Mrs. Nieswand is in no condition to be questioned, especially about the events of that day. Maybe in a month or so."

"I thought I might be able to gently..."

"No," Lippincott said. "She's just not up to it now."

Hannibal spread his hands in frustration. "Look, Doc, five minutes..."

"Have you forgotten who you're working for?" Lippincott crossed his arms, his lips curled in. "I will not endanger my patient, even if it might incriminate that little gold digger. Look elsewhere for your precious clues. Unless you would rather stop the investigation altogether."

"You think this is about your money?" Hannibal snapped. "This is about a teenager who might not get to be a man because Angela's got the family convinced she's the bone marrow donor Kyle needs. Have you forgotten Kyle? He ought to be your first priority too."

Hannibal clenched his fists, but Cindy's hand on his arm relaxed him a bit. She showed Lippincott her most reasonable courtroom face. "I don't work for you. My responsibility is to my client. And to the firm's clients, including the Mortimers. You appear to have a conflict of interest here, doctor."

"You're on dangerous ground, girl," Lippincott said, his finger thrust into her face. "I don't think the senior partner of your firm would appreciate your harassing his wife. You could be risking your career here."

Cindy's voice dropped but she responded with steely eyed resolve. "It wouldn't be the first time I went against the partners on a point of law."

Lippincott's jaw worked silently. Hannibal guessed he was not used to being challenged. Then his brows knit together and his teeth flashed. "Abigail Nieswand has been under my professional care for more than three years. She is a troubled woman, a confused woman, and I will not jeopardize her delicate mental condition with questions about the events which drove her to her present state. Mister Jones, your services are no longer required. I will forward a check to your office to cover two days work."

"You can't separate her from us forever," Cindy said. "She discovered the body. For all we know she may have seen the murder. Or the murderer."

"I am not in need of legal counsel," Lippincott said. "You may not see my patient, and if you don't leave this minute, I'll have security evict you from the premises."

Cindy rushed forward so quickly Doctor Lippincott stepped back and raise his arms defensively. "Don't play legal games with me, doctor. If your client has material knowledge I'll find a way to question her."

Hannibal took Cindy's upper arm and pulled her away from the doctor. "Not the time," he said. "Not the place." Cindy and Lippincott never broke eye contact until after Hannibal pulled her backward through the hospital's glass door. "You got things to do back at your office. I'm going to get this problem fixed. I'll call you in a few hours and we'll do this one together."

-28-

It would be hard to find a more direct contrast than a comparison of Doctor Lippincott's free clinic in Northeast Washington and his private offices north of Georgetown University. The waiting room was huge, furnished with a few comfortable chairs, all of which were empty at the end of the office day. The carpet was lush, a sandy beige color which complemented the muted earth tones of the walls. The paintings displayed a Southwestern motif, cacti at sunset and buttes in the dawn sun. The magazines in the wall racks would only interest an upscale clientele. Lippincott's receptionist bore more than a passing resemblance to Tyra Banks. Fresh flowers waved their sweet scent from tall vases on her desk. She offered Hannibal a broad smile despite Cindy's presence. He would have loved to talk to her, but instead he stood aside and let Rissik take the lead.

Orson Rissik chose to make his entrance in full police detective mode. Tan trench coat over gray suit, he stalked into the waiting room, jaw and badge thrust forward. The receptionist gasped quietly, her eyes cutting to a drawer on her left as if it was where she kept her stash.

"Where's Doctor Lippincott?" Rissik demanded. His sharp tone shook the young girl. Her hand moved toward the intercom. "No, don't call him. Just tell me where he is."

She waved a shaking hand vaguely down a narrow hall. "Consultation room," she stuttered. "Third door."

Rissik turned, winked broadly at Hannibal, and strode off down the hallway. Hannibal and Cindy moved quickly to keep up. Hannibal thought they must appear to be junior detectives, he in his usual black suit, Cindy wearing the navy blue skirt suit she usually reserved for courtroom battles. Rissik stopped in front of the closed door long enough for them to catch up. Then he turned the knob and burst in, slamming the door against the wall behind it.

"Lawrence Lippincott?"

Lippincott sprang to his feet behind his massive oak desk. Apparently he was going over his books, much as any businessman might at the end of the day. Although Rissik moved right up to his desk, Lippincott's eyes were on Hannibal and Cindy at the back of the room.

Hannibal would call the furnishings luxurious. The love seat, the easy chair, the coffee service on its own table, everything except perhaps the huge desk belonged in some rich man's study. Hannibal expected to see trophy animal heads on the dark paneled walls instead of the framed portraits of black leaders hanging there.

Lippincott's gaze eventually fell on Rissik who was too close to ignore for long. "And just who are you supposed to be?"

"Who I am is Orson Rissik, chief of detectives in the Fairfax police department," Rissik said, brandishing his shield, then putting it away. "I'm the guy these two came to with a problem earlier today. A problem that relates to a murder investigation I'm running. Who I'm supposed to be is the guy who questions Abigail Nieswand about the circumstances of that murder, since I have reason to believe she may have seen or heard something and could have material information."

Lippincott leaned forward, his fists on the desk supporting him. "I see. They've brought you here to intimidate me. They probably think that after the day I've had, one of the worst in my life, I'll just buckle under your pressure. Well mister detective, you can threaten me. You can bring out your rubber hoses if you choose. I will not jeopardize my client's emotional health. Not at this time."

Hannibal stepped to the side and into the room a few feet to watch the confrontation better. Lippincott was strong willed, but how long would he endure a staring contest with Rissik? After a full minute, he looked away from the detective's dangerous eyes. Then Rissik stepped back, lifting the left side of his jacket. Lippincott's eyes widened as if he feared the policeman might actually shoot.

"Don't worry," Rissik said. "I don't need my gun. I've got much better weapons." From his inside suit jacket pocket he pulled a handful of folded papers. They separated into two small packets, one in each of his hands.

Cindy stepped forward. "I checked with Charter," she said "You haven't committed her. She's signed in voluntarily. And that means we can require her presence. Of course, you could have her committed I suppose, which is why we also have a writ of habeas corpus requiring you to bring her before a court."

Lippincott's mouth opened and closed twice, then he slumped into his chair. Now it was Hannibal's turn.

"None of us wants Mrs. Nieswand cross examined in a court of law," Hannibal said. "That kind of pressure can damage the healthiest minds."

"Even if I let you talk to her," Lippincott said, "a clumsy approach could send her farther into her psychosis."

"Or," Hannibal offered, "You could tell us what she knows. We think we know what happened that day. We're really looking for confirmation." Lippincott looked up, startled. His hands settled on his desk and he now looked ready to listen.

"My client, Sloan Lerner, is accused of the murder of Patrick Louis, also known as Ike Paton," Cindy said. "I believe him innocent, but he was on the property that day." She started pacing in front of Lippincott's desk, and Hannibal imagined her working a jury. "My client went to the Nieswand home that day to see Abigail Nieswand. It seems she borrowed money from someone last year and never repaid the debt. Mister Lerner is a collection agent, whose job it was to recover the money. But instead of seeing Mrs. Nieswand, he encountered Ike Paton, whom he knew years ago as Patrick Louis. And Louis was quite protective of Mrs. Nieswand."

Cindy stopped in mid stride and turned a penetrating gaze on Lippincott. Suddenly she was not handling a jury, but dealing with a hostile witness. "Did you know Mrs. Nieswand and Pat Louis were lovers just a year ago in Atlantic City, Doctor? I see by your face that you did. Did you think no one else would ever find out?"

Without actually moving, Lippincott appeared to be backed into a corner. He looked from one accusing face to another. "You don't know. I mean, you don't understand the situation. Mrs. Nieswand is prone to addictive behavior. Alcohol. Barbiturates. This man. That was addictive behavior too."

"Yes, well we do know my client confronted Louis outside the Nieswand house and never got to speak to Mrs. Nieswand," Cindy continued, not letting any of the pressure escape. As she paced, her hair flipped over her conservative collar, snapping at Lippincott like a whip. "They fought. Louis pulled a knife. He cut my client, who fought back and managed to knock him out. And then," she turned and slapped her palms down loudly on the desk, "And then he left. Left Louis lying there, unconscious. A car pulled up, then pulled away. She had to hear. She was alone in the house. Her lover never came back in. She must have gone out to see what was the matter."

While she described events, Cindy slowly leaned toward Lippincott. Now he stared forward as if the lion cage was open and he was next to be eaten. Hannibal and Rissik exchanged admiring glances. Then Hannibal stepped forward, took her arm and gently pulled her back.

"It wasn't just the dead body of her lover that drove her over the edge," Hannibal said. "She saw something, or maybe heard something that shocked her."

Lippincott looked down but could not hide the pain on his face or in his gut. "No. She saw no evidence of another person."

"No," Hannibal said, "nothing she told you."

Lippincott looked up. "You think she'd tell you something she didn't tell me?"

"You don't know what to ask," Rissik said.

"Think about this," Hannibal went on. "We followed a pretty thin trail of clues to get this far. We told you all this to let you know we can put things together the untrained person might miss. I know if we can talk to her, even through you, we'll get something to incriminate Angela, to implicate her in this murder. Isn't that what you want?"

Lippincott's arms were wrapped around him now, as if to hold him together. His head moved slowly back and forth, and a thin sweat broke out on his bare head. "That's just it. She won't say anything to implicate Angela or anyone else."

Hannibal bared his teeth and clenched his fists. "How do you know that?"

"Because she's confessed to the murder herself."

-29-

Lippincott huddled in the corner of the back seat behind Hannibal, clutching his little black bag on his lap. Hannibal did not think he had any need for it, but figured it was the doctor's security blanket. Rissik, beside him, had been pretty rough getting him into the car and was undoubtedly capable of more coarse behavior if Lippincott said or did anything he considered warranted it. Hannibal thought the doctor was probably lucky they had decided to travel together to the office. If Rissik had arrived in a police car, Lippincott would likely be handcuffed to it now. But although he was clearly intimidated, Lippincott continued to try to explain on their way to the hospital.

"It's an expression of guilt you see. On some level, she knew her relationship with this Pat Louis was destructive, that it would destroy them eventually. When she found him dead, her mind took a quite predictable leap of fancy, to thinking she was responsible for his death. Anything else she saw or heard was blotted out by that twisted perception."

Rissik shrugged his shoulders and sat back. "Or she shot him," he said. And that was the bottom line, Hannibal thought as they pulled into a parking space at the Charter Behavioral Health System Facility. People came here when they needed specialized care of a type not available almost anywhere else in the area. And while Lippincott's scenario was credible, it was equally likely he was too close to his patient after years of nursing her through her fantasies.

In his years as a Secret Service agent, Hannibal had seen people who believed their government representatives were communist spies, demons, or even escaped Nazis who had run concentration camps in World War II. He had protected his charges from the most sincere patriots in the country, people who believed the only way to save the nation, sometimes the world, was to destroy a particular politician whose only real sins were the usual ones of greed, vanity and sloth. Was it such a stretch that a woman whose grasp on reality had loosened would decide to destroy her lover? He unlocked the car doors, but touched Cindy's hand to keep her inside for a second.

"How could a woman kill the man she loved?"

Cindy's smile was grim. "How could an apparently sane mother lock her own children in a car and roll it into a lake?"

The atmosphere in the hospital did not seem so repressive before, but now Hannibal and Cindy stayed close as they entered. The small group moved silently across the lobby, and no one else spoke when Doctor Lippincott asked to have Mrs. Nieswand brought to the visiting area. The nurse at the desk recognized them and, to her credit, showed none of the confusion she must have felt seeing them together. Instead she smiled and spoke to the doctor in quiet, professional terms.

"I'm afraid Mrs. Nieswand has left," she said.

Lippincott blinked rapidly and turned his head at an angle as if he must not have heard correctly. "No, you don't understand. I'm her attending physician. What do you mean she's left?"

The nurse was unmoved. "She signed herself out sir. Her husband came and picked her up. You only missed them by a few minutes."

"Her husband," Lippincott whispered. "Oh God no." His face turned the color of old parchment. He walked toward the door and the others followed. Once outside, he stared out across the wooded grounds. He was a lost boy, wondering which path would lead him home.

"Where would they go?" Rissik asked him.

"He's frightened and desperate," Lippincott said. "They could be anywhere."

Behind them, Cindy said "They went home."

Hannibal saw the hard set of her jaw and knew she was serious. "Darling that's the last place they'd go. He wants to hide. Guy with that kind of money, I'll bet he's got a place out of the country."

She shook her head. "A doctor trained in psychology, a detective, an ex-cop, but your problem is you're all boys. And boys never stop being boys. Of course he wants to hide, but they just left and he doesn't know she's been missed yet. Look, this guy's taking his wife somewhere. A guy who says his wife disappeared and he never found out where she went. A guy who probably doesn't even know he hired her lover. You think he'd know what to pack for her? Hell, he probably doesn't even know which toothpaste she likes. Fellows, they went home to pack."

* * * * *

Hannibal's car had no siren, but Rissik made no comment about their speed. And the white Volvo 850

GLT had plenty of guts for the run. Luckily most of the distance down into Virginia was covered on the beltway, where they did not even start passing cars until Hannibal pushed it over seventy-five. Only reckless driving or extremely bad luck would get them pulled over.

It was an eerily quiet drive. The evil clouds were back, glowering overhead in silent threat. Hannibal left the music off. In the back, Rissik and Lippincott slumped in their respective corners, wrapped in their own private thoughts. All Hannibal's senses were tuned into moving his vehicle at the maximum speed maintaining a reasonable safety margin. Occasionally he would glance toward Cindy, her brow wrinkled and lips tight. He knew she was grateful to the partners of her law firm for giving her a chance at the big leagues right out of law school. And he knew how much she respected them. He had heard her describe Nieswand as the most effective attorney she had ever seen, not as emotionally deep as Balor, the other partner, but more creative and aggressive. Now she undoubtedly felt she was betraying him. At the same time, she had to be reforming her view of him in light of the unavoidable facts.

Hannibal had only learned three things of importance in his time in Washington. You should not see how sausage is made, even good sausage. You should not know how laws are made, even good laws. And you should not know too much about your leaders, even good leaders. It only reduces their value to you, and makes you miserable.

As Hannibal pulled into Nieswand's driveway a slow drizzle started. They all got out of the car, ignoring the gentle tap of droplets on their heads and shoulders. The house looked the same as when

Hannibal paid his first visit. He saw no sign anything had changed since then, except for a barely visible stain on a cement garage floor. Nieswand's car was parked over Pat Louis' death spot.

"They're home," Rissik said, stalking toward the door like Dick Tracy. In recognition of his authority, the others followed in single file. The rain washed the sweet scent of the flowers out of the air, leaving the clean smell of ozone. The smell that comes before a storm. It also rustled the leaves of surrounding trees, almost talking aloud, warning them.

A much louder crack followed. It was not thunder. A bullet drove asphalt skyward two feet from Rissik and he dived backward, landing prone beside Hannibal's car. Three others joined him there in less than a second.

"Go Away!" Gabriel Nieswand shouted from a second floor window. Hannibal looked over the Volvo's hood, but shadows hid Nieswand's face.

"Put that away," Rissik told Hannibal, "and give me your phone."

Hannibal realized he had reflexively drawn his own weapon. He lowered it, but since Rissik was holding his own gun, Hannibal held his. "Before you call this in," he asked, "what is it? A mad sniper? Two suspects resisting arrest? Or do we have a hostage situation here?"

"Does it really matter?" Cindy asked.

Rissik nodded. "He knows it does. What I call it will determine the reaction, I mean the procedure for the backup I get. Everybody from a SWAT team to a negotiating team could get called into play, and they'll do this by the numbers on the page I determine when I call in. You don't treat a mad sniper the way you treat a desperate hostage taker."

"Abby could be damaged beyond repair by all this," Lippincott put in. "I need to get to her as soon as possible."

Rissik shoved a hand back across his head. He looked at Hannibal with a pained expression. "You were a cop?"

"Yes. More recently I worked for the treasury department. Personal protection."

"Secret Service?" Rissik asked. "Well, I'm open to suggestions. What do you think?"

"I think the wrong call could cost lives, blow my case and ruin your career." Hannibal said. "Or, you could let me handle it. Nieswand's an amateur. I could slip in and disarm him."

Hannibal knew Rissik was conservative, a company man, the kind of guy who plays by the rules, even if the game gets weird. He met many like him in his twelve years of law enforcement. Sometimes his dedication to proper procedure would run headlong into his devotion to human life and his infatuation with justice.

"Do you know what you're asking?" Rissik asked.

"Yes, I do. I'm asking you to back my play."

Rissik considered Hannibal carefully. "I could do this myself."

"Yes," Hannibal conceded, "but I know the house. And I know Nieswand."

A long, quiet minute passed. When Rissik's agreement came, it was in the form of a hand waved toward the building. Hannibal nodded his thanks, tossed Rissik his keys and moved off at a crouch up the driveway. Behind him he heard his engine roar. Then the sound shrank away from him. He knew Rissik would take the car out of sight of the house, hoping Nieswand would believe they all left.

Inside the garage, Hannibal took a moment to remove the cap from the stem of Nieswand's left front tire. Pressing a pen into the valve mouth he released the air, flattening the tire. If Nieswand somehow got past him, he would not drive off very quickly. Smiling grimly, he quietly opened the door into the house.

He was prepared for a confrontation if he met the Nieswand is leaving. But the kitchen was empty. The room smelled of leftover food not put away properly, and counters no one had wiped off. A half eaten bowl of soup on the table spoke volumes of Nieswand's loneliness and helplessness when left alone. Hannibal felt sorry for the man, but his sympathy was tempered by the fact Nieswand shot at him.

Leading with his gun, he quickly surveyed the first floor. It was large, well appointed, and unoccupied, so Hannibal moved upstairs. With his back to the wall and his pistol held close in to his belly, he stepped upward slowly. The carpeted steps accepted his weight without a sound. Not that it mattered. From above he heard suitcases slamming, closets banging open and closed, and the strident voice of a desperate man.

"Look, just tell me which of these you want to take," Nieswand shouted. "We don't have much time, honey. They'll be back soon and they'll want to separate us for good. You don't want that, do you?"

Abby Nieswand sounded groggy, like she was badly confused and disoriented, or partially drugged. "Gabe, can't I go back to the hospital. I don't feel too good. I think the people there can help me, maybe get me back on track, you know?" Then, after a short pause, "The pantsuit. The pantsuit is fine. I need the darker bra with that."

Both voices came from the same bedroom door. Once on the second floor, Hannibal inched toward it with his automatic pointed skyward. Less than a minute after reaching the top step he stood against the wall outside the door, listening to suitcase latches clicking shut. He tried to imagine the layout of the room, where the players would be. With any luck they would be at opposite ends of the room. The woman would be seated next to a large piece of furniture. And Gabe Nieswand would be standing, facing the door, his hands filled with suitcase handles. Hannibal took a deep breath, a second, and spun to face into the room, his Sig Sauer pointed forward with both hands.

He would have to wait for another day for luck. The Nieswands were walking toward the door side by side. Each was carrying a suitcase. Gabe's right hand held a small revolver, the kind of hideout wheel gun people who don't really like guns carry for protection.

As Hannibal came into view, Nieswand dropped his suitcase and pushed his gun forward. Oddly, to Hannibal, his wife did not scream, which probably helped both men overcome the temptation to fire immediately.

Hannibal had been here before. He waited a second for his heart to slow to only twice its normal speed, and spoke in deep tones to disguise the trembling in his voice.

"Put the gun down. Step away from your husband, ma'am." Abby Nieswand, looking unsure of what was going on, carried her suitcase back to the bed and sat down. A tall canopy bed dominated the huge room. It was decorated with pink lace, and the pictures on the walls were all elves and unicorns. Did they have separate bedrooms? This must be hers.

Gabe Nieswand looked marginally braver behind a gun. "I told you to go away."

Butterflies had commandeered Hannibal's stomach, but this was no new feeling to him. The trick, he knew, was to make them fly in formation. His answer was both strategically correct and sincere. "I'd only be replaced by a squad of nervous policemen who might hurt Abby. You don't want that, do you?"

"I've done a lot to help you," Nieswand said, taking a step forward. "You should be helping me, not stopping me."

"I am trying to help," Hannibal said, lowering his gun to waist level, but keeping it pointed forward. "Gabe, you've made some mistakes here. A couple of serious mistakes, but they're not irretrievable. I'm trying to keep you from making a bigger one. You know how this works. I'll bet you've had some clients who were in pretty big trouble."

"Yeah, but I always talked them out of jail," Nieswand said, "or at least got them lighter sentences."

"Right." Hannibal could hear the blood rushing behind his ears, but he held his gaze steady on Nieswand's eyes. "Did you ever advise any of them to run?"

"Of course not. Once you're a fugitive, a jury can take that as an admission of guilt." As he said it, Nieswand heard it as if for the first time. His mouth opened as his face registered the shock of recognition. Unsure of his next move, he turned toward his wife who was watching the drama play out before her like a television show beamed in from hundreds of miles away.

As Nieswand's head turned, Hannibal stepped in quickly, grabbing his right wrist and jamming it

241

upward. The gun fired, the blast a foot above his head, savaging his ears. He turned his face down to avoid the plaster littering his head. He dropped his own gun to wrap his left hand around Nieswand's gun hand, above his own right. Then he sharply twisted his arms out and down, slamming Nieswand to the carpeted floor. As he kicked the gun across the room and under the bed he started panting. He had not noticed, but he stopped breathing the instant he grabbed Nieswand's arm.

"Gabe?" Abby Nieswand suddenly looked shocked and ran to her husband. She crouched beside him, her hands on his chest, either to comfort him or hold him down. Or maybe both. Hannibal leaned back against the wall and got control of his breathing.

"Nice work." It was Rissik, walking into the room, handing Hannibal his gun. "I just called in backup, but now I don't have to worry about anybody getting hurt. You know, you're pretty good at that stuff."

"Good training," Hannibal said. Then Cindy hugged him, while Doctor Lippincott crouched beside Abby. She stood up while he spoke to her in low tones. But she backed away when he opened his bag.

Rissik was handcuffing Gabe Nieswand and reading him his Miranda rights. Cindy's head was buried in Hannibal's chest, but his attention was on Abby. She looked numb when he walked into the room, as if her reality radio was tuned to a different station. Now she was rising toward the manic end of a manic-depressive cycle. Lippincott had come prepared with a syringe of comfort and offered it to her now.

But Abby leaned against the far wall, saying "No, no, no" in an endless loop, shaking her head back and forth.

"It's okay," Lippincott said. "This will relax you, and dull the pain of what you've seen."

Water was streaming from Abby Nieswand's eyes. "Please. I don't want to be relaxed."

Hannibal looked at her face, so much more animated than he had ever seen it. Then he looked at Gabe Nieswand, then Lippincott, and a series of tiny switches closed in his brain circuitry. This case had been a mass of wires running nowhere, but suddenly, a circuit connected.

"No!" Hannibal broke free of Cindy's grip and dashed across the room. Lippincott had Abby's arm turned forward and was about to place the needle against her skin. Hannibal grabbed his arm, much as he had Gabe Nieswand's earlier, and twisted until the syringe hit the floor.

"Have you gone mad?" Lippincott snapped, yanking his arm out of Hannibal's grasp and, surprisingly, swinging a left into Hannibal's jaw. Barely pushed backward, Hannibal grabbed the doctor's jacket and slammed him against a wall. There he clamped his right forearm across Lippincott's throat and hung his left fist, cocked back, in front of Lippincott's face.

"You back off and leave the lady alone or I will smash your teeth down your throat," Hannibal said. "Do you believe that? Do You?" Lippincott blanched pale, but managed to nod. When Hannibal released him he scampered to the wall next to the door.

"Now what the hell was that all about?" Rissik demanded. "The woman needs help."

"Maybe," Hannibal said. "But I suddenly realized that everything I know about this woman I heard from somebody else." He faced Abby Nieswand, unsure what to expect. Her face was jittery, but she sat on

243

the bed, up near the pillows. Hannibal sat at the foot of the bed and slid his dark glasses off. Eye contact seemed important. "Based on all that input, I interpreted your actions in here as manic-depressive behavior," he told her. "But the truth is, you were just a lot calmer before your doctor came at you with a needle. Can you tell me why?"

The tears came again, but she was not sobbing. In fact there was no crying sound at all. "I was frightened. He calls it sedatives, what he gives me, but it makes it hard for me to think and feel. I don't want to hide anymore. I want to face the truth."

Lippincott said "Abby, you're confused."

Gabe Nieswand said "Honey I tried to protect you."

Hannibal said "Ignore them," while maintaining eye contact. "Look at me. Listen only to me, all right? I want to help you face the truth. But maybe the truth looks different to you than it might to me. Will you tell me what you know?"

Abby nodded. Hannibal heard her husband call her name and then grunt in pain. He assumed Rissik had taken care of the situation.

"Can I call you Abby?" Hannibal asked. She nodded again.

"Abby, that man behind me is a police officer. His name is Orson Rissik. The lady's name is Cindy Santiago."

"She's in my husband's firm," Abby said. "Good lawyer."

"Yes," Hannibal said. "She won't let you do anything that puts you in danger. If it looks like you might be in trouble, we'll handle it correctly. Do you believe that?"

Another nod. She seemed stronger.

"Abby, you know Ike Paton's name was really Pat Louis."

"Poor Pat," Abby said. "He's dead, you know."

"Yes, I know," Hannibal said. "But I think you mixed up how that happened." Lippincott tried to say "stop" but interrupted himself with a yelp. Hannibal figured Cindy kicked him or something. "Doctor Lippincott says you confessed to that crime. Did you really kill him?"

The transformation was frightening and fascinating and thrilling all at the same time. Hannibal could see connections being made behind her eyes, as he had made them moments ago. Abby Nieswand's mind traced the wires down to their source, putting it all together. Her eyes not only widened, but cleared. Her mouth dropped open, and the tears came again. She never reached to wipe them away.

"No," she said, just loud enough for everyone in the room to hear. "I loved Pat. That's why he did it, don't you see. Out of jealousy. I was upstairs in the window. Pat fought with Slo. Slo left just before Gabe came home. He got out of his car, walked into the garage and shot Pat in the head."

-30-

Hannibal was on his feet, facing Gabe Nieswand, who shrank back into Rissik's arms. Hannibal's face reflected not simply rage at the killer, but self-hatred, for accepting what he was told at face value.

"You knew," Hannibal said, his voice turned down in disgust. "You knew they were lovers. You probably knew where she was when she ran away."

Abby dropped to her knees on the floor, sobbing quietly. Cindy stared hard at her boss, her mentor, no longer her superior in her eyes. Rissik slipped out from behind Nieswand, letting his back bump against the flowered wallpaper. Hannibal's shadow covered him as he sank to the floor, then Hannibal's powerful hands gripped his collar and dragged him to his feet against the wall.

"You filthy bastard. A helpless man. In the back of the head, with no remorse. You must have known for months. What happened? Did it just become too much for you, thinking about them together when you were away from home? Just didn't have the guts to confront him, did you? So instead of firing him and sending him away, you waited for a chance to dust him. And you got your wish, right? You came home and there he was, helpless."

246

Nieswand stared up into Hannibal's eyes with more contempt than fear. "Any man might have done the same. She's my wife, for God's sake."

"The hell of it is, he'll probably duck the chair with that line of defense," Cindy said.

"I didn't know this man before I hired him," Nieswand said. "How was I to know he'd take advantage of my wife?"

"Liar!"

All heads turned toward Abby, now holding her husband's gun which she retrieved from under the bed. The barrel was trained on Hannibal's back, but as he slowly stepped away it stayed in place, focused now on her husband's heart.

"You knew the condition I was in," she screeched, her voice cracking with emotion. "How could you do this? For a while, you had me convinced I killed poor Pat. The liquor. The pills. Then the sedatives. I couldn't think. But hearing you say it, now I know it was you. You shot him, but you said it was me so many times I..." She swallowed hard, then went on. "But you said you didn't know Pat. Now you tell them the truth."

"Darling," Nieswand began, "You're confused. I never knew this man."

The gunshot was deafening in the small room. Nieswand must have felt the wind from the bullet hitting the wall five inches from his face. He dropped to his knees, leaning back, his chained hands in front of his face.

"You came and got me last year," Abby shouted. "Tell them."

"Yes," Nieswand croaked. "Yes, I came and got you." Then he turned to Rissik, as if seeking salvation. His eyes finally flashed fear. "She ran away from me.

Just disappeared. I was frantic. The police never got anywhere. I ran newspaper ads offering a reward for information. I called all her family I knew. I hired a detective. Then, three weeks she's gone, I get a phone call. This guy, he knows where she is, and he wants to know about the reward."

"That's a lie," Abby cried again.

"I'm sorry darling, but it's the truth," Nieswand said, still on his knees. "I went to that dirty hotel room he had you in and I paid him." Then turning back to Rissik, "I bought my wife back from that man for five thousand dollars."

"Oh my God."

Hannibal stepped slowly back until he stood on the opposite side of the bed from Abby. He could see her hands shake with the weight of the revolver. "Oh my God," he said again. "You knew him. You knew who he was when he came here. So you must have known about the scam with Angela all along. You let him do this, even knowing Kyle might die if it worked."

"Kyle?" Abby asked.

"Kyle Mortimer has cancer, Mrs. Nieswand," Hannibal said. "We think your Pat Louis brought in Angela Briggs to fool the Mortimers into thinking she was a close relative who could give Kyle the bone marrow transplant he needs to live."

Abby turned again to her husband, staring as if she was not sure she recognized him. "Is that true? Is that what you and Louis argued about in the night? This girl?"

Nieswand, apparently in control of himself again, turned to Rissik. "You have to protect me, and I have no intention of incriminating myself further."

"No," Abby said, moving one step closer but keeping her husband's chest in her sights. "Pat told

248

me he knew Harlan Mortimer's son years ago, and he was dead. You must have been in this with him. You tell me the truth now."

Nieswand stared into his wife's face and seemed to shrink into his clothes. Perhaps he realized it was over. Possibly, he believed his wife would shoot him if he didn't talk. Maybe he just ran out of energy and gave up. Finally he said "It was all Louis' idea."

"What was?" Rissik asked, pulling a pad from his pocket.

"He knew Jacob Mortimer was dead. He found this girl somewhere who bore a strong resemblance to him, and she was the right age to be his daughter. He wanted to slide her into Mortimer's family and when she got a big inheritance, he'd take it from her. I had no choice but to go along. He was right here watching me, and if I told anyone what he was doing he'd have told the world about his affair with my alcoholic, drug-addicted wife. I figure he must have something on Angela too, to keep her in line."

"That won't wash," Hannibal said, sitting on the bed. "Lots of people in this town have survived lots worse scandals. Besides, he might have gotten close, but he couldn't talk to the Mortimers. Only you could have planted the idea in Camille's head to look for Jacob as a bone marrow donor. So you had to have an active part in this. In fact, I'll bet it was your idea to use me."

"Yeah, why bring you into it at all?" Rissik asked from the doorway.

"Well, Angela couldn't just stroll up and ask 'are you my grandpa' could she?" Hannibal said. "They set me on the trail knowing I'd find Jacob's grave, and they simply positioned Angela where I'd have to fall over her. Most private detectives would have been happy to take the credit for finding the lost heir and dropped out of the picture."

"Thank God you didn't," Lippincott said. Then to Nieswand, "I've known you a lot of years, you sniveling bastard, but I didn't think even you could be capable of such pernicious villainy. You would have let Kyle die. And what you did to this woman. What you had me do." He turned to Abby, pain etched on his face. Rissik took the doctor's arm and guided him out of the room, into the hall.

"Okay, you got the picture," Nieswand said from the floor. "Abby, could you put the gun down now?"

"I should kill you for shooting Pat," Abby snarled. "There was no reason to kill him. Didn't you know I still loved you?"

Cindy stepped forward until she was within arm's reach of Abby's gun hand. The pistol's focus never left Gabriel. "You had nothing to do with the reason Pat Louis is dead," she said. "They were business partners. He didn't care who you slept with. In a sense those two were already in bed together."

"So did Louis try to squeeze you out?" Hannibal asked Nieswand. "Or did you just decide you wanted it all?"

Nieswand stared at the carpet. "The bastard got greedy. I wasn't going to let him cut me out. His plan worked just fine without him. I saw a chance to blame his death on his old mob contacts. I just didn't know Abby was watching."

"Sounds like a confession to me," Cindy said. "I have no doubt, Mrs. Nieswand, that your husband will spend a great deal of time in jail. Why don't you give me that gun now?"

Abby took a step back. "No, I don't think so. I think maybe I'll kill him." Her clear eyes and her smooth unwrinkled brow chilled Hannibal more than her steady hands wrapped around the small revolver. Abby had reached a point where she could calmly kill the man she loved. Across the room, Nieswand was changing again. His jaw shook, his eyes spread round and his breathing was labored. He sat back on his heels, a dark stain spreading from his crotch. Aside from trembling he held very still, his mouth silently forming the word "no" again and again. Like he finally realized if you tell a person they are insane often enough, they will eventually fulfill your expectations.

Bed springs squeaked as Hannibal leaned to his side, trying to position himself for action. "I know this sounds like a cliché, but you can't get away with it," he said. "You may not have noticed, but several more policemen have joined Detective Rissik in the hall. If your gun goes off, one of them will kill you."

"No, I'll shoot my way out."

Cindy reached out slowly. "You don't want to."

"Yes, I do," Abby snapped. "You get over in the doorway. That way they'll have to shoot you to get me." The gun barrel moved toward Cindy's face and she backed into the doorway. Rissik watched over her shoulder. Hannibal saw Rissik's gun peeking out under Cindy's arm. His heart drummed triple time in his chest and cold droplets rolled down his spine. This could get awfully messy awfully fast, and Nieswand was not worth his wife's life.

"Let's think about this," Hannibal said as calmly as he could. "Old Gabe here shot at me out the window. Then he made that hole there in the ceiling. And you made one over there in the wall. Now I figure that leaves you just three bullets. Hardly enough for a shootout."

Abby smiled in spite of herself. "Not quite a blaze of glory, is it? Him, you, maybe your girlfriend."

"Not really," Hannibal said, leaning a bit farther. "You don't kill anybody with one round from a thirty-eight. That thing won't handle thirty-eight specials or magnums. Just regular ball ammo. You'd use up all three bullets on your husband."

"Yeah. But he'd be gone," Abby said, her voice as cold as the grave she planned for her husband. He seemed to feel the chill clear across the room.

"Maybe. And maybe you too when the jury's through. This is cold-blooded, premeditated murder."

Abby seemed to consider his words. Her brow furrowed a bit, and her head tilted to one side. The tip of her tongue poked out a corner of her mouth. Then her lips pressed together and she shook her head once decisively, and turned to Hannibal.

"Consider what's written in my medical records. Think I could win with an insanity plea?"

As she turned back to face her husband, Hannibal knew she would do it. Her finger tightened on the small chrome-plated trigger as he launched himself across the bed. In slow motion, he saw the little gun's hammer move back as he fought against inertia and gravity to push himself across the queen size space. He could see the tip of Abby's index finger whiten as she squeezed.

-31-

Hannibal's gloved hand pressed against Abby's forearm as the concussion rocked his ears and the world returned to full speed. He landed on Abby's soft body, both his hands struggling to keep hers over her head on the floor. Acrid smoke choked him and the familiar metallic taste of cordite filled his mouth.

Abby actually growled as she grappled with him, and her head snapped forward, banging into him above his right eye. Blue floaters danced in front of him and his ears were still ringing but he leaned forward, pinning Abby's hands in place. Then a foot crushed down on the gun and strong hands jerked him to his feet. Three policemen rushed in to get Abby under control. And Lippincott was there too, close beside her, talking to her in soothing tones. Hannibal sat back on the bed and turned his head, setting off a pulsing headache. When he zeroed in on Nieswand Cindy was kneeling in front of him. Another bullet hole hung two inches from his head.

Cindy bent her head toward her one time mentor. "I am truly sorry I had to be part of this. To a great extent, I feel I should have been defending you. Instead, I helped bring you down."

Hannibal watched them with more than casual curiosity. He did not understand this man at all. Now he appeared quite reasonable, clear and lucid, the

253

man Cindy had described in the past. Nieswand put a hand gently on Cindy's shoulder and held her gaze.

"Don't you ever regret what you've done here today," Nieswand said. "I wish I had earned your loyalty, but in truth I didn't. And today, when it mattered, your loyalties were in the right place. You remember forever that your proper fidelity, allegiance and faithfulness is to the system of justice we, all lawyers worship. Or should."

A uniformed officer stood on either side of Nieswand and slid him to his feet. Abby was again quiet, standing in the opposite corner of the room. Nieswand watched her as the police began to guide him out of the room.

"Hold up a minute please," Hannibal called. When they turned, he held Nieswand by an arm. "Listen, there's still one thing that just doesn't make sense. You took a big gamble here, but I think you knew the stakes all along. You're not crazy, and you're not stupid. You might have talked your way out of all this today, got Lippincott to sedate Abby again and just got yelled at for taking your wife out of the hospital. Nobody even suspected you. So why on earth did you take that shot at me?"

"I got scared," Nieswand said. "I thought you were Angela and Malcolm coming back to get me."

"Whoa." Hannibal's head started spinning again. He pulled Nieswand back into the room. "Angela was here? When?"

"This morning, early. They came pounding on my door at the crack of dawn."

"What could she have wanted with you?" Cindy asked.

"Just like you, she wanted to know who killed Pat Louis. The girl was crazed, I'm telling you. And she had a gun. I was the only other person she could talk to, since I knew what Louis was up to. She figured I must know him well enough to know who'd want to kill him."

"Okay, so you were scared," Hannibal said. "And guilty. So what did you tell her?"

Nieswand seemed to be reliving Angela's visit. "I had to think fast. They were desperate and not real rational. I told them it must have been his ex-wife. He told me about her once. She was the real baby's governess or something I guess, so I said I figured she might hate Louis enough to do him in, especially if she thought he did something with the real baby."

"You stinking son of a bitch," Hannibal said. "You set those lunatics on Daisy Sonneville?" Before anyone could stop him, Hannibal slammed his right fist into Nieswand's midsection. The lawyer doubled over, and spit his last meal down onto the carpet. Hannibal stalked out into the hallway and grabbed a young uniformed officer. "Rissik," he said. The youngster blinked and pointed toward the stairs. Hannibal jogged down them. He found Rissik in the living room using the telephone. Lippincott hung at his shoulder, bouncing from one foot to the other like he had to go to the bathroom. Rissik hung up as Hannibal reached him. He seemed too calm for Hannibal's tastes, like he had days like this all the time.

"Where is she?" Hannibal demanded. "Where's Angela?"

Rissik looked at him the way policemen do, as if whatever your problem is, is not important. "Lost her."

"Lost her?" Hannibal's pitch rose with his frustration level. "Lost her? How the hell could you lose her? Did your boys fall asleep or what?"

"Look," Rissik said, as if explaining a simple concept to a child, "we only had her while she wasn't in a hurry. Wherever she decided to go, she was very much in a hurry today. I'd like to blame somebody too, but the fact is, I got nothing in my motor pool that could chase down that Porsche."

Hannibal turned away, fighting to contain his anger. As much as he hated it, he knew what Rissik said was the ugly truth. In her vehicle, Angela could have disappeared whenever she wanted to. He had no way of knowing where she might be. But he did know one place she went. While he contemplated this, Lippincott tugged on his sleeve.

"She has my son. Can you bring him back?"

"I don't know," Hannibal said. "All depends on if I can find them." He turned toward the door.

"I'll pay you," Lippincott said, laying a hand on Hannibal's arm. "I'll hire you on the spot to find my son and bring him back."

Hannibal shook free of Lippincott's grasp. "I don't exactly think he's a captive here." Then he scanned the room for Cindy. Not seeing her, he scanned his memory. She passed him, he recalled, while he was trying to speak to Rissik. She had passed through the door, as had a dazed and handcuffed Abby Nieswand. Hannibal went to the door and leaned out. A new sprinkle had commenced. Cindy stood beside a police car, consoling the woman who minutes ago threatened to shoot them all. He trotted out into the lengthening shadows and tapped her shoulder.

"By now Bonnie and Clyde must have paid a visit to Daisy Sonneville," he said. "She might know something. You coming?"

* * * * *

Racing down the highway, Hannibal considered he had done way too much traveling on this case. The sun was a dull red fireball low in the sky on his left. A persistent busy signal drowned out the whine of his tires on the asphalt. He reached up and pressed the button to stop the noise.

"It's too long. They've got it off the hook."

"They must be terrified," Cindy said. "Sure hope those kids haven't done anything stupid."

Hannibal pulled out left to pass a tractor trailer. "Little late for that."

"And Malcolm Lippincott is as much a part of it as Angela now," Cindy said. "His father's heartbroken. What would make a person betray their own flesh and blood that way?"

"He's no worse than his old man if you ask me," Hannibal said. He cut off a Camry to get onto the off ramp, raising a blare of horn which he ignored. "Lippincott's about the same age as Harlan Mortimer. He's been hanging around the Mortimers for decades, waiting for a fat inheritance to finance his clinic downtown when he's gone. His legacy, I guess. He hired me to bust Angela, not because he cared about Mortimer, but because she threatened his golden egg. And don't forget, he kept Abby Nieswand drugged and hidden as best he could at her husband's request, without ever once questioning why."

Cindy stayed quiet as they entered suburbia. Hannibal knew the way to the Sonneville house by heart, but he did not remember the neighborhood looking so much like a prison. Each house as much like the next as cells in a penitentiary, and providing each family about as much privacy. Many of these people, he knew, hardly ever went beyond this little community, except on their daily run to work and back. Even then, they usually took the same route. They were not locked in by others who feared them. Their own fear kept them prisoner. Prisoner to their routines, their jobs, their four walls with a television in every room.

Hannibal parked around the corner from the Sonneville house, which apparently got Cindy thinking.

"You don't suppose they're still there?" she asked. "Oh, God, maybe the Sonnevilles are hostages."

"Not likely," Hannibal said, opening his door. But standing outside the car, he bent his head back inside. "Why don't you sit tight while I see if they're home?"

"Like hell," Cindy snapped, bouncing out of the car. "This is not one of those movies where the woman stays behind."

Despite her bravado, Cindy hung well back from Hannibal as he approached the front door. Once on the welcome mat bearing the Sonneville name he rang the bell, then pivoted so his back was to the wall beside the door. He drew his pistol and held it down at his side, wondering if any of Daisy's neighbors were watching. While he waited for an answer, his mind ran every possible scenario, including those which stopped with him calling the police and letting them knock on the door. None looked better than the others to him. Then he focused on the doorknob, watching it slowly revolve.

"Who's there?" a man's voice asked. The door opened a crack and an eye pressed to it, staring over a heavy security chain.

"It's me, Mister Sonneville. Hannibal Jones."

"Go away," Phil Sonneville said, staring up into Hannibal's face. "We've had enough trouble."

Hannibal slid slowly forward, so he and Phil could make eye contact. "Are they still in there?" he asked.

"Nobody here but me and my wife," Phil Sonneville said, "and she's been scared enough."

"Mister Sonneville," Cindy called from the end of the cement path leading to the door. "We're here to help. May we please come in?"

From inside Hannibal heard Daisy's voice. "Oh, Phil, let them in. What more could they do?"

The door slammed and Hannibal was not sure what was happening, but he slid his gun back into its holster. He heard muffled conversation from inside, then the chain slid away and the door swung slowly open. Phil's lips were pressed together and his hands clenched and opened rhythmically. He said "Come in" in the same cadence and hard tone a person might usually say, "screw you."

Hannibal nodded his head, showed his empty hands as a sign of friendship, and eased past the man of the house. There was nothing to be gained by challenging him. Cindy followed Hannibal inside. Daisy Sonneville sat on the sofa, her hands clasped desperately, her blonde locks hanging forlornly around her brown face. Hannibal stood against the front wall, backed by the bay window, hoping to present a less intimidating appearance. He even considered removing his dark glasses and gloves, but he would be too uncomfortable. Instead, he looked to Cindy, wordlessly telling her she should speak first.

"We're looking for the girl calling herself Angela Mortimer," Cindy began. Daisy nodded without looking up. "We think she came here, with a man."

259

Another nod. "And I guess they frightened you. Can you tell us what happened?"

"I'll tell you what happened," Phil shouted. "They had a gun. I sent my little girl to stay with friends in case they come back for more trouble."

Daisy released a loud sob and started pouring tears on the floor. "I don't know where they came from, but they were crazy. I came home from work like normal. Soon as I unlocked the door, they came up behind me, pushed me in the house and slammed the door. She didn't look no more than a teenager, but she had this gun." Then Daisy's tears overwhelmed her voice and she started crying. Phil sat beside her, wrapped an arm around her shoulder, and shook with her weeping.

Hannibal dropped to his haunches to be at eye level with Daisy. "Did they hurt you?" Daisy shook her head.

"What did they want?" Cindy asked.

"The baby," Daisy wailed. "They wanted to know about the baby. The family. All about Bobby Newton and his family, only she said Bobby's real name was Jake something. She was fanatic, frantic. It was like she thought I was a criminal or something. Yelling, yelling, yelling, demanding details about everything. It was so long ago. I thought it was over."

"Yeah," Phil said, sneering at Hannibal. "And you brought it all back."

"Did they say where they were going?" Hannibal asked.

"She just said she was going home," Daisy replied.

Phil gave Hannibal an even harder look. "Why don't you just leave her alone?"

Hannibal stood. "I'm trying to end this. I need to find this Angela. If you want, I can get somebody to watch the house for a day or two until..."

Phil was off the sofa and in Hannibal's face in a second. "Look here. I love my wife. I'll take care of her, and I don't give a damn about her past or her ex-husband or any of that stuff."

"Don't tell me, tell her," Hannibal snapped back. "Don't worry about seeing me again. As of now, I'm out of your life. Her first husband is dead. Jake Mortimer, the man she knew as Bobby Newton, is dead. And once I catch up to the girl, the two of you can bury the past for good. I promise you that."

Hannibal wanted to tell Phil Sonneville what a good man he was, how his love would heal all of Daisy's old scars, how men like him made up for the weak and evil and selfish men he saw every day in his business. But it was not something to say, just to know. With a nod and thank you to Daisy, he waved Cindy out the door. They walked all the way to the street before he escaped the sound of Daisy's crying. Without any conversation he strapped in, started his car, and headed back toward Washington.

Daylight was fading quickly, the shadows slowly but inevitably growing and stretching until soon they would take over. While focused on the road ahead, Hannibal was aware of his seat mate. Cindy stared at him a long time before she spoke. He wondered what she was reading in his face, but was afraid to ask.

"What if she's there? I mean I can't imagine you calling the police," she said. There, he knew, was the Mortimer house. "You've got no more evidence of her guilt now than before. And she has a lot more detail of her supposed childhood and family. Do you think they'll give her up?"

"Got to try," Hannibal said. "If they have all the facts and still choose wrong, well, that's their problem. Her only real crime is fraud, and if Mortimer won't charge her, there's nothing the police or anybody else can do. Maybe I can at least shake Malcolm Lippincott loose. Angela's crimes aside, he's twice her age for God's sake."

In the dark, Great Falls looked very much like any other neighborhood. True, the streets were a little wider, and the space between dwellings greater than a lot of places, but young men still hung out under street lamps and half lit windows still harbored deep secrets. Mortimer's house was dark and quiet, the opposite of the way Hannibal found it on his last visit. He imagined everyone was settled into a quiet game of cribbage or Parcheesi, or whatever wealthy families did on weekday evenings. Or maybe they were all crowded around a big screen television, watching the latest Merchant Ivory film.

Hannibal rang the doorbell and waited. Time passed slowly until someone approached the door. He heard a latch reluctantly release, freeing the deadbolt lock. Then the door slowly swung inward, revealing Harlan Mortimer's face. Hannibal could not hide his surprise. From past visits he thought answering the door was one of Camille's assigned duties. Yet here was the master of the house himself, in smoking jacket and slippers, his salt and pepper beard looking straggly. He was visually testing Hannibal's face like unfamiliar waters. Hannibal felt Harlan's gaze burn right through to the back of his skull. He was about to ask if he could come in, but Harlan spoke first.

"You wear those things at night?" He asked, then turned and walked back into the house, leaving the door open. Hannibal took this as an invitation, and he and Cindy followed Harlan in. A library silence filled the house, prompting them to move quietly. They paused at the door to the cavernous great room. Harlan continued on, dropping heavily into an overstuffed chair and staring straight ahead at the fireplace. Hannibal entered slowly and walked around to stand left of Harlan's visual target.

"We're looking for Angela," Hannibal said. "Has she been here?"

"Oh yes. She's been here all right," Harlan said, nodding toward the fireplace.

Cindy moved forward until she stood beside Hannibal. "Mister Mortimer, we have reason to believe Angela is involved in a carefully developed fraud targeting you."

Harlan snorted one silent laugh. "Oh, I don't think so. She's gone now, and she won't be back. Like father, like daughter, you know."

Harlan's grim smile made Hannibal think he was missing something. He followed Harlan's gaze to the fireplace. What he finally saw there turned his blood to ice water and for a beat of time his heart ached in sympathy with Harlan's.

Cindy squeezed his hand and whispered "What's wrong?"

"The mantle," Hannibal said. "It's empty." The rare coin display cases which had stood in a row, on guard like stiff beefeaters above the fireplace, had all deserted. Or been taken prisoner in a war without rules. Hannibal knew their absence would not dent Harlan Mortimer's fortune, but it would tear open an old wound which had barely begun to heal.

"I'm sorry," was all Hannibal could think of to say.

Harlan looked at him with more curiosity than malice. "You must be happy to be proven right," he said. "You've been busy, I understand. My attorney, my friend of many years, is under arrest. As I understand it, he was also busy trying to rip me off. But you stopped that, didn't you? And now," Harlan looked back at the emptiness over the fireplace, "now I'm alone."

Alone. Hannibal had almost forgotten. "Harlan, where is Camille?"

"Bedside," Harlan said, then looked up in surprise. "You don't know, do you?" Hannibal moved his hands apart, palms up, signaling his ignorance. "Kyle had a serious attack this afternoon. Just as we were sitting down to lunch. Larry checked him into the medical center in Herndon. It's not the greatest, but it's nearby and it's close to Dulles. At first he was talking about flying the boy out to some specialist, but now I don't know. He says Kyle's probably only got three or four more days." A silent sob shuddered through Harlan Mortimer, his voice tightened and his eyes slammed shut. "I know I should be there but I just couldn't. I couldn't stay. Then I get back and, and this."

Hannibal listened numbly until Harlan ran down. This morning they had argued with Larry Lippincott, trying to get to talk to Abby Nieswand. This afternoon they dragged him from his office to see Abby, and then to Nieswand's house. Through it all he said nothing about Kyle's condition. Probably he, like Mortimer, assumed Hannibal already knew.

"Better get over to that hospital," Hannibal said to Cindy, who nodded.

"What good do you think you can do there?" Harlan asked. Hannibal headed for the door, wishing he had an answer.

* * * * *

As much as Hannibal hated lying in hospital rooms, he preferred it to being in one for any other reason. He never knew what to say or what to do with his hands when he visited people. He stood at the door to Kyle Mortimer's private room, staring into the darkened space, feeling helpless. The soft whoosh of oxygen would have been a soothing sound if not for the transparent tent it supported over the top of Kyle's body. Camille sat as still as her chair, bent under the weight of her anguish, clutching Kyle's hand through the plastic.

Cindy walked past him to wrap her arm around Camille's shoulders. The women shuddered together, perhaps crying, perhaps chilled by the spirit of death wafting through the room. When Hannibal did enter, he walked to the foot of the bed so he could face Kyle. Hannibal wanted to tell him about his efforts during the last week, about the false trails he ran down, about his complex case filled with aliases, rumors, and the basest human motivations. But all he could manage to say was "I'm sorry."

"Don't be," Kyle said. His bald head bobbled on a drinking straw neck. His eyes were sunken but bright. His face was wan and gaunt, but his voice was full of energy. "You found my father, and that's all you ever promised to do. And you found Angela. That's got to count as a bonus. I know we don't have the results yet, but she's still a possible marrow donor, right?"

Swallowing part of the truth, Hannibal simply said "Angela's gone."

"I know," Kyle said, his smiling asking Hannibal what his point was. "You'll find her."

"Kyle," Hannibal said, walking to the far side of the bed to take Kyle's hand. "Doctor Lippincott told your grandfather we didn't have much time."

"Three to four days," Kyle said with a matter of fact smile. "A lifetime if you're a fruit fly. Besides, you'll find her and bring her back in time. Or Doctor Lippincott will turn up another compatible donor."

Hannibal's chest squeezed his heart. What in this young man's life had bred in him such courage, such indomitable optimism? "You're not giving up, are you?"

"Nope," Kyle said. "You?"

"Not until it's over. Not until the day after it's over." After meeting this teenager, Hannibal felt no one in the world could ever have an excuse for quitting again.

* * * * *

Hannibal did not drive wearing his dark glasses at night, and now the world around his car was as dark as his mood. He had failed to bring any real comfort to the Mortimer family, because the truth does not always set you free. He might have saved Abby Nieswand from her own madness if he had seen the problem sooner. Not now. He may have saved Malcolm Lippincott from being taken in by Angela, but his attention was elsewhere at the time. He might even have saved Daisy Sonneville from being sucked into the cesspool this case had become, but he was too busy chasing his holy grail, the truth.

Most painful of all, he had failed to save Kyle Mortimer. As he parked in front of his home, he tried to add it all up in his mind and concluded he had brought everyone involved a lot more pain than help.

He was aware of Cindy grasping his hand as he walked toward the door, but he barely felt the pressure. He recognized the numbness as a cowardly defense, but he could do nothing about it.

"Welcome home." Jewel popped out of the office as Hannibal was closing the building's outer door. He figured she must have been listening for him. Her smile dropped off when she saw his face, and she took a small step backward.

"Don't mind him," Cindy said. "He's just in a pissy mood because the world won't do what he says. Come on over to his apartment for a moment. I've got something to tell you."

The last thing Hannibal wanted was company, but he said nothing. Besides, he hardly recognized the girl. The skirt she wore reached halfway to her knees, easily the longest he had seen her in. And she was in flats, not heels. And, most obvious, her face was scrubbed clean. Without makeup, she looked a lot closer to her real age.

When he opened the door, Cindy led Jewel to the kitchen table. Hannibal found three glasses and pulled a bottle of white zinfandel out of the refrigerator. He poured for each of them, then sat behind one of the glasses. Most people he knew would consider this a humorously mild reaction to needing a drink, but alcohol affected him more than anybody he knew.

"Jewel, remember my telling you I'd help you find your family back in Jersey?" Cindy asked. "Well, it turned out to be a lot easier than I expected."

Hannibal could only stare, and Jewel asked "You found my Mama?"

Cindy sipped her wine. "You told me you were from New Sharon, outside Trenton. Not exactly a bustling metropolis. And you said your mother was a secretary."

"Yeah," Jewel said, "but she never held a job very long."

"So I tried the obvious first," Cindy said.

"Kelly?" Hannibal asked.

Cindy nodded. "I started there, today while you were dealing with Rissik and the judge he went to for the warrants we needed to confront Lippincott. She's not a Kelly Girl, but I tried all the temp agencies in the area. All those places are on the World Wide Web as it turns out, and they were very cooperative."

Jewel was panting now, eyes round and shiny as new quarters. "You mean it was easy as that?"

"Well, I wouldn't call it easy," Cindy said, fishing a notepad out of her purse. "But I managed to make some headway sitting there in my office. She's moved around quite a bit in the last two years, but here's what her agency believes to be a current address."

Jewel's face crinkled with joy as she accepted the paper. Hannibal's mood lifted a bit and he reached to squeeze Cindy's empty hand. At least one of his clients would find what she needed, even if he was not responsible for her happiness. A few more years seemed to drop from Jewel's face as she stood to hug Cindy and, for the first time, she looked to Hannibal like a girl under twenty.

"God bless you, Miss Santiago," Jewel squealed. "Thanks to you, I can finally go home."

Home. Home for Jewel was someplace she had never been. Home was not a location filled with memories and personal history, but rather, the place she would find unconditional support. Home for her was wherever her mother was.

Hannibal looked at Jewel, looked at Cindy, and drained his glass.

"Of course," he mumbled, "how stupid could I be?" His chair fell over as he bolted for the wall phone. He felt Cindy's and Jewel's stares on him but he did not care. His head ached with the obvious revelation which had struck him.

"Who in the world are you calling?" Cindy asked.

"Lippincott," Hannibal said, punching buttons on the receiver. "I think he'll buy our tickets to Corpus Christi."

"Our? Why are we going to Corpus Christi? And why in the world would he buy the tickets?"

Hannibal impatiently listened to the phone ringing at the other end. "Because, babe, he wants me to bring his son back. And I'm sure the boy's travelling with Angela. And the last thing she said to anybody was she was going home."

-32-

TUESDAY

A huge, angry sun stabbed into Hannibal's eyes from his left as he drove his rented Ford Tempo out of the United States. A Tempo because it was the car available when he arrived at the airport. Each pothole jarred his frame and rattled the car, but slowing down was not an option he considered. The air was still crisp, and he drove with his window down, allowing a chilling wind to blow the road noise into his face. The cool air tasted sweet, and more importantly, the breeze kept him sharp and alert. Cindy, dressed as she was on their first trip to Mexico, wrapped her arms around herself against the slight chill. He knew higher temperatures would come soon after dawn, and later in the day his white, loose fitting jeans would be collecting sweat. He wore a light blue polo shirt, but his jeans and hiking boots were clear concessions to the fact he expected a good deal more action on this trip south of the border than the last.

The road turned slightly left, allowing his Oakleys to block the cruel sun's rays. He searched for a dust plume ahead, or skid marks on the side of the road, any sign the road was recently traveled. All he saw, so far, were donkey carts and ancient pickups strategically placed to delay his progress as much as possible. His mouth was set in a grim line, his mind repeating his failures like a litany. He could not save Abby Nieswand's mind. He could not save Daisy Sonneville's peace of mind. He could not save Kyle Mortimer's life. But he could save Malcolm Lippincott's future. And he would bring Angela Robinson, AKA Angela Briggs, AKA Angela Mortimer to justice.

"What are you looking for?" Cindy, sitting beside him, stared into his face as if she suspected he forgot she was there.

"Signs of passage."

"You can't be serious," she said, although she had to know he was. "They can't possibly be in front of us."

"Can't they?"

"Do the math," she said. "We flew. They're driving. It's got to be more than sixteen hundred miles. And they only left the Sonnevilles' house about fifteen hours ago."

"Okay," Hannibal said, his voice implying a patience he did not feel. "Let's look at this logically. Angela's a young kid. Malcolm's about my age, but he's foolish, and acts like a kid. And they're in a hurry, running scared. So I think it's reasonable they might take turns at the wheel and drive all day and all night. And they're not going to be worried about safety margins or scheduled rest stops, because the young and foolish just don't. Oh, and they're not just young and foolish, they're young and foolish in a brand new Porsche that'll probably push a hundred eighty miles an hour on the straightaway. If the drivers were up to it, the machine could certainly average over a hundred miles an hour. So yeah, I think it's just inside the realm of possibility they might be ahead of us."

271

Good job, Hannibal thought as Cindy crossed her arms and slumped into her seat. One more thing he regretted saying as soon as it came out. Well, she would get over it after he had Angela and Malcolm under wraps, and he could salve her wounds with dinner and a show.

By the time they rolled into the dirt road town of Esmeralda, Hannibal had the window up and the air conditioner blowing full blast. People moved slowly but purposefully into and out of stores. He supposed morning was the time of greatest activity, before the heat moved from objectionable to unbearable. As he rolled through, he noticed the same heavy jowled man on the chair in front of the small grocery store. He looked like he had not moved since they were last in town. In fact, he wore the same canvas pants, tee shirt and thong sandals. Like everyone else on the street, he ignored Hannibal's car.

Hannibal pushed the car into park and turned to face his passenger. "If I say I'm sorry and admit my ignorance of local language and customs, will you go in and get us something for lunch? And coffee, please."

Hannibal drove the Ford over the narrow wooden bridge and turned left at the fork. Less than ten minutes later he passed Scooter Johnson's whorehouse and, about a hundred yards later, managed a three-point turn and parked in the shade of a giant spreading oak. Having long since gulped down his coffee, he sipped from a bottle of water, tipped his seat back and started fiddling with the radio. Cindy laid a hand on his shoulder to get his attention.

"What are we doing?"

"Waiting for Angela and Malcolm," he said. "I want to see them as they approach. Then we go in right behind them and snatch them up."

"Wait a minute," Cindy said. "We can't just sit here all day and all night."

Hannibal smiled as he settled the tuner on a soft acoustic guitar melody. "Sure we can. Done all the time. That's how you catch the bad guys." He tilted his seat back and settled in. But his smile melted as he heard Cindy's breathing deepen and watched her start to shudder, building up steam for a major outburst.

"Damn it, Hannibal," Cindy shouted. "I'm a lawyer, not a cop. I don't do stakeouts! Let's wait in the house. I don't think Scooter or her husband will give us away."

Hannibal put a hand on her arm, trying to calm her. "Look, suppose we waited inside like you say. They pull up, right. Angela opens the door, and there we sit. Don't you think she'd turn around and beat it out of there? Then what? I'm jumping in this thing and she's firing up a brand new Porsche. What do you figure the odds of catching her then, huh?" Slowly, he pulled her toward himself, until finally she rested against his shoulder and he could kiss her hair. "Just hang out here with me a little while, okay? When they show, we can go in behind them, be between them and the car. And maybe we can talk Malcolm into coming back on his own. If we can do that, I've got handcuffs in my pocket to hold the girl with."

Smiling in spite of herself, Cindy asked "You don't think the girl's parents will kick about us taking her back to the States?"

"Honestly, I think it's a split decision," Hannibal said. "Mama will want to protect her baby, Papa will want his girl to pay the consequences of her actions. Don't forget that killer scar. So I figure it's a wash there."

"Got it all figured out, haven't you?" Cindy asked, nuzzling his neck.

"Not quite. I've got no idea what you got us for lunch."

Even with all four windows down, the inside of the car was an oven by noon. Not even a hint of a cloud tempered the effects of the blazing bright sun overhead. Hannibal had opened the driver side doors, and his legs hung out, away from the road, while he munched on a fat burrito. The homemade tortilla was rolled around more beans than meat, but the sauce was hot and greasy and delicious.

Cindy ate with a shade more dignity, and drank a bit more water. "Hannibal," she asked between bites, "be glad when this is all over?"

He stopped chewing for a moment. "Glad? No, I don't think I'll be glad exactly. This is just cleanup after all. I failed."

"That's not fair," she said, wiping his sweaty forehead with a towel. "You did the job you were hired for. You found Kyle's father."

"People keep saying that," Hannibal said, sitting up straighter. "Jacob Mortimer was never the job. He was just the projected means to the end. Kyle was the job. And even though I ended up in this thing because of a con game, Kyle never stopped being the job."

The rest of their meal passed in silence, Hannibal alternately lost in his own thoughts and wondering what Cindy's might be. He knew he was not a good man when he was on a case, at least not in the boyfriend sense. She deserved better, he thought, but he was too old and stubborn to change. He watched her wipe her mouth on a paper napkin and straighten her tee shirt. She licked her lips and smiled. Right then he wanted very much to hear her say she loved him.

"Know what?" she asked.

He looked into her pretty brown eyes. "What's that?"

"I'm going up to the house."

"What?" He sat bolt upright. "You can't, not now."

"Afraid I've got to," Cindy said. Then in muted tones, "I've got to go to the bathroom."

"Well, there's plenty of privacy here," he said. "Just wander over around that huge tree."

The backs of Cindy's hands rested on her hips and her head moved loosely on her neck. "I am not going to the bathroom behind some tree where people can drive by and see me with my ass hanging out."

"Okay, fine," he said. "Come around to the other side of the car. With both doors open, it makes a stall, sort of. And the trees straight ahead. Nobody could see you."

"I don't think you're listening," Cindy said, opening her own door. "I am just not the piss in the outdoors type. I'm going up to the..."

The roar of a car engine cut her off. An old Grand Torino skidded to a stop in front of the two story Georgian house. The car outdid the house, for while the house boasted peeling paint on every side, the Torino was down to the gray primer all around. Its throaty roar told Hannibal the car was tuned for racing in the streets, as was common all over the South where weather and salt did not attack old cars the way it did in Germany and New York. It growled two or three times before shutting off. Instinctively,

Hannibal yanked Cindy back into the Ford. It couldn't be them, but he knew it must be.

And it was. Even a football field away he recognized Angela's form as she climbed out of the driver's door and marched stiffly toward the house. Malcolm Lippincott trailed like an adoring puppy behind her. He carried a pair of Gucci overnight bags. She carried a revolver as big as her own arm.

Hannibal's mind swirled with questions, but he knew all the answers were within reach. Thinking no words were necessary, he climbed out of the Ford and jogged toward the house. At the wraparound porch he stopped and started again, this time very slowly. He stayed at the edge of the old steps, where he was least likely to make them creak. At the door he turned to watch Cindy step up on the first wooden stair. It would be easier for her, in tennis shoes, than his boots had made it for him. But he was sure no one inside could have heard him.

The door was not quite closed, and he stared into the room, allowing his eyes to adjust to the relative darkness. Without the red lights on, the room looked quite ordinary. The sofa left of the door faced into the house, he remembered. Further to the left, against the wall, stood a chenille love seat. The stairs leading to the second floor went up along the right side wall. A big sofa leaned back against the staircase. Straight ahead, he was looking at Malcolm's back. Beyond him, Scooter Johnson stood at her counter/room divider, her face a mask of worry. Between them, Angela stood staring into her mother's face, her handgun hanging at her side. Her posture said she was in charge, and willing to do whatever was necessary to keep control.

"Quit stalling, Mama," Angela said with uncommon force for such a small body. "Where is he?"

Scooter spoke with her hands, her lower chins vibrating with her actions. "I don't know what's wrong, but let your Mama help you, baby. You ought to know you're always welcome back home, Patty."

"Don't you call me that!" Angela hoisted her revolver with both hands. "Don't you ever call me that name, you old whore. My name is Angela, understand. You people aren't my parents. You couldn't be. I feel it in my blood, in my bones. You're too stupid, too common to be my parents. You must have taken me from my real family when I was an infant. But I need a place to stay, and this is the only safe place I know. But I won't stay here with him."

Scooter started around the counter and Angela turned to her right slightly to keep the bigger woman in her sights. Hannibal looked closely at the gun Angela's slender arms were supporting. A Taurus Model 607, three and a half pounds of stainless steel, a seven shot .357 Magnum. A big enough gun to support anybody's ego. He could also see a glimpse of Angela's eyes. They told him she was the loose cannon in the room, not the gun in her hand. She would shoot if driven to it, and once she started, she would not stop until she stood alone in the room. He took a couple of deep breaths. Maybe if he entered slowly and easily, he could talk her out of violence.

His plan disintegrated when Nelson Johnson ducked under the arch and walked out from the kitchen. He wore coveralls and carried a big hammer, but without the work gloves he had on the last time Hannibal saw him. He took three steps into the room before he realized Angela was there. His reaction was shock, and reflexively he raised his hammer.

"You!" Barely ten feet from him, Angela swung her weapon on line, pointing its gaping muzzle at the old man's chest.

Hannibal's options had shrunk to zero. There was no time for talk or even thought. With a scream meant to spur himself into action as much as freeze Angela, he dived through the door. Shoulder first, he smashed into Malcolm's back. With a grunt of pain, Malcolm flew forward. His bulk crashed into Angela from behind. Her left arm swung forward to break her fall. Her right arm swung farther right as the gun discharged, the bullet smashing into the wall below the stairs. The flash dazzled Hannibal, but he could see the gun's natural muzzle rise snap it up and back. The revolver twisted Angela's arm as it swung up and over her head, then flew over Hannibal to thump to the floor in the doorsill.

Still barely in the room, he pushed himself up to survey the scene. Malcolm had rolled onto his back. He was staring at the ceiling, breathing through his open mouth. He was probably looking through floating blue dots and his ears were probably ringing, like Hannibal's. Angela's head snapped back and forth, as she searched for the cause of her fall. Scooter leaned, collapsed, against the counter.

But Nelson Johnson, Angela's hated father, was still standing. He pulled his lips back away from yellow, crooked teeth. "I know you'd killed me if you got the chance, you little black bitch. Now you missed your shot, and I'm taking mine."

Three long steps brought Johnson to hover over Angela's prone form. He bent at the knees as low as his stiff body would allow. Maintaining eye contact with his target, he raised his hammer into the air slowly, as if he wanted to savor this moment forever.

Angela stared defiantly back into his eyes. No fear showed on her face. In fact, she was eerily serene, like she was anxious for closure, ready for an end to this grim drama regardless of which ending it had. As the hammer reached its apex, she swung her head down then back up, and spit upward. She spattered his chest, falling short of her target.

"Missed my face," Nelson said, "Just like that day with the hot coffee." Rage lit his eyes, and he screamed as he drove the hammer head downward.

Before Hannibal could react, Johnson was swept aside by an angry mass of pent up resentment. Scooter's body hit him like a freight train, her three hundred plus pounds sweeping the slender man halfway across the room. The two rolled once and stopped with Scooter straddling her husband. She thumped her bulk down on him, like a scene in a most disgusting porno film. Nelson's long legs danced around to no effect, his boot heels clacking on the floor. Scooter was wailing out years of pain, swinging her heavy arms back and forth, slapping him in a bizarre, fascinating rhythm.

While the couple wrestled like sadistic lovers, Scooter's baggy flowered dress rode up around her bulbous rump. Hannibal reflexively turned away, then looked again to check his memory imprint of the picture. Below her graying, once white panties, he saw scars. Scars he recognized as the remnants of cigarette burns, scattered around her buttocks and the upper part of her legs. His stomach clenched, and he could barely breathe for the weight of the truth pressing in on his chest.

Scooter's weight kept her husband immobile, but his arms were free. His right hand was still wrapped around the hammer and he seemed to have gathered enough of his wits to raise it. Hannibal got to his feet, jogged across the room and kicked the man's wrist. The hammer dropped and he pushed it out of reach with his foot. Then he rested a hand on the woman's shoulder. His touch seemed to short circuit her arms, which hung limp at her sides as she looked up.

"Don't you think that's enough?" Hannibal asked. "No matter how much you hurt him, your pain won't go away. And after all, you agreed to this life, didn't you?"

Scooter's head slumped down onto her broad chest, and the sobbing began again. Hannibal was about to ask her to stand when a movement behind him drew his attention. Cindy had come in, and was helping Malcolm to his feet. He looked like a man in shock. Hannibal guessed he was having the adventure of his life, and had only now realized it was totally out of control.

"Hey Malcolm," Hannibal said, "What'd you do, wreck the Porsche?"

"Actually, about half way here, Angela started to worry we'd get traced down by the car," Malcolm said, still leaning on Cindy for support. "We sold it in Memphis and flew from there to Corpus Cristi. Bought this junker there, because Angela thought it would be inconspicuous."

"So that's how you got here so fast," Cindy said. "Sounds like Angela thought of everything. Have you done any thinking in the last day or two?"

"No, cause he's a faggot." Angela burst forward in a rush of action, shoving Cindy aside as she bolted out the door, swinging it closed behind her. Hannibal was stunned for a second by the abrupt action, then he started after her. As he pulled the door open he saw Angela had scooped up the loose pistol. He ducked back, pushing the door closed but a heavy bullet thudded into it, slamming the door back open. As it swung by, Hannibal darted outside.

Angela had already fired up the engine of the Gran Torino and was trying to maneuver it around on the road to face back toward north. Considering his options on the run, Hannibal steered his feet toward his own rented car. Angela was a good driver, but the Torino did not handle like a Porsche and if he was fast enough, he might catch her.

He had to now.

Hannibal was a track star in high school. At one time, he pushed his hundred meter dash time to a hair above ten seconds. But that was at the apex of his physical ability under perfect conditions. Now, in boots and jeans, on a dirt road instead of a paved track, he was panting hard, driving his legs to forget the years between then and now. Sweat stung his eyes as he ran hard toward his car, now only fifty yards ahead. His arms pumped hard as he dragged blazing hot air into his lungs.

He could hear his heart pounding when his hand snatched the Ford's door handle. The aluminum burned his palm but he ignored it, consumed with getting into his seat. The car started quickly and he pressed the accelerator to the floor. Dust spewed up behind him and after an annoying second of hesitation the car burst forward.

The little Tempo was an automatic, so Hannibal simply kept his foot mashed to the floorboards and prayed the car would stay on the road. He roared past Cindy waving on the porch, and within seconds he had the Gran Torino in sight. Angela's car had a lot of power, but the dust covered, pot holed road made it almost impossible for her to put her advantage to good use.

He had never turned the radio off and now he recognized the guitar tune coming from it. It was an intricate piece called Malaguena, which he had heard on a school vacation to Spain. Back then nothing was life and death to him, and he had almost recovered from the serious emotional blow of learning, at six years old, how the Viet Cong killed his father. Thank God he had his mother all those days, months, years to hold him together. Knowing the pain of losing a father tempted him to slow down, let Angela go. Knowing how family could ease the pain of loss made him will his car to move faster.

He was within a couple of car lengths of the Torino when the wooden bridge came into view. The road beyond it was smoother and a little wider. A good driver could lose him on a well-paved straightaway. He had to stop her now. He pulled to his left and, to his surprise, began to gain on his quarry. She was slowing slightly. They were closing on the bridge. Her left hand came out her window, pointing the big revolver backward. Hannibal swung his steering wheel left, then right.

Angela fired. Hannibal reflexively ducked. He heard a burst of crackling white noise and his windshield became a mass of white spider webs, except for the fist-size hole almost dead center. He jerked the wheel right again, hoping to be in the middle of the road. An impact jarred him. The screech of metal on metal, like chalk on a blackboard. Then his car crunched into the bridge's left side wooden railing and his head snapped into the steering wheel and everything stopped.

-33-

Quiet. No roaring engines. No tires whining on the dirt track. Hannibal shook his head and watched shards of crumbled safety glass shower down onto his lap. He was sore, but not aching anywhere the way you do when a bone is broken. He did not smell gasoline, did not see blood.

"Any wreck you can walk away from," he muttered. His door opened easily enough, and the front of the car did not look too bad. All four tires held air. He might even be able to drive this heap. Then he clamped his eyes shut as he realized he was alone. Angela must be halfway to Texas by now. He slammed a fist into his car's door. He had done his best, but it was not enough. Time ran out, the buzzer sounded. It was over. He lost.

He turned to start his walk back to the bordello when a scream froze him in place. He stared around, trying to find the source. Then he heard it again, a woman's voice, shrill with fear. Running around the Tempo he followed the sound to the edge of the bridge. No one in sight. A third scream. Very near. And down. Under the bridge?

The gray trunk of a car stuck up out of the shallow river the bridge crossed. The picture formed at once. He had sideswiped the other car. It swerved right, he swerved left. The bridge stopped him. But Angela had gone past the bridge and down the seven foot bank into the water.

At the water's edge, Hannibal found Angela sticking halfway out of the Torino's driver's side window. Her door would not open. The dirty water was over the edge of the window and poured into the car, which was still sinking. Her eyes were panicked, but as she saw him the fear increased. He stretched as far as he could, planting his right foot as far into the river as he could, leaving his left on dry land.

"Give me your hand, girl," he said. "Now, or you'll be sucked under with the car."

Incredibly, Angela hesitated. "I lost my gun, damn it. I'm not going back, understand. I won't go back and I won't go to jail. I know what jail does."

"Just give me your hand," Hannibal said, pleading rather than ordering. But both her hands were on the door, trying to push herself out of the car. Then the Torino shifted, sliding on the muddy river bottom, and she reflexively reached out. Hannibal had a good grip on her wrist and yanked hard. Angela slid free of the car, splashed up through the water, and scrambled to her feet. In less than a minute she and Hannibal were kneeling on the ground beside the bridge's railing. Tiny tears started in her eyes, but her mouth was set in a defiant line. Hannibal leaned forward and Angela's forehead fell onto his shoulder.

"I'm not going back," she whispered.

Hannibal took her shoulders in his hands and held her at arms' length. "There's no more need to run, girl. Please believe me. Everything you know is a lie. Everything you dream is true."

The Tempo made more noise than its earliest relative, the Model T, but it carried Hannibal and Angela back to the house where it all began. He stared at the peeling paint and missing shingles, and saw the house's abandoned appearance as an analogy for the lives it had contained.

Hannibal climbed out of the car and helped Angela out through his door, the other being jammed shut. He held her by the arm as they marched slowly up the porch steps. More than her waterlogged clothes weighted her down, he knew. She was burdened with a lifetime of resentment, a load almost as difficult to put down as it is to carry. Exhausted, he pushed the door open and took three steps inside before he realized something was wrong. Cindy and Malcolm shared the love seat on his far left, their faces twisted in horror.

"You come right on in."

Hannibal turned right toward the voice, and stared into two wide gun barrels. Johnson stood at the base of the stairs, aiming a long double barreled shotgun down at Hannibal's head. His yellow teeth shone triumphantly. Hannibal looked close, confirming what he knew must be on the back of the man's left hand. Then he gently pushed Angela toward the others and turned to face the gun.

"If you put that down, all the evil can end right here," Hannibal said.

"Put it down?" Johnson almost laughed. "I ain't putting shit down. Not till I'm done rid of that bitch."

"You mean Angela?" Hannibal asked. He waved the girl toward the sofa without turning, and was rewarded with the sound of her footsteps moving away. "I don't see the point of that. I'm taking her back to the States and out of your life for good. Why kill her now?"

"It'll make me feel good."

Hannibal stepped farther into the room. The shotgun pivoted to follow him, leaving the others behind. "I can't believe you'd kill your own daughter. But then, she isn't yours is she?" Another step forward. "In fact, there's not a drop of your blood in her, is there?" Another slow step, but he still faced the gun. "If I'm right, I dug up her father's bones in a cellar in Baltimore."

"Guess I got to kill you too." Johnson took one menacing step forward.

Hannibal faced him squarely, stepping back slowly toward the kitchen. "They used to call you Killer, didn't they? You are Killer Nilson, right? And Scooter, she used to be Barbie Robinson. Figured that out when I saw those old scars on the backs of her legs. Doctor Lippincott told me about them when I asked about the young girl who took Jacob Mortimer away."

"Oh God," Cindy moaned behind him. "She didn't have any more imagination than Jacob did. He called her Dolly, as in Barbie doll. And Barbie's best friend was Scooter."

"I figure you met her in your bar, Killer," Hannibal said. "She's the girl Detective Dalton told me about, the one you and Pat Louis fought over. I guess you won, eh?"

"We was married," Scooter said from the sofa. "Long before my baby we was married."

"Sure," Hannibal said. "You got married, then you went to jail. Scooter, Barbie, must have met Jake Mortimer while you were in stir. They fell in love and she got pregnant. From what I've heard they were pretty happy until you got out."

"She was my wife," Johnson shouted. "She belonged to me."

"Right, and you were the well known Killer," Hannibal said. "So how much of that was hype? Were you really so dangerous? Well, we know you killed one man. Angela's father."

Behind him, Hannibal heard Angela cry out "No! No!"

"I killed lots of men," Johnson said. "Should have drowned that bitch in the tub when she was too small to cause trouble."

Hannibal controlled his breathing, but he could not stop the sweat breaking out on his forehead through force of will. "Yeah, but you didn't, did you? From what I've seen, I'll bet her mother wouldn't let you."

"I begged him," Scooter said from the sofa. "I swore I'd do anything he said if he'd spare my baby. I swore I'd never leave him if he'd just leave her be. He didn't know who Bobby was but I told him he was Jacob Mortimer and his family was important. The police, they look for peoples what kills important people. So we come down here to get away from the police. But he always hated Angela, always mistreated her."

Scooter was rocking now, fighting her grief. Angela held her arm with two hands. "Momma, why didn't you tell me? Why'd you tell me my name was Patty?"

Scooter's voice was a squeal now. "Your father named himself after two Black Panther leaders, Bobby Seale and Huey Newton. So I named you after the only woman black liberation leader I could think of. Angela Davis. When we got down here, Killer said we all had to have new names. Best I could come up with, only other woman revolutionary I knew was Patty Hurst."

"Shut your face, woman," Johnson shouted, "Or I swear to God I'll kill you."

"And who you going to kill after that?" Hannibal asked. "Me? Angela? You only got two barrels. Malcolm over there's young and strong. Once that gun's empty, he'll just get up and kick your big black ass."

His heart had climbed halfway up his throat, but he was still focused, waiting for the instant of action. He knew it would be soon. The man he faced had stopped being Killer Nilson long ago, and Nelson Johnson was not nearly the same man. Hannibal could almost see Johnson's spine being eaten away by years of paranoia.

"He ain't going to do nothing," Johnson said, but his eyes wavered. "He'll sit there and watch me blow you in half."

Hannibal stopped at the end of the counter. "You know something Johnson, or Nilson, or whatever the hell you call yourself? I don't like your attitude. Now!" With the shout, Hannibal pointed toward Malcolm. And Johnson's fear made him move the shotgun toward the sofa for an instant.

Knowing he had only a second, Hannibal relaxed his legs and spun, to drop behind the counter. He reached down under his left pants leg. A swarm of twelve gage hornets burst through the counter, leaving a hole the size of a man's head inches above Hannibal's back. But he had the little Colt Commander out of its ankle holster and in one smooth movement he swung his arm around the counter and fired. Johnson jerked as if someone had punched him in the left shoulder and blood burst up from his sleeve. He slumped against the wall, the shotgun's barrels swinging toward the floor. Hannibal leaped to his feet like a berserker and charged through his own gun smoke. Johnson began to slump, but Hannibal held him up with his right hand around Johnson's throat. He pressed his pistol's short barrel into Johnson's neck and breathed the hell fire of retribution into Johnson's face.

"You murdering bastard," he said through clenched teeth. "You killed him didn't you? You stabbed the man you knew as Bobby Newton and dumped his body in the cellar."

"Yes," Johnson gasped. "I did him. I did him for her."

Behind him, Hannibal heard Scooter burst into tears, wailing louder than ever. She probably never forgave herself for the tradeoff she made. Hannibal felt her pain. He felt Angela's pain, and his swirling mind reached out to all those who had suffered because of one act of greed so long ago. The entire Mortimer family, who lost a son, a husband, a father. In some twisted way it also resulted in Nieswand's corruption and his wife's eventual breakdown. All their pain converted easily to anger. And he could dispel his rage with one bullet fired into Johnson's hated brain. His finger tightened on the trigger. Johnson relaxed, as if he knew what was coming. Maybe he had been waiting for it for decades.

"Hannibal," Cindy shouted. "You don't want to."

"The hell I don't," he screamed back. "He's nothing but a cold-blooded killer."

Cindy walked to within four feet of her man. "He is," she said. "But you're not."

Teeth grinding together, Hannibal felt the anger boiling in his belly again. He must learn to control that.

And he did. The red haze passed from his eyes and he heaved a heavy sigh of partial regret. For a moment he had wanted this man to die by his hand, but he had to face the facts.

"You're not worth the bullet," Hannibal said, lowering his gun. "You're a hateful old man, an evil old man, a vicious old man. But after all that, you are still just an old man."

When Hannibal released him, Vernon "Killer" Nilson, now known as Nelson Johnson, dropped to his knees and silently wept. He could never be punished enough, Hannibal thought, but fate had certainly made a good start of it.

-34-

MONDAY

Kyle Mortimer looked up from his bed into Hannibal's hazel eyes. Kyle was shaved bald, emaciated and heavily sedated, but his eyes looked unnaturally clear and sharp. He was riding down a hospital hallway, pushed by an orderly, his mother Camille gripping his right hand as they traveled. His grandfather walked beside the orderly, watching the IV tubes and occasionally telling the orderly to be careful. On his way to surgery, Kyle's concern was for those walking along with him.

"You don't look too good," he told Hannibal. "You getting enough sleep?"

"You kidding?" Hannibal said. "Never been more relaxed. Why, it's been almost a week since anybody took a shot at me." He knew the deep circles under his eyes contradicted his words, but how could he claim to feel bad next to Kyle's weakened condition? When they reached the door to the operating room, Kyle said "I knew you'd come through. Thanks."

"Thank me when it's over," Hannibal said. The wide, white double doors bounced open and Kyle disappeared into the mouth of fate. The small group stood for a moment, each with their own private thoughts, then they turned together and walked back to the waiting room.

The room was way too white, with a large screen television speaking softly at one end and a coffee urn gurgling at the other. In between was a collection of the most uncomfortable chairs and couches Hannibal had ever seen in the United States. Stuck among them in a corner, the biggest visitor looked no less uncomfortable. Scooter Johnson, now again known as Barbie Robinson, kept looking around like she was guilty of something and was sure someone would suspect. Cindy, seated beside her, patted her arm occasionally, in a reflexive comforting motion. Even at six in the morning her hair was perfectly waved and she looked professional in heels and a tan suit. And while a new dress and shoes could not hide Barbie's girth, she clearly had worked at looking as nice as she could.

Malcolm Lippincott sat staring at the floor on the other side of the room. Hannibal was surprised to see Camille take the empty seat beside Barbie. He considered how much alike their bodies must have looked eighteen years ago, before Barbie left her own country and took up the most degrading profession she could think of. How much did she grow to hate herself, he wondered. Was that why she had gained so much weight? Or was Barbie Robinson hiding in there under the perfect disguise of Scooter Johnson's obesity?

The way Camille looked at Barbie, it seemed clear she saw nothing except another mother in pain. "What your daughter is doing for my son, there are no words," she said. "Thank you just seems so inadequate. It was pure luck that her blood and bone marrow matched his, even though Kyle would tell you it had to be. Still, she didn't have to agree to the transplant."

"Of course she did," Barbie said. "After what she tried to do to you people. She knows how wrong she was. Just as wrong as I was for not telling her who she was. By keeping her away, I almost killed your little boy."

Camille did not pull away, although she was obviously taken aback. "You never told her you were my husband's..." To her credit, Camille stopped and started again as if she had not made a major gaff, as if she was correcting her grammar. "You never told her who her father was? Then by what miracle did she find her way into our lives? Were we right the first time? Did Mister Jones provide our salvation?"

All eyes turned to Hannibal who was drawing a cup of coffee from the urn. "My mother used to say the Lord works in mysterious ways," he said. "Actually, Pat Louis should get the credit. True, he's the real villain of this piece. He corrupted Gabe Nieswand, and drove Abby Nieswand over the edge. But he's also the reason Angela came face to face with her grandfather."

Hannibal sat in one of the plastic covered, sponge rubber cushioned chairs. "You see, when Killer Nilson went south across the border, his house became known as a hideout for thugs on the run from up north. All his old buddies from Baltimore knew that, for a price, they could get a room there until the heat died down. Years ago, Pat Louis went down. Killer figured he got rid of the competition for Barbie, but Louis still held a grudge. Now I figure anybody could see the way things were between them, so the most disruptive thing he could do was to tell Angela that Killer wasn't her father. He knew who Bobby Newton really was and who killed him. So he came up with the scheme of scamming the Mortimers. He told Angela if she'd come to Virginia with him and do what he said, she'd get rich. Of course, he would too."

"But Angela was gone a long time before she came up here," Barbie said.

"That's because on their way back to the states, Louis got busted," Hannibal said. "That's when Angela got herself adopted by a nice man in Corpus Cristi and got her education. When Louis got out he found her, and figured all she had done during that time was build herself a stronger back story. His scheme would go forward, even easier."

Cindy nodded. "And to cement things, he seduced Abby Nieswand, got her to go to Atlantic City with him, and then called Gabe Nieswand to come get her. I guess it wasn't that hard for him to get Mister Nieswand into the plot."

"He had the poor girl masquerading as herself," Camille said. "Never let on the truth."

"He couldn't," Hannibal said. "If she knew she really was the girl she was pretending to be, she'd have no use for him. That would have done Louis out of any money. As it is, Nieswand cut him out anyway, permanently."

Cindy checked her watch. "Afraid you've got to get a move on, lover."

"Okay," Hannibal said, "but I'll be back in an hour at the most. Take care of Scooter, I mean Barbie, okay?"

Harlan Mortimer's voice rumbled up from the seat by the door, and he stood to face Hannibal. "You don't have to worry about Miss Robinson. I'll make sure she's well cared for. She's family now. After all, she's the mother of my granddaughter. My granddaughter who, right now, is in there sharing her blood and bone with my grandson. Can't get any closer than that."

"And I'll take care of Angela," Malcolm said from his corner. "I know she's confused right now, but we'll work that all out. Even if I have to fight my old man."

"Don't worry about Larry," Harlan said. "He knows what's in the girl's heart. "He's in there assisting with the operation, isn't he? He'll see her different after this."

"We're fine here," Cindy added. "You just hurry back, lover."

Hannibal crossed the room again to drop a kiss on Cindy's cheek, then headed out. Downstairs he was greeted by lark songs and the first rays of dawn. The cloudless sky was a shade of blue he had only seen once or twice except in dreams. He filled his lungs with a great gulp of air and jogged into the parking lot to his car. No one could tell it had ever been damaged. He would have to remember to send that repair shop a Christmas card.

He pulled his door open and peered inside. Jewel sat nodding in the passenger seat, looking fresher and younger than he had ever seen her. Her straight black hair gently embraced her dark face, the face of a Nubian princess, Nefertiti or Cleopatra. At first her face seemed incongruous resting above an oversize flannel shirt. But as he looked more closely, it seemed perfect there, much more natural than the leather and miniskirts he was used to seeing her in.

He sat without waking her, but she stirred when he shut his door. She offered him a relaxed smile which he accepted gratefully. "You ready?" he asked.

"I think so," Jewel said. "Never thought I'd be nervous about a plane flight."

He started the engine and pointed his car toward Reagan National Airport. "I wouldn't worry. No one on earth has the capacity to forgive and forget like your mother does. Just keep thinking that tonight, for the first time in years, when you lay your head down, you'll be home."

Jewel leaned back and closed her eyes, conjuring a scene Hannibal could only imagine. "Home," she said.

Author's Bio

Austin S. Camacho is a public affairs specialist for the Department of Defense. America's military people overseas know him because for more than a decade his radio and television news reports were transmitted to them daily on the American Forces Network.

He was born in New York City but grew up in Saratoga Springs, New York. He majored in psychology at Union College in Schenectady, New York. Dwindling finances and escalating costs brought his college days to an end after three years. He enlisted in the Army as a weapons repairman but soon moved into a more appropriate field. The Army trained him to be a broadcast journalist. Disc jockey time alternated with news writing, video camera and editing work, public affairs assignments and news anchor duties.

During his years as a soldier, Austin lived in Missouri, California, Maryland, Georgia and Belgium. While enlisted he finished his Bachelor's Degree at night and started his Master's, and rose to the rank of Sergeant First Class. In his spare time, he began writing adventure and mystery novels set in some of the exotic places he'd visited.

After leaving the Army he continued to write military news for the Defense Department as a civilian. Today he handles media relations for a division of the DoD. He has settled in Maryland with his family, including Princess the wonder cat.

Austin is a voracious reader of just about any kind of nonfiction, plus mysteries, adventures and thrillers. When he isn't working or reading, he's writing.

Keep up with all of Austin S. Camacho's latest accomplishments at www.ascamacho.com

Other Hannibal Jones Mysteries
By Austin S. Camacho

The Troubleshooter
A Washington attorney buys an apartment building in the heart of the city, but then finds the building occupied by drug dealers are unable to empty the building for use by paying residents. No one seems willing or able to take on this challenge until the lawyer meets Hannibal Jones. He calls himself a troubleshooter, but he finds more trouble than he expected finds himself facing off against a local crime boss and his powerful, mob-connected father.

Collateral Damage
Bea Collins is certain her fiancée wouldn't just leave without telling her. Troubleshooter Hannibal Jones is skeptical until the missing fiancée turns up dazed, confused and holding a knife over a dead body. To find this killer Hannibal will travel to Germany, Vegas and through Dean's past, which includes the murder of Dean's father, his first childhood crush and brings Hannibal face to face with Dean's convicted mother.

Damaged Goods
The death of Anita Cooper's father crushed her dreams of a better life. Then a hard man named Rod Mantooth stole her innocence and her father's legacy, a secret that could have rebuilt her life was lost until she encountered another hard man - the professional troubleshooter named Hannibal Jones. Like a rolling mass of icy fury, Hannibal follows a trail of corrupted human debris leading to Rod Mantooth and a final showdown in the icy waters of the Atlantic.

Russian Roulette
Hannibal Jones is forced to take a case for a Russian assassin. He must investigate Gana, who has stolen Viktoriya, the woman his new client loves. Evidence connects Gana to the apparent suicide of Viktoriya"s father. Then more deaths follow, closing in on Viktoriya. To save the Russian beauty, Hannibal must unravel a complex tangle of clues and survive a dramatic shootout side-by-side with his murderous client.

Also available by Austin S. Camacho
The Stark and O'Brien Adventures

The Payback Assignment
While fighting for their lives, mercenary soldier Morgan Stark and jewel thief Felicity O'Brien learn they share a psychic link that warns them of danger. They then combine their skills to get revenge on the man who double-crossed them both and left them to die in South America.

The Orion Assignment
Ex-mercenary Morgan Stark follows retired jewel thief Felicity O'Brien to her native Ireland to defend her uncle's Catholic parish from Ian O'Ryan, and IRA terrorist. Trying to separate patriotic mercenaries from heartless terrorists leads them to a sniper mission on the rocky Irish coast, a deadly high speed motorcycle race in Belgium, and a final confrontation on an island off the coast of France where Morgan could die by slow torture if Felicity doesn't find him in time.

The Piranha Assignment
The CIA asks security specialists Stark & O'Brien to go undercover to investigate The Piranha Project - construction of a stealth submarine that will give the U.S. total command of the seas. The project is run in Panama by eccentric genius Francisco Bastidas, but may have been infiltrated by terrorists. If stark and O'Brien can't stop them, America's new super weapon could threaten the world with nuclear destruction.

The Ice Woman Assignment
Federal agencies ask security specialists Morgan Stark and Felicity O'Brien to use their underworld connections to help stop the import of a new drug called Ice. That ignites a war with The Escorpionistas, a Columbian cartel led by a female mystic known as Anaconda. The action moves from California to Texas to a climactic battle in Columbia pitting our heroes' psychic link against natives who can see the future.